Patna Blues

Praise for *Patna Blues*

'Abdullah Khan manages to bring together a heartfelt simplicity in his prose style with delicate personal and cultural observation and humour. His writing is lit with a love for the world.' – **Amit Chaudhuri**

'Reading *Patna Blues* is like pedalling your way through a little-known India. It is certain to fill you with inexplicably candid and absolutely stunning tales. *Patna Blues* marks an impressive debut and brings us an important voice.' – **Anees Salim**

'[A] stunning debut novel . . . sometimes hilarious and at others, heartbreaking . . . *Patna Blues* is a successor of the tradition of Raja Rao, R.K. Narayan, Mulk Raj Anand and Ruskin Bond.' – ***Business Standard***

'A heartbreaking, engrossing read.' – **Scroll**

'An important novel and a timely one . . . *Patna Blues* heralds the arrival of a powerful new voice.' – **Rakhshanda Jalil, *Friday Times***

'An unputdownable saga of life.' – ***Hindu Businessline***

Patna Blues

Abdullah Khan

JUGGERNAUT BOOKS
C-I-128, First Floor, Sangam Vihar, Near Holi Chowk,
New Delhi 110080, India

First published in hardback by Juggernaut Books 2018
Published in paperback 2022

10 9 8 7 6 5 4 3 2 1

P-ISBN: 9789393986269
E-ISBN: 9789393986276

Typeset in Adobe Caslon Pro by R. Ajith Kumar, Noida

Printed at Thomson Press India Ltd

To Dadi, Late Amirunnisa,
and Amma, Late Shaheeda Khatoon,
from whom I inherited the art of storytelling

Aur bhi dukh hain zamaane mein mohabbat ke siva
Rahatein aur bhi hain vasl ki rahat ke siva

(There are many other sorrows in this world
Besides the agony of love
There are many pleasures in the world
Besides the joy of one's union with the beloved)

Faiz Ahmad Faiz

Dream

ONE

Arif shivered when a gust of wind hit him. *I should have worn a jacket*, he thought as he stopped his bicycle in front of a two-storeyed yellow building. He had just returned home from college. Parking his bicycle in the stairwell of the building, he pulled a notebook from its carrier and climbed up a flight of stairs. The banister of the staircase was broken in places and cobwebs hung from the ceiling.

On the first floor, Arif pushed open a door and entered the balcony of his family's flat. He placed his notebook on a tangerine wooden chair. Next to the chair was a cheap grey-coloured three-seater rexine sofa. Arif bent to remove his black leather shoes. Holding them in his hands, he clapped them together to free them of the mud. Placing the shoes in the corner next to the entrance, he rubbed his palms to get rid of the dust, picked up his notebook and walked to his bedroom.

Arif was tired and wanted to rest for a while, but he turned back from the door of his room when he saw two strangers there. One of them, a short, stocky boy with closely cropped hair, probably in his early twenties, was sleeping on his bed, and the other, a pot-bellied, middle-aged, bearded man, was sitting on a chair, and intently going through the latest issue of *India Today*.

Arif went straight to his mother, who was chopping vegetables in the kitchen.

'Who are these people, Amma?'

'The old man is a distant cousin of your father's. He has come to Patna to get his son treated at the Indira Gandhi Institute of Medical Sciences. They will be staying with us for the next four or five days,' Amma said as she placed the chopped vegetables in a big bowl.

'Guests again! Is this a house or a serai? Every second day we have guests,' Arif said, pulling his hair. 'We have just three rooms and that's not enough even for the eight of us.'

'Keep your voice low, beta. They'll hear us,' Amma said in a whisper as she washed the chopped eggplants, potatoes and radishes in running water.

'So what!' Arif said and stomped out of the kitchen to a tiny room at the end of the corridor.

The storeroom with its three gunnysacks of wheat and rice also held a small bookshelf, a table and chair, to serve as Arif's backup study. The smell of pesticides from the sacks aggravated Arif's allergies and made him sneeze. There was no window and he had to keep the door propped open. He could not sit there for too long; the odour was overpowering.

Guests were a perennial problem in his house. Relatives visiting Patna always stayed with them. Who would spend thousands of rupees on lodging when it was available for free? Most of them came for medical treatment, some to participate in mass recruitment of police constables or to appear for a case at the Patna High Court. Some of their guests were so distantly related that Abba and Amma had never met them before. They came with references, either a letter from his uncles or a call made to Abba's office.

Abba too resented this incessant flow of guests. 'These people think that my house is a dharamshala,' he would say in a fit of anger, once the guests had left. However, while they stayed, he was the perfect host, which probably encouraged them to come again.

Amma was always overburdened with work. At times she cooked for as many as twenty people on the coal chulha. Abba had been trying to buy a gas connection for the last three years. He had applied for a connection the previous year, but his turn had not come. Even a single-cylinder connection was expensive in the black market. Every morning Amma left her bed early to light the chulha. Because of the heavy black smoke that it emitted she took the brick-and-mud chulha to the terrace, filled it with raw coal, lit it there and then brought the lit chulha back to the kitchen. She never woke her children up to help her. Even if her children were awake, she did not allow her daughters to lift the heavy chulhas. 'Carrying weights can affect the menstrual cycle in young girls.' She couldn't come up with an excuse for her sons, so Arif and Zakir did help her on the few days they woke up in time to do so. 'Starting tomorrow, I'll wake up early to help Amma. At least I can help her with the chulha,' Arif had resolved last year, but most mornings Amma would have lit the chulha before Arif woke up.

Arif and Zakir shared a room. The second room had

two small-sized beds placed at a distance from each other where Abba and Amma slept. It also had a plastic table and four chairs and functioned as a drawing room during the day. The third and largest room with a big balcony had a wooden chowki for Dadi. On a double bed all three of his sisters – Rabiya, Nazneen and Huma – managed to fit in. Whenever a male guest arrived, Amma slept on a mat in the corridor and the guest shared the room with Abba.

'Amma, I'll sleep in the corridor. You sleep in my room,' both Arif and Zakir would tell her, but she never agreed. If the number of guests increased, Arif and Zakir had to give up their room as well. Arif didn't mind giving up his room if it meant Amma wouldn't sleep on a woven straw mat spread on the floor, with a bundle of clothes made into a pillow. But he felt annoyed about his studies suffering as a result of this.

Arif returned to his room. The bearded man was busy reading a book in Urdu, absent-mindedly scratching his salt-and-pepper beard. The young man was still asleep.

'Assalam alaikum,' Arif greeted him.

'Walaikum assalam rahmatullahe barkatahu,' replied the bearded man, extending both his hands out to him. Arif reluctantly shook them.

'Are you Abdul Rashid sahab's younger son?' he asked warmly.

'No, I'm the elder one,' Arif replied.

'Oh! But your brother Zakir looks older than you. Mashallah! He has got the physique of real Pathans, he is so tall and fair. How old is he?' The man continued scratching his beard.

'Twenty,' Arif replied. At five feet ten inches, Arif was tall by Indian standards. But Zakir was even taller.

'And you?'

'I am a year older than Zakir.'

The man paused for a while and then asked, 'Isme Sharief, your sacred name please.' This time he had spoken in sophisticated Urdu, almost in old Lakhnavi style.

'Arif Khan.' Arif was already exhausted with the seemingly never-ending questions. He was only too familiar with this routine.

'Nice name. How are your studies? Are you doing a BA?'

'B.Sc. Chemistry, Honours, third year,' Arif said as his eyes scanned his desk.

'Which college?'

'A.N. College.'

'Zakir and your sisters?'

'Zakir is in his second year, BA, at A.N. College. Rabiya is in J. D. Women's College. My other two sisters are studying at the Bihar Military Police High School.'

'Arif babu' – the bearded man's tone changed suddenly – 'if you aren't busy, would you like to come with us? The city is completely new to me. If it were Motihari, I would have had no problem.'

'I'm afraid I can't,' Arif said. 'My final examinations are just two weeks away.' He walked towards his bed and picked up a windcheater from a stainless steel wall hanger next to it.

'We don't come visiting every day,' the man said in a hurt tone.

'Sorry,' Arif said as he collected a slim book, a blue diary and a pen from the table and walked out of the room.

Ten minutes later, Arif sat on a green patch of grass in Nehru Park with a blue diary and the *Diwan-e-Momin* lying next to him.

'Instead of studying for my exam, I am here with a poetry book,' Arif muttered to himself. The park was desolate except for a few kids playing on the swings in a distant corner. Flower beds with roses and marigolds flanked the pebbled paths that criss-crossed the park, with a marble bust of Jawaharlal Nehru in the centre.

A gust of wind shook the plants and Arif felt a slight chill. Zipping up his windcheater, Arif picked up the book. He was flipping through the pages when the sound of footsteps distracted him.

An emaciated old man wrapped in a white shawl and a tall, slender woman in a black sari walked slowly in his direction. Her long hair was dishevelled, her eyes swollen and smeared with kohl. She had been crying. Arif couldn't help looking at her.

'Subhanallah!' he murmured and went back to his book as he saw her helping the elderly man settle down on a bench nearby. He opened his diary and couldn't stop himself from scribbling two lines in Urdu about her.

Syah zulf uska syah parahan uska
Maninde sang-e-marmar hain badan uska
Misal kya doon is husn-e-bemisal ki
Chand se bhi haseen rukh-e-roshan uska

(Her tresses are black and so are her robes
Her body is like marble

Her beauty is incomparable
Her face more beautiful than a full moon)

'Babuji, how are you feeling now?' Arif heard the woman's voice and raised his gaze again. There was no response from the old man. She held him by his shoulders and looked around, confused and anxious.

'Babuji! Babuji!' Her voice became shriller. With one hand, she touched his forehead and cheeks, and then bent her head to place her ear on his chest. She started to shake him frantically.

Clutching his diary and book, Arif got up and rushed to them.

'Please help!' she cried, trying to hold back her tears. Arif dropped his things on the bench, grabbed the old man's wrist and searched for a pulse.

'Please call an ambulance,' the woman said, wiping her nose with the back of her palm.

'It takes ages for an ambulance to arrive in Patna. I'll get a taxi instead,' Arif said and hurried towards the telephone in the paan–cigarette shop nearby. The swarthy shopkeeper with a handlebar moustache was all alone, busy clipping the tips of paan leaves. Sharda Sinha sang from a tape recorder, '*Le le haiye O piya choliya bangal ke* . . . (O my dear husband, get me a blouse made in Bengal . . .)'

'Local call,' Arif said, handing him a two-rupee coin and stepping into the booth to dial the taxi number.

It took almost twenty minutes for the taxi to arrive. Arif asked the driver, Habib, who knew Arif from having ferried his family every now and then, to help carry the old man to the car. Poking his ear with his little finger, the driver glanced nervously at the old man and the woman in black by his side before saying 'Yes, Arif bhai!'

The woman followed them and extended her arms to support her father's head as they laid the old man on the back seat. She accidentally brushed Arif's chest with her arms. Arif felt a strange sensation run through his body. He kept staring at the woman as she got into the car and placed her father's head in her lap.

'Let's go,' the woman said with urgency.

Shaken out of his stupor and embarrassed for the way he had stared at the woman, he climbed in the front and sat next to the driver.

Turning to Habib, he said, 'Patna Medical College and Hospital, Emergency Ward.'

On the way to the hospital, Arif looked in the rear-view mirror. The elderly man was still unconscious and the woman was rubbing his palms and chest as tears rolled down her rosy cheeks. *Ya Allah, help this old man*, Arif prayed silently.

Near Dak Bunglow Square, the car stopped with a jolt.

The road ahead was blocked. A makeshift barricade had been created in the middle of the road using plastic chairs, bicycles and scooters. Sixty to seventy young men, some of them squatting on the ground, chanted slogans in Hindi:

V.P. Singh Murdabad

Mandal Commission Wapas Lo

Paper and cloth banners were hung on the nearby electric and telephone poles.

Mandal Commission Will Not be Accepted
Say No to Reservation! Say Yes to Merit
Stop Vote Bank Politics
No Appeasement on the Basis of Caste

The taxi was blocked by vehicles queued up behind their car and they were unable to take a different route. Arif got out of the taxi and looked around. On a cycle rickshaw, a dhoti-clad middle-aged man with a pencil moustache was discussing the politics of reservation with a short, plump young man on a motorcycle.

'After twenty-seven per cent reservation for the backward castes, we upper castes will be left with no option but to beg on the streets,' he said in an agitated voice.

The woman had rolled down the glass and was looking outside distractedly. She didn't say anything, but her brimming eyes beseeched him to get her father to the hospital somehow.

Unnerved by her tears, Arif desperately wanted to find a way out of there. 'Habib bhai, we should talk to the students,' Arif said to the driver.

'No point, Arif bhai.' Habib was again poking his ear. He cleared his throat, rolled down the glass, stuck his head out, spat and said, 'They'll not let us go.'

I have to face them alone. Arif stole a brief glance at the woman.

'Should I come with you?' she asked.

'Stay with your father. I'll talk to them,' Arif said, rubbing his chin with his fingers. He was afraid of facing the protesters because he knew how far a mob of students could go in a charged situation. Mustering all the courage he had, he exhaled and began to make his way through the crowd to the other side.

'What's the problem, mister? Don't you see the road is blocked?' One of the protesters, a well-built, bearded man with a red tilak on his forehead, rose from the ground.

'Sir,' Arif entreated, 'an old man is seriously ill. Please allow us to go. He'll die if he doesn't get timely medical help.'

'No, it's not possible. Go away.'

'Please, brother. It is a question of life and death,' Arif implored.

'When the future of millions of youth is at stake, we don't care about an old man,' said a swarthy man in a grey safari suit as he emerged from the crowd.

'Just go away!' the bearded man said threateningly.

'No! I won't. What you're doing is illegal,' Arif began to lose his temper.

Suddenly, a sturdy-looking twenty-something jumped out of the crowd and punched Arif, who fell to the ground.

'Abey saale, are you here to teach us what is legal and what is illegal? Fuck off or we'll beat the shit out of you. Bloody rascal.'

Arif knew he couldn't fight alone with this mob of students.

Other protesters had begun to surround him. And one of them held a hockey stick. There was complete silence.

Arif was frightened and confused. He didn't know what to do next.

'Please don't hurt him,' a female voice said. Turning around, he was surprised to see the woman in black standing behind him with her palms folded in request. Her hair was covered with the pallu of her sari and her eyes were brimming with tears.

The bearded man shook his head and told his fellow protesters, 'Let him go.'

The students surrounding Arif stared at him with angry eyes, and then began to move aside indicating that Arif could pass. Rising from the ground, Arif looked intently at the woman. He rubbed the dust off his palms and turned to go when he heard Habib shouting and gesturing frantically towards the car. Arif's heart sank. The woman in black had already started running. Arif followed her.

The old man was muttering something indecipherable. Habib was fanning him with a folded newspaper. Arif heaved a sigh of relief. The woman got into the car, placed her father's head in her lap, started gently rubbing his chest and began reciting the Hanuman Chalisa:

Pavanatanaya sankata harana mangala murati rupa
Rama lakhana sita sahita hridaya basahu sura bhupa . . .

(O son of the wind god, one with an auspicious form and the destroyer of adversities. O king of gods! May you dwell in our heart along with Rama, Lakshmana and Sita . . .)

In a few seconds, the old man fell silent. The woman continued with the recitation. Arif looked around to find a way to get away. But there was none.

Barely a few minutes had passed when a white Ambassador car and two anti-riot police buses stopped on the other side of the road. Thirty to forty policemen emerged from the buses and moved towards the protesters. The helmeted men were armed with lathis. A senior police officer got down from the car and made announcements on a hand-held loudspeaker, asking the students to clear the road.

The students responded by pelting stones at the policemen. Sensing trouble, Arif swiftly got into the taxi. A few stray stones fell on the crowd stuck in the traffic jam. People panicked and many of them left their motorcycles and rickshaws and ran for safety. Those in cars and taxis cowered.

The policemen went after the protesters. Arif saw the students scatter. Some fell on the road and the policemen beat them up mercilessly before dragging them to the police van.

Soon, the road was cleared. Habib sped through the Dak Bunglow Square.

The old man was wheeled inside the hospital on a stretcher and the woman went in with him. Arif stayed to settle the taxi fare. Luckily, he had received his monthly pocket money from his father that morning.

Entering the waiting hall of the Emergency Ward of PMCH, Arif spotted the woman sitting in the waiting room, the loose end of her sari pressed against her mouth, probably trying to control her sobbing.

'Where is your father?' Arif asked as he sat down on a chair beside her. The hall smelt of dettol and phenyl. A lanky middle-aged man was wiping the floor with a piece of soggy cloth.

'They have taken him for some tests,' the woman said in a low voice. 'They asked me to wait here.'

She had barely finished her sentence when a sturdy man with a thick moustache came and asked her to accompany him to the ICU. Arif also rose to go with her.

'Only one person allowed,' the man said matter-of-factly.

'Please wait here till I return,' the woman said to Arif.

'Okay.'

An hour later, the woman was back. 'Thank you very much for all your help. You saved my father's life. It was a heart attack,' she said, her face shining with gratitude. 'He is much better now.'

'I am happy I could be of help,' Arif said shyly, trying not to look at her face. 'What's your name? And where do you study?' She had used the respectful '*aap*' instead of the informal '*tum*'.

'My name is Arif Khan. I am doing my B.Sc. Honours from A.N. College.' He thought of asking her name as well but checked himself. It was impolite to ask a woman's name if she was older than you. 'You live near Nehru Park?' Arif asked tentatively.

'Yes, in Swagat Nagar. But we are planning to move to some other rented accommodation very soon. My husband is a manager at the State Bank of India,' she replied. 'I . . .' she began to say something and then stopped suddenly.

'Yes?' Arif asked.

'I am sorry to bother you again,' she said hesitantly. 'Could you do me one last favour? Could you go to Danapur to fetch my cousin? I tried his phone but I couldn't get through. Tell him Sumitra sent you.' She held out a scrap of paper. 'This is his address.'

Sumitra! What a beautiful name. He silently recited her name many times as if it were some kind of hymn.

'I'll go immediately,' Arif said, looking at her face guardedly. She seemed comforted by the fact that her father was doing well. She even smiled while thanking him again and the world's most beautiful dimples appeared in her cheeks.

'Arif, this is for the taxi.' Sumitra held some money in her hand.

'No! No! I have already paid him,' Arif said.

'You are a student. And students are always short of money.' She came closer, gently held his arm and pushed the money into his breast pocket. When her hands touched him, Arif froze. He couldn't breathe during those few blissful moments.

Arif exhaled deeply as he walked out of the hospital. He thought of the moment her hands had touched him and he got goosebumps.

Ashok Raj Path was bursting at the seams as it did on weekdays. The traffic moved at its own leisurely pace. Arif caught a yellow-and-black Bajaj autorickshaw to Gandhi Maidan from where he would change to another autorickshaw going to Danapur.

Two hours later, Arif reached the address. The house was locked. The neighbours didn't have any idea about the whereabouts of Sumitra's cousin or his family. It was eventually ten past five when Arif returned to the hospital, but Sumitra was not there.

'Some relatives of the old man came here and they have

taken him to a private hospital for further treatment,' the woman at the reception informed him.

Arif asked her if they had left any message for him. The receptionist said no. Arif was exhausted and had eaten nothing since morning. He decided to return home, wondering how Sumitra could disappear without leaving him a message. His heart ached with an unusual kind of pain. The thought that he might not see her again saddened him.

Later that night, he wrote a poem. *A Beautiful Lady in Black.*

TWO

One Saturday morning in 1992, almost two years after his encounter with Sumitra, Arif was strolling on the terrace of his home in Police Colony. Taking in the fresh air, he felt good. A cold he had been nursing for many weeks had finally vanished. Pressing one of his nostrils with his index finger, he blew his nose. No snot. He also coughed to clear his throat. No phlegm. Dr Ganguly's prescription had worked.

Arif had other reasons as well to be in high spirits.

The result of the preliminary examination for the civil services had been published that morning. His name was among the successful candidates. He was confident of getting through the mains and the personal interview as well.

Abba's dream to see me as an IAS officer will soon be a reality. He fantasized about his photograph appearing on the cover of *Competition Success Review*. 'A Tête-à-Tête with IAS Topper Arif Khan.' His parents would be proud of him.

Once he became an IAS officer, first he'd employ a full-time domestic help for his mother. Amma had spent her entire life taking care of the family. She deserved to take it easy. Then, he would arrange for Dadi's pilgrimage to Mecca. He wondered how Dadi would react when he told her that she was going for hajj. Then, he would find good alliances for his sisters. Who on earth wouldn't want to have an IAS officer for his brother-in-law? *How sweet my three sisters are.* He thought of each in turn. *They deserve the best in life.* But of course, Nazneen was the sweetest among them. Then he'd insist that his father apply for voluntary retirement. Abba had worked enough late hours. He should spend the rest of his life in peace.

For his brother, Zakir, he'd convince Abba to allow him to pursue a career in the movies. If his brother needed money, he'd provide for him. But, to succeed in the mains, Arif needed to study harder. Nothing less than ten hours every day.

Thinking about his plans made Arif smile in contentment. When was the last time he had been in such good spirits? He tried to remember but couldn't.

In the backyard of the building, Arif saw two old ladies worshipping a peepal tree: they marked the trunk of the tree with a vermilion-like substance, offered potfuls of water and then stood still for some time with their hands folded in prayer. He found it strangely pleasant to watch the women go through the rituals, almost like sunbathing in winter. Once they had finished and walked away, Arif was just about to go back downstairs when he saw another woman approaching the tree. She was tall and fair, in a black sari and a matching sleeveless blouse, her black hair cascading down her back. She carried a dolchi, a small bamboo basket, in which she had things essential for performing the rituals of her puja. When she turned around after finishing the puja, he could see her round face, large eyes and plump lips.

Oh my God! Sumitra!

He kept looking at her till she walked away.

'Beta, breakfast is ready.' He heard his mother's voice from the balcony.

Things around him had changed as he climbed downstairs. The day had become brighter. The breeze had become cool and pleasant.

He relished the breakfast of chapattis and hot aloo-istoo as if they were delicacies from paradise. As he finished his breakfast, Dadi brought a plateful of sliced mango. From its sweet fragrance and golden-yellow colour, he knew it was jardalu. His face lit up as he inhaled the fragrance of his favourite fruit.

'These mangoes are from our own orchard. Your Badke baba sent them from Jamalpura,' Dadi said, smiling, as she settled next to him.

'No mango in this world can be as delicious as jardalu,' Arif said as the sweetness of the mango pulp permeated his taste buds. Closing his eyes, he thought of Sumitra and imagined kissing her. *It must be like tasting a fully ripe jardalu mango.*

What a day! First the UPSC result and then Sumitra, he thought to himself and retired to his room.

The books for the mains lay open in front of him, but he was thinking of Sumitra.

That night Arif dreamed of her.

The next morning he woke up quite early, even before the muezzin of the nearby mosque called out azan. Zakir slept fitfully on the other side of the bed. The Shiv mandir inside Police Colony was yet to start the bhajans on its loudspeakers. Everyone was asleep, except Amma, who was washing dishes. He could hear the sharp clink of utensils as they scraped against each other. And Dadi was reciting from the Holy Quran, her soft, mellow voice carrying through the house.

Arif shaved and bathed before going upstairs.

On the terrace, leaning against the parapet, he waited for Sumitra for the next couple of hours, but she didn't come to worship the peepal tree. Nor did anyone else. As the sun ascended the horizon, he looked dolefully towards the tree, and then went downstairs. The area around the tree was still deserted. It was already nine o'clock.

The next four days rolled by restlessly. Sumitra didn't show up at the peepal tree.

Why am I waiting for her? She is married, Arif reminded himself again and again.

'Peepal trees are worshipped only on Saturdays,' his friend Mritunjay, who was a Kanyakubja Brahmin, told him later that week, when Arif casually enquired about the ritual. 'In Sanskrit the tree is called ashvattha,' his friend went on. 'According to the Brahma Purana, Ashvattha and Peepla were two demons who harassed innocent people. Ashvattha would take the form of a peepal and Peepla would take the form of a Brahmin. Peepla would then advise people to touch the tree, and as soon as they did, Ashvattha would kill them. They were both killed by Shani devta, the god of

Saturday. Because of his influence, it is considered safe to touch the tree on Saturdays. Also, Lakshmi, the goddess of wealth, is believed to inhabit the tree on Saturdays.'

So, I will have to wait till Saturday to see Sumitra again.

~

On Friday Arif went to see Mritunjay, who had also cleared the prelims for the civil services exam. They often studied together.

Mritunjay was plump and short in contrast to Arif's tall and athletic stature, and had a thick Jackie Shroff-like moustache. In Mritunjay's fifteen foot by ten foot room, populated by a wooden bed, a Godrej almirah, a study table and a couple of chairs, they sat discussing their study plan. A tangerine bookshelf hung on the wall.

'Arrey Arif, please help me with decision-making theory. I find Herbert Simon and Chester Barnard a bit heavy going,' Mritunjay said as he pulled out a book on administrative thinkers from the stack of books on his table.

'Of course.'

Mritunjay's mother called out to him from the kitchen.

'I will be right back,' Mritunjay said as he tossed the book on the table and hurried to the kitchen.

Arif stood up and walked to the window. He saw a woman drying clothes on the terrace of an adjacent building. He could not believe his eyes. She was so close, he could even see the upturned tip of her nose. Her long tresses were tied in a loose bun. Arif was stunned to see Sumitra again, and even more so to learn that she was his friend's neighbour.

Sumitra caught him staring at her, and gave him a magical, dimpled smile. Arif felt overwhelmed and was unable to smile back. Then she disappeared. Mritunjay returned with tea and a plate full of vegetable pakoras, sprinkled with chaat masala.

Should I go out and say hello to Sumitra? Arif wondered.

No, he decided emphatically.

What do I call my infatuation with her, and where might it lead me, Arif wondered. He heard the answer in a beautiful Gulzar song carried by the wind from a radio or TV somewhere:

Sirf ehsaas hain ye rooh se mahsoos karo
Pyaar ko pyaar hi rahne do koi naam na do

(This is a feeling and your soul can feel it
Let love be love, don't give it any name)

THREE

The following Monday morning Arif was in his room, engrossed in a book on the Indian freedom struggle by Bipin Chandra, when Abba walked in, dressed in his police inspector's uniform, his green cap askew on his head. Sitting next to him on the bed, Abba patted Arif on his back gently.

'Wah beta! I am really happy that you are working so hard for the mains.' Abba's face was lit with hope. 'Inshallah, you'll clear the exam in your first attempt.'

'Inshallah,' Arif seconded his father's words.

'Accha, take this cheque and get it encashed from SBI, Judges Court Branch. Ahsan uncle's son has sent the money for his treatment.'

'All right, Abba.'

'Do you know where this branch is?'

'Yes, Abba. Near the Gandhi Maidan bus stand.'

'Yes,' Abba said as he took off his glasses and rubbed his eyes.

As Abba walked out of the room, Arif looked at the wall clock. He had two hours before the bank opened. He could rush through 'The Rise of Communalism in Nineteenth-century India'. Just then Dadi entered the room. She had a steel bowl in her right hand.

'What is my grandson doing?' Dadi smiled.

'Studying, Dadi.'

'Here is your favourite chatpata chana,' she said as she bent to place the bowl in front of him.

Arif beamed at the bowlful of crispy, spiced chickpeas.

'Thank you very much, Dadi.' Arif rose to hug her.

~

It was ten past eleven when Arif reached Gandhi Maidan. Even from outside he could see that half the Maidan was covered in colourful canopies, thousands of men and women sitting on the ground, chanting 'Jai Shri Ram! Hail to Lord Rama! Vidya Devi Zindabad!

He pedalled his bicycle through the crowd of the Bharatiya Janata Party supporters on the road. Vidya Devi had not arrived at the Maidan yet. He saw police personnel all around the place. A deputy superintendent of police was on a walkie-talkie. Arif was a little nervous; being a Muslim, he could never feel safe or comfortable in the presence of members of the Hindu fascist party.

He heard Vidya Devi's voice over the loudspeakers.

'They kill cows because we venerate cows as our mothers. And they always try to instigate Hindus. You see what happens when India loses a match to Pakistan. They light firecrackers. They celebrate. They live in India but sing songs of Pakistan. If our party opposes these traitors, the Congresswallahs brand us communal. The Congress party has appeased them to an unreasonable extent. If India is a secular country, why is there no uniform civil code? If India is a secular country, why do they get a subsidy for the hajj pilgrimage? All these things have been happening because we Hindus have forgotten our glorious past. A thousand years of slavery has made us cowards. When Hindus awaken, the traitors will be shown their place.'

Vidya Devi was famous for her venomous speeches against Muslims. Arif felt a chill run down his spine. He pedalled faster.

'Saali randi!' he muttered.

From there Arif went to Mritunjay's house instead of going home to collect a photocopy of notes on public administration by Vaji Ramarao. Thanks to Mritunjay, Arif got them cheap – Rs 450 was nothing compared to the Rs 6200 for the original. As Mritunjay came out to see Arif off, a blue Premier Padmini car stopped close to them and a tall man in his forties with a narrow moustache got out.

'Pranam, uncle,' Mritunjay greeted. 'Meet my friend Arif.' He turned to Arif and added, 'This is Ramesh uncle, our neighbour. He is a manager at the State Bank of India.'

So, this must *be Sumitra's husband. What are the chances of another SBI manager living in the same neighbourhood as Sumitra and her husband.*

Arif did a quick namaste.

'May Lord Shiva bless you,' Ramesh Kumar said.

Arif took an instant liking to him.

'Is your father at home?' Ramesh Kumar asked Mritunjay.

'No, uncle.'

'Okay, I'll come by later then,' he said and waved to them.

A few hours after reaching home, Arif realized that the money was missing from his pocket. He couldn't imagine how and where he had lost the money. He remembered taking the money from the cashier at the bank and stuffing the notes into the left pocket of his trousers.

The money was for Ahsan uncle's treatment. The old man had come all the way from his native village, Jamalpura, to be treated for stomach ulcers. The doctors had prescribed surgery, scheduled after two days.

Arif searched his pockets, looked for it in his bedroom and study room. The money was nowhere to be found. Ten thousand rupees was a big amount. His father's monthly salary was less than that. What could an honest police inspector like Abba, who didn't take bribes, earn? Just enough to stay alive. Mr Verma, his father's colleague, who lived just one block away, lived a lavish life.

If I don't find the money, how would Abba manage to get such a large amount at such short notice? Maybe he had dropped the money at Mritunjay's place. *Ya Allah!* Arif prayed.

Mritunjay was surprised to see Arif back again. 'Have you forgotten something here?' he asked.

'No yaar! I've lost ten thousand rupees,' Arif replied in a choked voice, and explained what had happened.

Arif was not worried that Abba would scold or beat him for his carelessness. As a matter of principle, Abba never slapped his children. Arif was more terrified of having to see his father's expression of horror and defeat when Arif told him about the loss.

'You must tell your father at once,' Mritunjay said. As Arif was about to leave, he heard Sumitra's voice. She was in the adjacent room talking to Mritunjay's mother.

By the time he reached home, Arif had decided to call up Abba and tell him about the loss of money. But he was shocked to see Abba at home in the middle of the day. *Something must be wrong, otherwise Abba would never be home so early. Perhaps he was unwell.* Arif grew alarmed. Normally, Abba left the office after 9 p.m. Arif registered the expression on his father's face; it was blazing with anger and there was no sign of illness. Amma stood silently in a corner with a glass of water, looking anxious, and Zakir stood in another corner.

'This bloody rascal from the National Intelligence Department says he can't hand the file over to me because it contains sensitive information about the ISI's activities in Bihar, and I am a Muslim. This is the reward for my integrity and honesty. Tiwari, who would happily sell his own mother for a few rupees, is considered more trustworthy than me.'

'Please drink some water,' Amma said as she held out the tumbler. Abba took a sip and threw the tumbler to the floor.

'You can't even keep a glass clean.' Abba was fair-skinned, tall, with broad shoulders, small eyes and a prominent nose. Whenever he lost his temper, he stood erect with his chest out, appearing taller than he was. His nostrils flared. His broad forehead had furrows. Dadi entered the room, her head covered with the pallu of her white sari. Her narrow brown eyes looked worried. She came straight to Abba, gently placed her hands on his head and said, 'My son, you shouldn't get angry with your wife for whatever happened at the office. Our holy Prophet, peace be upon him, has told us to treat our women with respect. Poor Hamida, she spends the entire day taking care of her family.'

Abba didn't say anything. He just closed his eyes. Dadi was stroking Abba's hair, trying to calm him down, when the doorbell rang. Ram Chandra Upadhyaya, a senior accountant at the police headquarters, was at the door. Having been Abba's mentor since Abba joined the police department twenty-eight years ago, and knowing the family well, he walked straight in. Abba stood up.

'Rashid, come, let's go to the office. Bade sahab has sent me to fetch you.' Ram kaka spoke with authority and affection. 'Bade sahab scolded the intelligence officer.' Arif knew that Abba and his colleagues referred to Bihar's Director General of Police as Bade sahab.

Arif knew Abba wouldn't say no to him, and after a little persuasion, Abba accompanied Ram kaka back to the office.

Once in his room, Arif fretted over how to break the news to his father. He knew Abba would borrow the money from his friends. However, for the next few months, this additional expense would destroy the equilibrium of the precariously balanced monthly budget. They would stop their subscription to the *Times of India* and *India Today*, and they would take only half a litre of milk a day, instead of a litre, and potatoes would be cooked more frequently. Fish, mutton and chicken would disappear from the kitchen till the money was paid off.

Overcome with self-loathing, Arif wanted to scream at himself.

'Any problem, bhaiyya?' Zakir asked, noticing Arif's anguished face.

Arif told him the whole story.

'What! Have you told Abba?'

'No, I'll tell him tomorrow.'

'Don't get upset, bhaiyya. Just rest for a while and then try searching for it again. I'll go to a PCO to call the bank and ask if you left the money there. My friend's cousin is a clerk in the same branch.'

Zakir left immediately. Arif took off his shirt, lay on the bed and closed his eyes. Outside, he heard Amma welcoming some woman, 'Namaste, behenji.'

Minutes later, Amma called out to him, 'Arif beta!'

It was customary for Amma to introduce her children to every new visitor. Arif would be introduced as the eldest, Badka baua, who was preparing for the civil services examination. And while performing the ritual of introductions, his mother's pale face would glow with maternal pride.

Not in the mood to be introduced to anyone, he pretended to be asleep. But he leapt up as he heard footsteps approach. As he hurriedly threw his shirt on and started buttoning it up, Sumitra walked in. What was she doing here! If he hadn't been in such low spirits over the money, his heart would have jumped with joy.

'This is Sumitra aunty,' Amma said. She had no idea that they had met earlier.

'Sit here, Sumitraji, and talk to Arif.' Amma pointed to a chair and left the room.

'This is your book and diary. You gave it to me the day

you helped me get my father to the hospital. I kept it in my bag and forgot to return it,' Sumitra said, pulling out the *Diwan-e-Momin* and his blue diary from her rather large brown handbag.

'There is something for you inside the book,' Sumitra said, smiling.

Is it a love letter? Arif thought and got goosebumps.

Arif could feel something stuffed between its pages. Keeping his eyes on the room entrance, he opened the book. There was a brown envelope. He gingerly peeked in. It was stuffed with money.

Arif looked at her in surprise.

'I know you lost some money. I heard you at Mritunjay's house. So, I thought . . . Please treat this as a loan. You can return it when you become an IAS officer.'

'Thank you very much. But I can't accept this. Sorry.' He held the envelope towards her and saw her smile vanish.

'Please don't be offended. I didn't mean to hurt you,' Arif apologized.

'Don't worry, I understand your dilemma. I am impressed with your self-respect.' She smiled again. Her smile, that same dimpled smile, overwhelmed Arif, and he had a sudden impulse to kiss her.

Remember, Arif, she is married. Think of your family's reputation. Think of the consequences of pursuing her. He hated himself for his feelings.

'Did you say something to me?' Sumitra asked.

'No,' he replied quickly, making eye contact for a split second. Up close Sumitra was even more beautiful. Arif inhaled the fragrance of her talcum powder. Her lips were full and her breasts generous. *Tauba! Tauba! Ya Allah, forgive me for the sins of my eyes.*

Sumitra picked up a cassette titled *Hits of K.L. Saigal Volume One* from the table.

'One of the greatest singers India ever had. My father is a big fan of K.L. Saigal. When I was a child, he used to play Saigal on a gramophone. I still remember his favourite songs: "Gham diye mushtaqil", "Madhukar shyam hamare chor" and "Jab dil hi toot gaya". Nowadays, nobody listens to Saigal sahab. My husband says it's ridiculous how anybody can enjoy a song sung in a nasal voice.'

Arif smiled, but he was restless. He was still thinking of the lost money. 'How is your father?' he asked.

'He is fine. He is in Katihar now. He owes his life to you.'

'Only God is the saviour.'

Sumitra looked at the tennis rackets cross-nailed to the wall. 'So, you play tennis?' She seemed impressed.

'I used to play tennis. Not any more.'

'My husband also plays tennis. He goes to New Patna Club.'

She got Arif to talk more about his likes and dislikes, his ambitions and dreams. And when Arif spoke, she listened attentively. Arif noticed that Sumitra's pronunciation was impeccable, especially when she used Urdu words.

'Who is this handsome boy?' she asked as she lifted a photo frame from the table.

'My brother, Zakir. He wants to try his luck in films.'

'Mashallah!'

She was looking at a family photograph. Dadi, Amma and Abba were sitting on chairs. Arif, Zakir and their sisters stood just behind them.

'My family,' Arif said.

'You have three sisters?'

'Yes.'

'All of them are beautiful.'

Arif smiled in response.

They stopped talking as soon as Amma returned. Rabiya, his sister, who had come back from college, followed Amma with three cups of tea, plates of suji ka halwa and thick homemade potato chips.

'You must be a busy young man. I'll leave you to your studies,' Sumitra said and walked out with Amma.

In Sumitra's presence, Arif had almost forgotten about the lost money, and now it returned to haunt him. He wondered if he should have accepted the envelope from her. *But how could I?*

At last, he made up his mind to tell Amma. He got up from his bed and searched for his slippers. He stooped to look under the bed and noticed that his white handkerchief was lying there. Stretching himself a little, he caught it with two fingers, and as he pulled it towards him, he shrieked with joy. Inside it were the currency notes held with a rubber band.

Zakir had returned from the PCO and was just walking into the house when he heard Arif yell. Zakir came running to the room. 'What happened, bhaiyya?'

Arif brandished a fistful of 500-rupee currency notes and Zakir's face lit up. He moved closer to his elder brother and hugged him tightly.

Later in the night, Arif held the *Diwan-e-Momin* and

imagined Sumitra's touch. As he flipped through the pages, he was surprised to find his name written on the second page of the book in Urdu. It wasn't his handwriting and it hadn't been there before. It looked like a professional calligrapher had inked it. He wondered if Sumitra knew Urdu. How did a middle-class Maithil Brahmin woman learn a language that was now stigmatized as a 'Muslim language'?

He went through the book, curious to see if she had written anything else. He found a small piece of paper, folded into a square. His heart thudding, he unfolded it. It was an Urdu ghazal in four couplets:

The day began / Craving for a glimpse of a face
You didn't come / Depriving me of your grace
My heart aches / And is in turmoil
My restless soul / Has no peace, even for a while
Time stands still / The minutes become hours
The day loses its brightness / And the fragrance shuns the flowers
Maybe my desire will be fulfilled / Before I die
Or craving I have to go / To the alley of death, beyond the sky

She had signed it with her name.

Subhanallah! He was impressed that Sumitra was an Urdu poet. Her selection of words, the deployment of metaphors and imageries, the radeefs and the qafiyas, everything about her poetry captivated him. He read her poem over and over again, until Amma called him for dinner.

FOUR

Arif sat in one of the third-row seats of the Rabindra Bhavan auditorium, his eyes searching impatiently. Just a few minutes ago, he had seen Sumitra entering the hall. Dressed in a cobalt blue sari and blouse, she had entered through the door adjacent to his seat. But he lost her in the crowd.

Did I really see her or was it a figment of my imagination? He stood up and turned back to have a clear view of the hall, trying to scan the faces.

'Sit down, brother. You're blocking our view,' someone shouted from the row behind. He instantly sat down.

The hall was jam-packed for a Hindi adaptation of Shakespeare's *Hamlet*.

Zakir was playing the Prince of Denmark. The show was in its eighth day and was still drawing packed houses, a rare occurrence for a theatre production in Patna. The city editions of newspapers were replete with favourable reviews.

As the curtains lifted, Arif turned his attention to the play. The ghost of the king made an appearance onstage.

Machines spewed spooky smoke. And then Zakir appeared in a royal get-up, and Arif clapped enthusiastically. The man on his left looked at Arif in bemusement. Embarrassed, he stopped clapping.

After the show, Arif made his way to the make-up room. A guard tried to stop him, but when he learnt that it was Zakir's elder brother he let him into the room.

Sanjay Upadhyaya, the director of the play, a clean-shaven man in his early thirties, was congratulating Zakir. 'You are getting better with each show. This year you must try your luck with the National School of Drama. I am sure you will be selected.'

Arif was proud of how his brother had given life to the character. Zakir could be the next Dilip Kumar or Amitabh Bachchan. He imagined Zakir playing the angry young man Vijay in *Zanjeer*, Prince Salim in *Mughal-e-Azam* and Raj in *Qayamat Se Qayamat Tak*.

'You were stunning in your role! You will go a long way,' Arif said as he hugged his brother.

'Thank you, bhaiyya,' Zakir replied in an unenthusiastic voice.

'What is wrong? Are you okay?' Arif asked, concerned.

'Nothing to worry about, bhaiyya. I am perfectly fine. I have not slept properly for the last four days. Feeling exhausted.'

'Are you coming home with me?'

'No, bhaiyya. I have to discuss something with Sanjay sir. Anyway, the sponsors will drop me in their car.'

'Okay, Zakir. It's already nine forty-five. I must leave now.'

As he stepped outside the auditorium, he scanned the group of people leaving the venue. And there she was!

He walked up to her. 'Namaste,' he said, his voice trembling.

'Namaste.' She did not seem surprised to see him there. Maybe she had seen him inside the hall.

'You came alone?' Arif asked her.

'Yes. There's a day-and-night cricket match today, so my husband . . .' Before she could finish her sentence, a Bajaj auto stopped in front of them with a screech. Its silencer hissed and belched out smoke. The autorickshaw had two male passengers; one of them, a middle-aged man in a kurta, was rubbing tobacco leaves on his palm with his thumb. The other was a man in his early twenties wearing a T-shirt with a high collar.

'One of you, please come and sit in the front seat,' the driver said.

The young man scrutinized Sumitra and Arif before getting down from the vehicle and squeezing himself to settle down beside the driver. Arif got in next to the middle-aged man at the back and Sumitra sat next to him.

During the twenty-five-minute journey Sumitra didn't say anything. She was lost in thought and cracked her knuckles constantly. Arif sat frozen in his seat.

At Naya Mor, Arif insisted on paying the fare, which she reluctantly allowed. Arif looked at Sumitra and smiled. But she remained expressionless.

All the shops at Naya Mor were closed. The lone bulb on a nearby electric pole struggled to keep itself alive. Arif looked around and found that there was no cycle rickshaw. The road was deserted.

'I don't think we'll get any rickshaw at this time,' Arif said.

'Achcha!' she said and they started walking.

'Did you like the play?' Arif attempted conversation. The songs of the crickets from the wild shrubs along the road awkwardly punctuated the silence. He was aware that walking on the streets of Patna late at night was full of risks, especially for a woman.

'It was good and Zakir gave a sterling performance.'

'You shouldn't have come alone.'

'In fact, the girl who played Ophelia is my distant cousin. She insisted that I come. I wanted my husband to come too. But he doesn't miss a single cricket match.' Arif sensed some bitterness creep into her voice. He remembered his meeting with Sumitra's husband; he seemed nice. Arif decided to change the topic.

'Where do your children study?'

'My son Rahul is in St Karen's School in class three. My daughter is in class ten in Indira Gandhi Balika Vidyalaya, Hazaribagh.'

'Achcha. I read your ghazal. It was really good. Your Urdu is so good. How and where did you learn the language?'

'I'll tell you that story some other day,' she said.

They reached a small Sufi shrine when it began to drizzle, and there was a cold wind blowing. Arif saw Sumitra pull her sari pallu to cover her shoulders. There was a power outage and the roads were dark. An old man with a flowing white beard in a green kurta sat on the arched veranda of the shrine, smoking. His face shone in the orange light from a hurricane lamp.

Sumitra stopped before the shrine and offered her respects with folded hands. They had not walked even a hundred yards when the drizzle turned into a full-fledged shower. *Unseasonal October rain, a sure-shot way to catch a cold*, Arif thought and looked around for shelter. A motorcycle whizzed past and startled them. But as its headlight beam flashed, Arif spotted a shuttered shop with an awning and they ran towards it.

The raindrops drummed on the corrugated asbestos canopy. They could barely see anything on the road and there did not seem to be a soul in sight. Arif's watch read eleven. They would not be able to get out of their shelter in that rain. Even though he couldn't see Sumitra clearly, he could sense the restlessness. What if somebody saw them together out in the rain at this time of the night?

Despite the fear of a scandal, he felt a mild thrill. He wanted to say something, but was not sure it was the right time or place to do so. They were silent for a few minutes until Arif spoke.

'Why did you disappear from the hospital without leaving any message for me?'

'That's not true, Arif. I left a letter for you with my contact details. Half an hour after you left to fetch my cousin, another cousin of mine reached the hospital. He got the news of my father's illness from my mother, whom I had called just after my father started talking. My cousin insisted on taking my father to a private hospital in Kankarbagh immediately,' Sumitra said.

'Can I ask you a question?'

'Of course!' she said as she wiped her face with the pallu of her sari. A low voltage bulb flickered back to life overhead and Arif could see her face.

'What should I call you? Should I call you *aunty*?'

'No! Certainly not. I am not that old,' she said irritatedly. 'You can simply call me Sumitra.'

'Okay, Sumitraji.' When he uttered her name he felt like she had kissed him on the nape of his neck, sending a pleasant chill down his spine.

The rain slowed down to a drizzle.

'Let's start walking. I don't think the rain is going to stop.'

As soon as they stepped out on to the road, Arif saw a snake crawl near their feet. He flinched and was about to warn Sumitra when she spotted it too. She shrieked, turned back and grabbed Arif, wrapping her arms around him. Startled, Arif didn't react first. Then he placed his hands around her in a reassuring way and inhaled deeply the fragrance of her hair. The snake was gone, but Sumitra was still clinging to him. Arif felt his skin burn and he breathed as if his lungs had run out of air. He wanted to stay that way for eternity.

A few seconds later Sumitra let go of him, slowly and without looking at him.

'Sorry,' she said and continued walking. Arif followed her.

Within the next five minutes they reached the peepal tree Sumitra worshipped on Saturdays. A cobbled path branched out from the road next to the tree and led to Bank Colony. On the other side of the road was a big arched gate with a carved stone that read: Gate No. 2, Bihar Military Police, 5th Battalion, Patna – 800014. A uniformed constable, wearing a round green cap and a plume of red feathers, stood at the gate. Beyond the gate was a long array of two-storeyed buildings.

'You go home; I can go by myself from here,' Sumitra said.

'No, Sumitraji. I can't allow you to go alone at this time.'

'Okay. Thanks.'

They walked silently.

'Come to my place sometime. We'll share our poetry,' Sumitra said, as her house came into view. The light in her balcony was on; Ramesh was on the balcony, waiting for her. 'Bye.'

'Bye, Sumitraji,' Arif said. He stood by a neem tree not far from her residence and saw Sumitra walk to her house. She climbed the staircase, then appeared on the balcony of her first floor flat and for the next couple of minutes she stood there talking to her husband. Then they walked back into their house and the lights went off.

He tried to recall the last few hours he had spent with her. Was he going to seduce her into a sinful relationship with him? Was he going to wreck a happy family? He hated himself. He was aroused when she had hugged him. He had come too far, too soon. If he didn't stop himself now, he would be doomed forever. What if his parents came to know about his affair? She was a Hindu and this could cause a communal riot. *What if her husband comes to know? He'll certainly kill me.*

Arif stood in front of his house, closed his eyes and recited a verse from the Holy Quran, and decided to crush the bud of his desire before it blossomed into something sinister.

FIVE

On the windswept and moonlit banks of the Ganga, Sumitra, dressed in black, her head covered with the pallu of her sari, beckoned him. The pallu then slipped to reveal her hair, which shone as if it was made of metal. Something fell into the water; Arif tore his eyes away from Sumitra and saw Zakir drowning. He ran towards the river, but heard Sumitra singing in a melancholic voice. He couldn't understand the lyrics but the melody was compelling. Sumitra was now in front of him. She was wearing a sleeveless evening gown which revealed her ample cleavage. Desire began to uncoil inside him. His brother screamed but he couldn't move. He pulled Sumitra into his arms and kissed her passionately, leaving his brother to die.

'Tauba Astaghfar! Tauba Astaghfar! Tauba Astaghfar!' Arif woke up with a start. He sat up, unsettled, his feet tentatively touching the floor, feeling its cool indifference. Arif could hear his brother breathing by his side. Still, to reassure himself, he turned on the light and checked on Zakir. He seemed to be deep in sleep, right next to him, on the bed they shared, his left foot dangling out of the mattress. Bending a little, Arif gently lifted his brother's leg and placed it back on the bed, and affectionately ran his fingers through his hair. On the windowsill were a fat Penguin Classics paperback of *Anna Karenina* and a jug of water. He took a swig directly from the jug and picked up the novel, but then placed it back without opening it.

Getting back into bed, he tried to sleep, but he still felt disconcerted. Was it just a nightmare or was it something else? Didn't his grandmother once mention something about varieties of dreams?

'There are three types of dreams,' she had said. 'Celestial dreams or khwab-e-rahmani are from God, which give insight into future events. Khwab-e-shaitani, satanic dreams, are dirty dreams and nightmares. And psychological dreams or khwab-e-zehani are reflections of what you think about deeply when you are awake.'

Arif wondered if his had been a satanic dream. Or was it a portent of some future calamity? Or was it a divine warning to keep away from Sumitra? He closed his eyes and started reciting from the Surah Al-Baqarah, and slowly drifted off to sleep.

Arif was restless the next morning. He stood outside the bathroom waiting for his turn. With a creaking sound the door opened and his sister Rabiya came out, drying her waist-length hair with a towel, water from her hair dripping on her salwar-kameez. Arif was about to step inside when he heard Nazneen's voice from behind.

'Arif bhaiyya, I have to go to school a bit early. Please let me use the bathroom.'

'Okay, Nazneen,' Arif responded affectionately, 'just give

me my toothbrush and toothpaste from the bathroom. I can wait.' He moved aside to make way for his sister.

Brushing his teeth, Arif walked out on to the rear balcony of his flat.

'Bhaiyya!' Now it was Huma. At fourteen, she was tall for her age. Her features were similar to her sisters' but she was not as fair-complexioned as them. 'Yes, Huma?'

'I need your help with this algebra equation.'

'Of course, show me the problem.'

Arif was quick with maths and solved the problem in five minutes. As soon as Huma left, the nightmare returned to bother him. He thought of talking to Dadi and went to her room. She was reciting from the holy book. But his grandmother had also warned him not to talk about his nightmares, or their effects wouldn't be nullified.

Was he becoming superstitious? Was it really a divine warning to stop him from pursuing Sumitra?

Even thinking of a married woman is an immoral act. The Holy Quran says even the thought of adultery is a sin.

After freshening up, Arif settled down in a wooden chair in his room and began thinking of Sumitra again. He recalled the last time he had seen her, the way she had brushed a tendril of her long hair with her hand. *Ya Allah, what should I do?* He picked up the book on public administration from his bedside table.

'I have to discuss something with you,' Arif said as soon as Zakir entered the room, back from his morning walk in the police stadium.

'What is it, bhaiyya?' Zakir asked, surprised by Arif's serious tone.

'Come upstairs.'

Once on the terrace, Arif paced around for a while and then settled down on the parapet. Zakir stood in front of him.

'Zakir, I don't know if it's appropriate for me to share this with my younger brother,' Arif said, looking away at two sparrows frolicking on the terrace floor.

'Bhaiyya, I am your younger brother, and also your friend,' Zakir said and placed a reassuring hand on Arif's shoulder. 'Can I not be privy to your secrets?'

'How would you react if I tell you that I am crazy about a married Hindu woman with kids?'

'What?'

'Yes, my brother.'

'What did you see in a middle-aged married woman?'

'The woman is so graceful that I can't help myself. Everything about her is special: her confidence, her poise, the way she carries herself, the way she speaks and the way she smiles. But to tell you the truth, I don't know exactly what attracted me to her. I have never felt like this.'

'My dear big brother, the path you are treading is very dangerous. A married woman!' Zakir continued, 'Moreover, the lady is a Hindu. I hope you understand the consequences of pursuing a Hindu woman.'

'Yes, I understand, but my heart doesn't.'

'Think of Abba. Think of Amma. If they find out about this, they will die of shame. Think it over, bhaiyya; only you can draw your own moral boundaries.'

Arif was astonished by Zakir's maturity. He sounded like his elder brother rather than his younger.

'Tell me what I should do.'

'You have no future with that woman. You will only end up destroying the woman's life as well as your own. Forget her. Don't try to meet her again. Go away from Patna for a couple of months if you want.'

'You are right, Zakir. I will–'

But before he could complete his sentence, Amma appeared from nowhere, quite angry.

'What kind of habits have you developed? Breakfast at lunchtime. It is already nine o'clock. Come downstairs and have your breakfast at once.'

They silently followed their mother downstairs. At the entrance of his flat, Arif bent down to pick up the *Times of India* from the floor. His eye fell on the date: 31 August 1992, Monday.

Less than forty days left for the mains, Arif reminded himself.

Desire

SIX

During the month of September, Arif shut himself in his tiny study room, spending all his waking hours preparing for the mains. The previous month Amma had made Abba buy two large cylindrical steel containers to store grains, and these were then placed in the corridor outside his study room. A mason had been deployed to cut through the brick wall and construct a window that opened into the backyard. Amma had also got the study room whitewashed and the table and chair had been given a new coat of polish.

'My son needs privacy to prepare for a prestigious and difficult exam like this,' Arif had heard her saying to Abba.

He stopped going over to Mritunjay's place, fearing he might run into Sumitra. He knew that if she was around, he would not be able to stay away from her. Whenever Mritunjay complained about his reduced visits, Arif invented new excuses.

But Sumitra kept popping up in his mind. The scene from that rainy night played in his mind continuously. Whenever he conjured up the moment she had embraced him, he got goosebumps. At times he also recalled Simran, his childhood crush from Darbhanga, and felt nostalgic. He convinced himself that Sumitra would vanish from his memories the way Simran had.

October finally arrived and Arif felt that he had performed exceptionally well in the exam. He was sure to get an interview call. The very next day he went to Ashok Rajpath and bought the books required to prep for the interview. He also created detailed notes on his personal and academic backgrounds, the areas he would be questioned on during the interview.

'A part of our ancestral house in Jamalpura has collapsed in the rain. One of the walls requires immediate repair. I want you to go there and oversee the construction,' Abba told Arif.

Arif was eager to leave for Jamalpura instantly. This way he would be away from Sumitra. He also wanted to test Zakir's hypothesis – maybe staying away from her would help him forget her. He would also be able to concentrate on his studies. His ultimate dream to join the civil services was just one hurdle away and he couldn't mess up all his hard work and his family's dreams now.

'See, Arif, you are close to your goal. In Jamalpura, you'll have a comfortable space to study for the interview. Here, the continuous footfall of guests will distract you,' Abba said. 'Sometimes I feel guilty for not sending you to a good coaching institute like Mritunjay's father did,' he added with a heavy sigh.

'Don't say that, Abba. You have been a wonderful father.'

~

The bus crossed Gandhi Setu over the majestic Ganga and entered Hajipur. It turned and speeded towards Muzaffarpur. Between Muzaffarpur and Hajipur, there was no road, only a long stretch of potholes and cobbled paths. The bus jerked like a horse cart. A bespectacled old gentleman cursed the chief minister of Bihar, Lalu Prasad Yadav, for the condition of the roads and ridiculed Yadav for claiming that he would make Bihar's roads as smooth as Hema Malini's cheeks.

Often the driver drove through farmlands which were smoother than the uneven roads. The passengers felt a big jerk as the bus descended into a diversion, freshly dug to allow vehicles to pass. A small bridge had caved in for want of repairs.

'All the thieves and thugs are sitting in the assembly and Parliament. No one cares for the public; everybody is busy filling their own pockets. And now we have elected a joker as our chief minister,' remarked a bulky middle-aged man.

'What have the earlier governments done for the betterment of Bihar since Independence? The present chief minister has been here only for the last few years. He can't undo the wrongs of the previous regimes in such a short time,' responded a young man sitting next to Arif. 'The so-called upper castes are yet to digest the fact that a Yadav has become the chief minister of Bihar.'

'It is not a question of caste but of development and good administration,' the old man replied.

The argument continued and more people jumped into the discussion. Arif silently followed the heated conversation.

Just as the bus was about to enter Muzaffarpur, the driver stepped hard on the brakes. The road ahead had been blocked by hundreds of people squatting on the road. 'I think they are protesting the murder of that boy,' someone in the bus called out loudly. Most people were familiar with the story from the local newspapers. The boy, a class seven student, had been kidnapped for ransom. His father, a rich businessman of the city, had been asked by the kidnappers to pay a ransom of twenty lakh rupees. They had warned him not to call the police. But the father of the boy had informed the police. The very next day the boy had been found on the outskirts of Muzaffarpur, his throat slit.

All the passengers were leaning outside their windows, straining to see what was up, and some of them had gotten off the bus to stretch. There was a bus ahead of them and they could hear an argument. It sounded like the other bus driver was asking the protesters to move.

Suddenly, there was a loud crash and the sound of breaking glass. Just as Arif was considering his options, a big stone hit the windscreen of his bus. People pushed each other as they tried to grab their bags and get out of the bus. Clutching his own bag, Arif shoved through the crowd and managed to get out. The vehicle ahead of them was now on fire and people were scattering everywhere. Arif was stunned for just a moment before he came to his senses and, along with a bunch of fellow passengers, began to run away from the rioting crowd. He had no idea which way they were running, but it felt best to stick to a group. Finally they stopped at a small teashop, a few hundred metres away.

The owner had considered shutting down his shop but saw that the mob was focused on the bus and thought he could maybe do some business. There were no buildings in sight. Across the vast expanse of fields the burning buses and the mob were visible. The passengers watched the scene silently and fearfully, ready to run at the first sight of the mob proceeding towards them. Thick black smoke rose into the air like an apparition. For a few minutes the crackling of fire and the distant cries of the mob were the only sounds they could hear.

Surprisingly, police jeeps drove past them in less than five minutes.

'Did you call the police?' someone asked the young teashop owner.

'There is no phone here, bhaiyya. I don't know who could have called them. But it's good they are here.'

'I think the police must have already been on their way, even before the riot broke out,' someone remarked.

The silence broken and with the police headed towards the rioting crowd, the teashop owner started offering tea and locally made buns. The passengers discussed how they should continue their individual journeys. The teashop owner warned them that there was still news of buses being vandalized by the mob on the Motihari–Muzaffarpur road. Most buses had either been cancelled or were taking a detour to Sitamarhi. Arif was surprised that his bus had come this way. People asked each other and the teashop owner for suggestions.

'From Sitamarhi, you can take a train to Inayat Nagar,' one of Arif's fellow passengers suggested to him.

'That's a good idea, thank you,' Arif said as he looked at his wristwatch. It was 12.10 p.m.

By two o'clock, he was in Sitamarhi. After a hot meal of dal, bhaat, tarkari and bhujia at Bhargava Hotel, he reached the railway station and saw that the train was already whistling and puffing, and he ran to board it.

Two hours later, the Darbhanga–Inayat Nagar passenger train crawled to a stop next to a red brick building. 'Inayat Nagar (East)' was painted in black against a white background, the letters fading. A few hundred yards away, Arif could see the river Bagmati's zigzag trajectory. On its makeshift bamboo bridge, a man rode leisurely on his bicycle, seemingly in no hurry to get anywhere.

The river surrounded Inayat Nagar, a small town of three thousand people, on three sides. During the rainy season the town was totally cut off from other parts of India, as the floods would wash the bamboo bridge away. And after the floods the bridge would be built again.

Outside the railway station horse carts were lined up, their drivers yelling names of different villages. Making his way through the crowd of passengers and the people who had come to receive them, Arif came on to a brick lane flanked by shops selling puffed rice, jalebis and balushahi. He turned left into a narrow alley which brought him to a wide road just in front of the Clock Tower. He walked into a dispensary.

'Hakim Sahab ka Shafakhana' read the signboard. The blue lettering had lost its sheen and the once white background had turned the colour of mud. His mother's only brother, Hakim Ajmal Khan, sat alone in his clinic.

He was a short, thin man with a salt-and-pepper beard. The cabinet next to him had a dozen or so plastic jars. Arif instantly recognized one of them labelled 'Sualin' from which he used to steal sweet and fragrant herbal lozenges as a child.

'Assalam alaikum!' Arif greeted as he placed his bag on the floor.

'Walaikum assalam, bhanje.' Hakim sahab stood up and hugged his nephew with a broad smile lighting his face. 'Let's go home. Your aunt has been waiting for you.'

'But why are you closing your clinic so early, mamu? What about your patients?'

'Arrey bhanje, hardly any patients nowadays. Everyone is running to allopathic doctors.' Hakim sahab paused, and then added, 'And there is also the meeting of the Emarat Committee in the evening.'

Arif knew his uncle was the president of the Inayat Nagar Emarat Committee, a non-profit social organization and dispute redressal forum for local Muslims.

Arif did not say anything more and silently walked alongside his uncle.

In front of Hakim sahab's house, chairs and benches were being arranged by three men dressed in lungis and half-sleeved short kurtas.

'A married Muslim woman has been caught red-handed with a Hindu man. The Emarat Committee is going to decide on this matter,' a tall man in his early twenties responded to Arif's question on what the meeting was about.

A bearded man in his fifties greeted Hakim sahab. As the two of them sat down to discuss something, Hakim said to

Arif, 'Bhanje, go inside the house. Say hello to your mami, then have lunch and rest.'

'Yes, mamujaan.'

Inside, fifteen-year-old Farzana, Hakim sahab's only daughter, dressed in a blue salwar-kameez and head covered with her dupatta, wished Arif, 'Assalam alaikum.' Dragging a chair for him from a corner of the veranda, she asked him to sit down.

Arif unzipped the side pocket of his bag and pulled out the latest issue of the *Pakeezah Anchal*. He handed the magazine to her and she seemed genuinely happy.

'Thank you, bhaijaan,' she said softly, and went inside and returned with a glass of water and two poached eggs. The yolks were dark yellow and the eggs had been sprinkled with coarsely ground pepper.

Ten minutes later Farzana's mother, his mami, emerged from one of the rooms. After showering him with the choicest of her blessings, she settled on a chair next to him and asked about his family in Patna.

After a delicious lunch of mutton korma and pulao, Arif stepped out of the house. The townspeople had begun to gather in the lawn in front of the house.

The meeting started after the afternoon prayer. Hakim sahab had changed into a faded black sherwani and ankle-length pyjama, and sat on a wooden chair with an intricately carved armrest. Next to him was his childhood friend, Harihar Prasad Srivastava, a tall, thin man with a thick moustache. Settled on a cushioned wooden chair, he was a special invitee to the committee.

Arif stood under the neem tree at the far corner of the courtyard. His distant cousin from his mother's side, Bilal, a short young man with a scant beard, stood just behind him. By now about a hundred people had gathered to watch the proceedings.

Suddenly, a baby goat emerged from under the wooden chowki, on which some of the junior members of the committee were seated. Seeing the crowd, the goat panicked and started to run here and there.

'Whose goat is it?' Hakim sahab asked in an authoritative voice.

A frightened boy, around ten years old, came out of the crowd.

'Get it away,' somebody shouted.

The boy swiftly caught the goat by its ears and dragged it away, while the crowd made way for them.

Bilal whispered to Arif, voluntarily briefing him about the case, 'Sanjay Kumar Gupta, a teacher at the local primary school, is having an affair with Abida Begum, the wife of Sheikh Waris. Their affair, in fact, was the talk of the town for some time. But this was the first time they were caught together in an objectionable position in a sugarcane field. The elders have decided to resolve it before this becomes a Hindu–Muslim issue.'

Why did she cheat on her husband? Arif wondered, but did not ask Bilal.

Abida Begum, along with some women, was seated on a bench in the nearby veranda, shielded from the crowd by a semi-transparent makeshift curtain. The curtain flapped in a gust of wind and Arif caught a glimpse of Abida's round face and big eyes. He also saw two middle-aged women seated behind her point at her, whisper and snigger.

Is Sumitra attracted to me? Arif asked himself. But he didn't have an answer.

Turning to his right, Arif saw Sanjay standing silently, his head bent, his hands shaking. Next to him stood a dhoti-clad old man in his sixties, with a white stubble, looking anxious, perhaps Sanjay's father.

Abida's husband, Sheikh Waris, was not present.

A committee member asked if Sanjay had anything to say. Sanjay instead burst into tears, his head still bent, his shoulders shaking. In a swift move, his father took off his hawai chappal and started beating him. 'Abey chutia, speak now, why are you silent?'

Harihar Prasad intervened, 'Ram Prasad! Stop this immediately,' and snatched the chappal from him. Then it was the old man's turn to weep. 'The boy has brought shame to our family. I wish he had never been born.'

A tall man with a clean-shaven, pale face stood up to speak. 'Mohtarma Abida Begum, what do you have to say about this allegation?'

'That's Syed Hafiz Ahmed, sahab,' Bilal kept up his commentary.

Through the curtain, Arif saw Abida Begum stand up. 'If I have done anything wrong, Allah will punish me on the Day of Judgement.'

'If you want to live in our society, you have to follow its conventions,' Hakim sahab said. 'Your behaviour is against our religion and culture.'

Abida Begum's voice became acerbic as she replied, 'Where was our society when my husband was lying in the hospital? Where was our society when my daughter was married off to a man twice her age because we couldn't afford dowry for a younger groom? Is dowry not against our religion? I know that many among the esteemed members of the Emarat Committee also took dowry for their sons' marriages. Why didn't the Emarat summon them for an explanation? Let it be. As far as Sanjay sahab is concerned, I respect him a great deal. He has always helped us in times of trouble. I tried to pay our debts by being nice to him. That's all.'

A man with a soot-black beard stood up. 'Shut up, you shameless woman!' His body trembled in anger and his untrimmed beard fluttered in the breeze as he spoke.

'Mohammed Nasir Ali sahab gets angry easily,' Bilal whispered to Arif.

Hakim sahab silenced Nasir Ali and asked Abida Begum, 'Did you come to us for help?'

'Do you expect me to go from door to door with a begging bowl?'

Nasir Ali again rose and shouted, 'Shut up!'

This time Abida stopped talking. She covered her face with the loose end of her sari. There was agitated murmuring among the crowd.

What kind of a shameless woman is this? Arif thought. He did not like the idea of humiliating a woman publicly, but he also didn't like the way Abida defied the Emarat Committee. *At least she should show some remorse for what she has done.*

Hakim sahab turned and whispered something to Harihar Prasad. A few senior members joined in by pulling their chairs closer to them in a circle.

Bilal said to Arif, 'Sheikh Waris is really a eunuch. He has no control over his wife, nor is he able to fuck her; that is why she offered her pussy to this Hindu boy.'

A bemused Arif looked at Bilal, but said nothing.

The committee announced its decision: Sanjay Kumar Gupta had to atone for his improper conduct. He was asked to spit on his chappal and then lick it and promise the committee that he would not repeat the mistake. Abida was let off with a warning that if she did not mend her ways, the committee would take severe action against her.

Sanjay cried inconsolably. He bent to weakly spit on his pair of worn-out hawai chappals, with their webbed blue straps and white insoles, both of which had blue patches at all the pressure points. As soon as he licked the chappal, he retched. In the veranda Abida Begum shifted restlessly on the bench.

Harihar Prasad remarked, 'This is enough punishment for now.' Everyone nodded.

Arif felt sorry for the man.

He imagined himself and Sumitra in place of Sanjay and Abida, and shivers went down his spine. He wiped the beads of perspiration on his forehead.

~

The same evening Arif asked his aunt if she would accompany him to Jamalpura.

'Farzana will go with you. For months, Apa has been asking us to visit her. It is not possible for all of us to go but I promised to send Farzana,' his aunt said. She and Arif's paternal uncle's wife were sisters.

Part of the twenty-kilometre stretch between Inayat Nagar and Jamalpura was paved with loose bricks, but most of it was a kuccha road that sometimes ceased to exist, and instead a slushy bed, where drainage from houses opened directly on to the road, appeared. A Mahindra jeep plied twice every day between Inayat Nagar and Shamshad Nagar, from where Jamalpura was only five kilometres away, and people either walked the rest of the journey or arranged for a bullock cart. For the first part of the journey, people were stuffed into the jeep like cotton sacks in a truck, with four passengers instead of two in the front seat, the driver occupying only half of his own seat, his other half jutting out of the jeep. More people precariously held on to the jeep from the back, swinging to and fro through the ride. A few also sat on the roof. The jeep lurched and shook, jolting the passengers all the way.

To spare Arif and Farzana this tortuous journey, Hakim sahab had hired a bullock cart for the journey from Inayat Nagar to Jamalpura.

But Arif resented having to travel in the bullock cart with Farzana because he suspected that it was his aunt's scheme to get him to know Farzana so that he would agree to marry her.

The next morning Arif sat on the veranda with his cup of tea and his aunt waxed eloquent about Farzana. 'You know she has done so well in the Fauquania examinations.'

Even a table and a bench can pass the madrasa board examinations, Arif thought.

His aunt continued, 'She is an expert in cooking, knitting, sewing and embroidery.'

Arif knew two things. His relationship with Sumitra was not going to go anywhere. But also, despite Abba's word to Hakim sahab, he was not going to marry Farzana. Arif had faint memories from the day Farzana was born, when Abba had announced to the crowd of relatives that she would be his daughter-in-law. Arif had even clapped at his father's proclamation without having understood its future implications.

To change the topic, he asked, 'Mami, when is the bullock cart coming?'

'It is already at the gate. The bullock cart driver is tying the wahar.'

It was taboo for women to travel in an open bullock cart, so the driver had to tie a canopy over the cart. Arif was relieved as the wahar would also protect them from the sun.

Homemade sweets and snacks were packed in a bamboo basket and placed at the back of the cart, along with the travel bags carrying Arif's and Farzana's clothes and other personal belongings. Farzana sat inside the canopy. It was covered on all sides with thick cloth except in the front where a semi-transparent fabric had been hung as a curtain and tied with a string to allow air to enter. Arif sat with a part of his body inside the canopy and part out.

The cart driver sat on his seat outside at the front end of the cart, his legs dangling, his hands holding the reins of the bullocks. His name was Yaqoob Ali. A lanky man with a meagre beard, he was from the same locality of Inayat Nagar where Hakim sahab lived.

They started at 10 a.m. and by noon they were in Panchkurwa. It was unusually hot for November. Propped against one of the railings, Farzana was snoozing, sweating inside the canopied cart. To avoid the sun, Arif also took shelter under the canopy and immediately felt awkward to be so close to Farzana. She was fair with sharp facial features and looked older than her age. Her long tresses fell below her waist. There was no sign of make-up, but still she was attractive. Arif wondered for a moment if he should say yes. But the moment passed.

He remembered Farzana as a five-year-old girl clinging to him and asking him to buy her chocolate. Also, how could a future IAS officer have a semi-literate village girl for a wife? But whom would he marry in the end?

Just out of Panchkurwa, Yaqoob stopped the bullock cart near a neem tree and suggested that they should have lunch. At a hailing distance were half a dozen thatched shops selling tea, samosas, grains, vegetables and other items of daily needs.

'What have you packed for lunch?' Arif asked Farzana.

'Paratha, fried potatoes and roasted kulma,' Farzana said in a mellow voice. She took out three tiffin boxes kept in the back of the bullock cart.

As she opened the box of kulma, the idea of eating six-month-old sun-dried, spiced minced beef didn't appeal to him. Beef was never cooked in his house at Patna. His father had banned it from the kitchen a year before Arif was born.

'Many Hindu friends come to our house. We must

respect their sensibilities. Anyway, we have the option of eating mutton or chicken,' Abba would say.

When Farzana handed him a plate to pass to Yaqoob, the smell of the roasted kulma almost made him throw up. Arif cleared his throat and spat on the ground and then turning to Farzana, said, 'Please, give me the fried potatoes only. I don't eat kulma.'

Yaqoob began chewing his paratha and kulma contentedly.

After lunch Yaqoob suggested they order tea from an open-air teashop a stone's throw from where their bullock cart was parked. Arif didn't want to have tea, but guessed that Yaqoob needed a cup. He gave Yaqoob a five-rupee note for three cups.

Sipping the tea, Yaqoob said, 'You know, Arif bhai, this is a Bhumihar village. All bloody Jan Sanghis and communally minded. Only three Muslim houses in this village. Last month a poor Muslim's house was burnt down when he was caught with beef in his bag. The poor guy was beaten badly by the youth in the village. The Muslims of the neighbouring villages were very angry, and it looked as if there would be a riot. Finally, the police intervened and arrested the culprits.'

'Then what happened?' Arif asked.

'The police released all the suspects for lack of evidence and instead warned the Muslims in the area to refrain from eating beef or slaughtering cows. They say it is against the law of the land.' Yaqoob seemed agitated. 'What kind of law is it which prohibits people from eating their food?'

Tethered to the neem tree the oxen were munching on green bamboo leaves and dry hay. Yaqoob released them and then tied them to the yoke before taking his seat. As he prodded them with a bamboo stick, they heard a large crowd. The air around them reverberated with chants of 'Jai Shri Ram'. Arif saw fear dancing on Yaqoob's face as he pulled the bridle with all his might to stop the oxen.

A stocky, dark man with a handlebar moustache holding a triangular saffron flag hoisted on a bamboo stick was leading a group of around eighty people. They kept chanting 'Jai Shri Ram' in loud, passionate voices as they passed by. Thankfully, they didn't pay much attention to the bullock cart.

'What was that, Yaqoob bhai?' Arif asked when the procession was gone and the bullock cart started moving.

'I told you earlier; this is a village full of Jan Sanghis. And now Suresh Singh, a former smuggler and a BJP MLA, has started this programme called Prabhat Pheri to polarize the Hindus. The flag they were carrying is called the Ram Dhwaj, the flag of Lord Rama.

'Achcha.' Arif nodded.

'Even in Inayat Nagar, some Hindu youths tried to take out similar processions and there was communal tension. But Hariharji, the only sensible Hindu in Inayat Nagar, intervened and nothing happened. However, his son Shashidhar . . .' Yaqoob rambled on but Arif tuned out, sleepy from the meal.

As they entered Shamshad Nagar, three adolescent boys playing gilli-danda in the middle of the road stopped their game and moved aside. One of them called out to the others, 'See, Zulfikar, some bride is going. The bridegroom is sitting in the front of the bullock cart.' He pointed at Arif and giggled. Then they started following the bullock cart and began singing:

Lali lali doliya mein lali re dulhaniya
Piya ki piyari bholi bhali re dulhaniya

(In a red palanquin is a beautiful and innocent bride
This lovely bride is her husband's beloved)

Arif flushed. From the corner of his eye he saw Farzana blushing, her cheeks turning red.

Yaqoob scolded the children, 'Go away, you rascals.' But the children did not pay heed and followed the cart till the end of the village.

Remembering his own childhood in Jamalpura, Arif had to smile. Zakir, he and their friends had always run behind a bullock cart that seemed to be carrying a bride and had sung the same song.

The minarets of the Jama Masjid of Jamalpura loomed on the east, and the scene flowed into the domes of the mausoleum of Hazrat Baba Pir Jamaluddin Khan Rahamatullah Alaih. They were close to their destination.

A bicycle pulled up next to the bullock cart.

'Assalam alaikum,' Arif greeted Abdul Waheed Khan, his Badke baba, father's elder brother, and jumped out to greet him.

They followed his bicycle into the village. After a nap and another glass of tea at Badke baba's place, Yaqoob began his long ride back to Inayat Nagar.

In the evening, Arif sat down for dinner with Badke baba and his cousin Muneer. The rectangular courtyard where they sat on a wooden platform was flanked on two sides by four grain storage cylinders made of hay and mud. In the corner was a green-coloured iron handpump.

'Bhai told me that you don't eat mughal-e-azam.' Badke baba used the code name for beef. 'So, I had to go all the way to Shamshad Nagar to buy mutton. In our poor village only a handful can afford mutton.' Although Arif's father was younger to him, Abdul Waheed Khan held him in great regard for having completed his studies against all odds and getting a job in the police department.

'How are Azmati baji and Rahmati?' Arif asked after his uncle's daughters as he helped himself to mutton korma.

'Azmati is in Delhi. Her husband runs a lathe machine repair workshop. And Rahmati is in Kathmandu. Her husband has started a bakery shop. However, he has had some trouble with the Nepalis. They say Indians are Madhesias and have no right to live in Nepal.' He finished his dinner and burped as he drank water.

'Did you like the food, beta?' his aunt Saleha Begum asked him, standing in the veranda, trying to keep the pallu of her sari from slipping from her head.

'Delicious,' Arif remarked. His aunt responded with a smile and began to remove the dishes.

'Muneer bhai, let's go for a walk,' Arif turned to his cousin.

'Yes,' Muneer said, rubbing his tummy.

They came out on to the road leading away from the village. It was a full moon night.

'So how is Sadaqat?' Arif asked about one of his childhood friends in Jamalpura.

'He is as hopeless as ever. I heard he is having an affair with a chamar girl.'

'You don't say!'

'Married at ten and widowed at the age of twelve, Chameli is now Sadaqat's paramour. But one good thing is that he has stopped drinking tadi.'

'That is really good news.'

'Also, recently he got into trouble with the village elders for allegedly writing a poster.'

'A poster?'

'Last month, on a Friday morning, a poster written in Urdu was found pasted on the wall of the old bungalow facing the Jama Masjid. It read:

Hashim Khan – *Rangeen Mizaj* (The Flirt)
Sagir Khan – *Betichod* (The Daughter Fucker)
Raees Khan – *Chughalkhor* (The Slanderer)
Sartaj Khan – *Randibaaz* (The Whoremonger)
Saeikh Rahmat – *Aag Lagwa* (The Troublemaker)
This poster is written by Sadaqat Ali Khan

These were respectable and powerful people of the village. A meeting was convened in front of the mosque to discuss this mischief. Sadaqat denied his involvement in this episode and said, 'Do you think I am a fool to sign my name on the poster if I had actually written it?'

'People were not convinced. They asked Sadaqat to write whatever was written on the poster. And he did. Both the handwritings were different. He was exonerated.

'Achcha.'

'But the contents of the poster were mostly true,' Muneer concluded and chuckled.

They had walked almost a quarter of a mile away from the village. And as the call for the night prayer was heard on the mosque's loudspeakers, Muneer turned to Arif and said, 'Arif, I have to go for prayer.'

'Okay, Muneer bhai.'

Muneer started walking briskly towards the mosque.

Arif was following his cousin in a leisurely manner when he saw Sadaqat approaching from the other side.

After exchanging pleasantries, Arif began to walk with Sadaqat.

Sadaqat was carrying a hurricane lamp and water in a lota. Arif guessed he was going to the fields. In his village 'going to the fields' meant going to take a shit.

He asked Sadaqat about the poster episode. Sadaqat laughed and said, 'Don't tell anyone. I did paste the poster there. I had one of my friends in the neighbouring village write it.'

'I heard that you are in love with a village girl,' Arif teased his former classmate.

'How do you know?' Sadaqat blushed.

'Magic.' Arif laughed.

'Arif bhai, you are an old friend. I'll not hide anything from you. Her name is Chameli. She is a Hindu and that too from an untouchable caste. A chamar, to be exact. My family would never agree to this match. But I don't care; I'll marry only her.'

'That's good.'

'Let it be! Tell me about yourself. Surely, you must have a girlfriend in Patna?' Sadaqat asked, laughing.

He was tempted to tell him about his fascination for

Sumitra, but didn't. 'No, Sadaqat bhai, I am not as lucky as you are.'

'I don't believe you. Tall and handsome men like you can easily enchant any girl. I have heard that Patna girls are very liberal.'

They had reached the pulia, the tiny bridge over the Karpoori Thakur canal. Though built in the 1970s, there was still no water flowing in it.

'I'll be back in ten minutes.' Sadaqat descended into the dry canal and started walking towards the bhutia gachhi, the ghost orchard abutting the small piece of open land used as a cremation ground by the Hindus of the village.

Not even two minutes had passed when Arif saw a feminine figure silhouetted against the full moon walking towards the bhutia gachhi from the other side. Arif's grandma had told him that many years ago a rakash had been seen around here. A rakash was a type of ghost with a hundred eyes on its body. That's how the orchard came to be known as bhutia gachhi or the haunted orchard. But should an educated person like him believe in ghost stories?

Then he realized that must be Chameli.

Arif saw her climb into the canal and walk towards the bhutia gachhi. He was overtaken by curiosity and, without thinking, he got down into the canal and walked towards the bhutia gachhi as well, making his way through the wild growth. A shiver ran down his spine as he thought of the snakes and other creatures that lurked in the undergrowth. He ducked under the low branches of the litchi trees and reached a point from where he could see Sadaqat sitting in the orchard. He strained his eyes to see better, and in the light of Sadaqat's hurricane lamp, he could also see Chameli lying on his lap. As Sadaqat's hands strayed into her blouse, she slapped his hands and said, 'Not before marriage.' Their conversation was audible in the quiet night. Sadaqat kissed the girl on her cheeks and lips. His hands strayed into her blouse again, but she didn't stop him this time. Pushing her on the ground, he was on top of her. Arif imagined himself with Sumitra in a mango orchard.

'No, Sadaqat!' Chameli suddenly pushed Sadaqat away. Sadaqat was laughing. Arif was drawn back to reality, regretting his lustful thoughts about Sumitra. What Sadaqat was trying to do with Chameli was wrong, a sin. What he had fantasized about Sumitra was also wrong, a sin.

'Chameli, I have to leave early today. My friend Arif is waiting for me at the pulia.'

'But when are we going to Kathmandu?'

'Very soon.' Sadaqat got up.

Arif rushed back to the pulia.

~

The people of Jamalpura were early sleepers. Even in the month of November, when the weather was cool and the sky was clear, the village was in deep slumber by eight thirty. But Arif was awake. There was silence everywhere except for the singing of crickets that could be heard from the nearby fields, punctuated from time to time by the howling of jackals. Arif had acquired the habit of sleeping late at

Police Colony where nobody slept before eleven. His mind wandered to Sumitra again and he worried if he'd ever be able to erase her from his thoughts.

The bedroom in Jamalpura was huge, almost triple the size of the bedrooms in Patna. A 1960s'-style four-poster teak-wood bed with intricate carvings occupied one-fourth of the space. The bed was his mother's wedding gift from her father but despite the passage of many years, it still looked sturdy. The room also had a study table and a chair of shisham wood and an almirah. Two windows opened to a view of the main mosque of the village.

To distract himself, Arif opened the almirah hoping to find something interesting to read. Among the moth-eaten old copies of *Dastan-e-Amir Hamza*, *Tilsm-e-Hoshruba* and *Alif Laila*, he spotted a couple of his old diaries, buried beneath books from his school. Lying in his bed he began reading his diary entries on Simran. He could vividly remember the day he had seen Simran for the first time, almost ten years ago.

~

31 October 1984

Around eleven in the morning, one of Abba's collegues, Mr Mishra, came running to our house. He looked upset and spoke in a choked voice.

'Khan sahab, the Iron Lady is no more.'

Abba's face turned white and then he rushed to get his radio. All India Radio news confirmed the death of Mrs Gandhi.

By evening it was known that the prime minister's two Sikh bodyguards had assassinated her. Rumours were afloat that Sikhs were celebrating her death and were distributing sweets in the local gurdwara. I had also heard someone saying that this was revenge for Operation Blue Star.

The prime minister's death is like a news item from the papers to me: Two die in a road accident. Boat capsizes in river Sone, three persons missing. I don't understand why Father is so sad for somebody who is not related to or even known to us.

1 November 1984

Zakir and I came home from the playground in the evening. I was pleased that the electricity had not gone off as it usually did. Nazneen and Rabiya sat on the floor playing Ludo but my ladli little Huma sat on a chair, looking sad. When I asked her what happened, she complained that Nazneen and Rabiya were not letting her play as she was too young. I wanted to be the big brother. With mock authority I asked the other two: 'Arrey, how dare you not let my favourite sister play? Do ask Huma to join your game.' They didn't have a choice but to ask her to join. I felt great affection for my sisters as I watched Rabiya tell Huma, 'Don't cry if you lose.' Dadi lay on the cot reading a magazine in Urdu, The Huda Islamic Digest, *her glasses perched on the tip of her nose.*

Seeing me she asked, 'Does my grandson want anything to eat?'

'No, Dadi,' I said and hugged her.

'Should I cook your favourite potato snacks or halwa?' Dadi asked, planting a soft kiss on my forehead.

'This is not fair, Dadi! You reserve all your love for bhaiyya,' Zakir complained.

'That is not so, Zakir,' Dadi said, smiling. 'Just tell me what you want.'

'Halwa!' Zakir responded immediately.

I went inside, changed into a lungi and kurta and returned to the veranda with the day's newspaper. There was a huge photograph of the deceased prime minister dominating the front page.

'Please come inside, sir,' I heard Abba say. A jeep had pulled up in front of our house. Abba ushered Sardar Swarn Singh with his wife into our bedroom, which also served as the living room. Swarn Singh was the deputy commandant of the Bihar Military Police and Abba's senior. He looked grave and worried.

A middle-aged Sikh man in a dark brown turban and a plump woman in a maroon sari also walked in after Sardar Swarn Singh. A girl in a green salwar-kameez with Sadhna cut hair followed. As I looked at the girl, I couldn't breathe for a while. I had never experienced something like this before. The girl looked beautiful.

'Khan, meet Dr Balwinder Singh, his wife and their daughter, Simran. Doctor sahab is my wife's cousin.' Mr Singh introduced his brother-in-law and his family.

Simran. Simran. Simran.

Even as I was captivated by her, the conversation interested me. Why was this beautiful girl in my house?

'Dr Singh lives in Kathalbari where some shops belonging to Sikhs have been vandalized. So he took shelter in our house. There too ten to fifteen constables gathered in front of our bungalow and started raising slogans against Sikhs. My wife panicked and thought we would be safer in a Muslim officer's house.'

'Doctor sahab did the right thing,' Abba said.

'Bhaisahab, please don't tell anybody that we are here,' Mrs Singh said. Her hands were shaking. I felt sorry for her.

'Memsahab, don't worry. Nothing will happen in Police Colony,' Abba said as he picked up the radio from a wooden table and tried to tune it. He was probably searching for the news again.

'The anti-Sikh riots continue unabated in Delhi,' came a voice from the radio.

I stood in the corridor against the wall, looking inside the room once in a while, stealing glances of Simran's face. She looked tense, and beautiful.

By nine thirty in the night the electricity went out, engulfing the room in darkness. I heard the sound of gunfire from a distance. What if the neighbourhood Hindus decide to attack Simran and me and my family? I was terrified. I was reminded of that time in Inayat Nagar, five years ago.

There had been minor scuffles between some Hindus and Muslims over the organization of Durga Puja in the town. The rumour was that Hindus were going to attack Muslim colonies in the night. I can still remember how scared I was that Hindu mobs might attack us. I can still feel that fear.

Amma came into the room with a hurricane lamp and placed it on the stool. Around the same time, there was a knock on the door. I was startled and I looked at Abba. He looked alarmed too. Simran was holding her mother in a tight embrace, sobbing. My heart raced. I was sure the neighbourhood Hindus had come to know about our guests.

Abba gestured everyone to be silent as he went out of the room.

I automatically followed Abba. Holding the lamp in his left hand, Abba moved at a measured pace. He stood close to the door, trying to listen to the sound outside, and then unbolted the door. A tall young man with a clean-shaven face stood at the door, along with someone who looked like a bodyguard holding a Sten gun.

'Jai Hind, sir,' Abba greeted him.

'Jai Hind, Khan. Where is Singh sahab? I have come here to take him and his family to my house. I just returned from Muzaffarpur and found out about the afternoon incident. I'll take strict action against all the constables involved.'

Abba brought them inside.

'Singh sahab, the Commandant of Bihar Military Police Ranbir Singh is here to take you with him.'

Simran had been in my house only for a few hours, but her presence lingered on even after she left. I dreamed of Simran. This morning I feel inspired to dedicate my first poem to her. (See the last page in the diary.)

For the next one year, Arif began to follow Simran. He sat in a tea stall close to Simran's house for hours, just to get a glimpse of her. He stood outside her school as well. He visited the local gurdwara on Sundays. He filled his diary with poetry about her.

Despite his obsession for Simran, he couldn't muster the courage to talk to her. Even after pursuing her for three years, he couldn't even bring himself to say hello to her. Once he planned to hand her a letter, but at the last moment he changed his mind.

Then, his father was transferred to Patna and they moved immediately.

After arriving in Patna, Arif remained in the grip of a strange longing for Simran for many months. He wrote hundreds of ghazals and listened to sad songs by Mukesh and Mohammed Rafi.

One day, six months later, at a magazine stall, Arif saw the latest issue of *Sportstar* with a centre spread of Steffi Graf holding aloft the Wimbledon trophy. In a white Adidas tracksuit, she looked astonishing. She was the most beautiful tennis player he had ever seen.

Arif promptly fell in love with the glamorous Fräulein from Germany. Simran moved out of his orbit of daydreams.

It was his infatuation with Steffi that introduced him to lawn tennis. He wanted to play the game that she played. Borrowing a few books from Sinha Library, he tried to understand the basics of tennis. He watched matches on television regularly to learn the nuances of the game. He planned to start playing the game.

At the age of seventeen it was very unlikely that he could make it to the competitive level. Arif knew this, but still the incorrigible optimist inside him believed that he was going to be the next Boris Becker or Stefan Edberg. Sometimes he daydreamed of winning the mixed doubles title at Wimbledon with Steffi Graf, and hugging and kissing her after the match. He even sent a letter to her Mannheim, Baden-Württemberg address in Germany, asking her to be his pen friend.

Arif, of course, had no money to buy tennis rackets. He had visited Chhabra Sports at Fraser Road and Kohli Sports near Bakerganj police station. A good quality racket cost more than a thousand rupees. Even a Jalandhar-made local brand, Kay Kay racket, which was made of steel and was more of a mallet than a racket, cost three hundred rupees.

Disappointed, he returned home. He dared not ask his father for money to buy a racket, something he knew would be considered wasteful expenditure.

But luck was in his favour as the new commandant, the head of the Bihar Military Police Unit, was very fond of the game. The first thing he did after joining was to have the old red clay court refurbished. A tennis coaching camp was organized for the children of Police Colony. Amma convinced Abba to buy rackets for him and Zakir. One of Bihar's top tennis players, Chandra Bhushan, had come to train the children. Arif picked up the basics easily. Tennis became his obsession, pushing Simran to the margins of his mind.

Steffi regularly appeared in his dreams now, sometimes dressed in a beautiful chiffon sari or a pink full-sleeved salwar suit. He bought a poster of her from Book-en-Amee in Boring Road for a princely sum of twenty-five rupees. He inscribed AK+SG on all his books.

Three years of hard work fetched Arif a place in the Bihar Junior team. That year, 1989 to be precise, the Junior National Championship was to be organized in Patna. He was excited when he heard that some of the big names in junior tennis would be playing in the nationals – Leander Paes, Gaurav Natekar, Ashif Ismael and many more.

It was his first day at the New Patna Club.

All six grass courts of the club shone an emerald green. The ambience was electric. He saw Leander Paes talking to the chairman of the Bihar Tennis Association. Five girls stood a couple of yards away in their colourful tracksuits. A strange kind of uneasiness gripped Arif as he reached court no. 4 near the eastern end of the club. His heart was beating very fast and beads of perspiration began to appear on his forehead.

His first match was with a local player, Jagat Srivastava, who appeared to be a couple of years younger than him. Jagat was a bit plump and shorter than him.

Arif looked at his opponent and at the other players around him. Everybody was wearing branded T-shirts and shorts and carried graphite- or carbon-framed rackets, not only the well-known players but even other newcomers from Bihar, including his rival in the first match. Arif looked at his Symonds wooden racket and his cheap Power shoes, a factory second purchased from Bata's factory outlet at Digha, and his oversized fake Nike T-shirt. Even the spectators were well dressed. Arif felt like the odd man out. Embarrassed and uneasy, he lost the match even before it began. During the match he served one double fault after another. His service returns were so weak that his opponent killed them easily. From the stands Zakir kept shouting throughout the match to encourage him. But that didn't help Arif and the match ended with 6-1, 6-0 in favour of Arif's opponent.

After the match, Arif was heartbroken. He vowed he would never visit the New Patna Club again. He stopped playing tennis. The rackets were hung up on the wall. A black-and-white poster of Meena Kumari replaced the Steffi Graf poster. When he watched tennis on TV, he saw Steffi hitting her trademark forehand, lifting trophies and giving interviews, as millions of her fans did across the world. During those moments, he continued to be filled with yearning for Steffi and tennis.

He would forget Sumitra just as he had forgotten about Simran. He just needed a distraction, he convinced himself, as he fell asleep and dreamt of Sumitra again.

SEVEN

The construction of the wall was in the final stages. Arif sat on a cane chair near the worksite, with a book on the history of Bihar in his hands and the lovely Sumitra on his mind.

'Muneer bhai, the mason has told me that a pandooa has been seen in our village river. Is it true?' Arif asked Muneer to distract himself from Sumitra.

Muneer had just walked in with an aluminium kettle full of tea and a few small kulhads and placed them on a bench.

'Yes, it is true,' Muneer said as he handed a kulhad of tea to Arif. Muneer filled another kulhad for himself and settled on a chair close to Arif's. He gestured to the mason and other workers to come and get their tea.

'Now, Arif bhai will believe that pandooas are real.' The mason, a man in his early twenties, who had just walked in, said as he helped himself to a kulhad of tea.

'I don't believe in the river ghost. It's just a superstition,' Arif said as he rose from his seat and placed the book on the nearby bench where another worker, a lanky man in his early fifties, sat loudly slurping his tea.

'Arif, this is not a superstition. Many men from our village have seen a woman in a bridal sari, strolling along the banks of the river,' Muneer insisted.

'Really?'

'Yes.'

Arif remembered his Dadi's words about pandooas. 'See, they are departed souls who have committed suicide by jumping into the river. They try to kill whoever they find near the river at an odd time like noon or after dusk. They kill so they can have some company too.'

'Tell me, who has seen the river ghost?'

'Hasrat Khan saw it first some months ago. He had gone for an evening walk and saw a beautiful woman in a colourful sari. He stopped and asked her who she was. She didn't reply and looked straight into his eyes, a cold look, her face devoid of any expression. He felt a sudden shiver and started to briskly walk back towards the village. Two minutes later, he noticed his gamchha missing from his shoulder. He turned back and found it lying a few yards away.'

'Then?'

'Hasrat Khan thought it must have slipped off his shoulder. He went back and picked it up. But he had barely walked a couple of steps when the gamchha disappeared again. He turned around to find it but couldn't see it anywhere. Feeling something amiss, he started walking faster. As he was about to reach the outskirts of the village, he saw his gamchha hanging from a small fig tree by the road. He reached out to grab it, but then stopped himself. How did his gamchha get here? He was debating whether to touch the gamchha or not, when he realized there was someone standing near him. He turned and saw the same woman standing a few yards away, her face still devoid of any expression. Horrified, he started running as fast as he could. He reached Shoaib Khan's bungalow and then collapsed.'

'You very well know, Muneer bhai, that Hasrat Khan is not trustworthy. I am sure he made up this ghost story.'

'Okay. Now, I am going to share the experience of a man you'll certainly believe.'

'Let's see.'

'Last week Maulvi Murtuza, the sixty-five-year-old imam of the Jama Masjid, was returning from the neighbouring village. The sun had set. It was the time of the evening prayer. He decided to offer namaz at the bank of the river. After performing ablutions in the river, he spread his gamchha on the sand and stood up to pray. As he finished his namaz and bent to collect his gamchha, he saw her smiling. He had heard in the village that a newly married Rajput girl from a neighbouring village had jumped into the river. And here she was, dressed in bridal wear, bedecked with jewellery. He recited Ayat-ul-Kursi from the Holy Quran and started running at once. He stopped only after reaching the village.'

'I am not saying Maulvi sahab would lie but I think he must have mistaken some ordinary woman for a river ghost,' Arif argued.

'I know you won't believe unless you see a pandooa with your own eyes,' Muneer said, a bit annoyed.

'That's a good idea. Let's go to the river. I would like to meet the river ghost,' Arif said.

'You shouldn't make fun of ghosts and djinns.'

'So, you are not coming with me?'

'If you insist, I'll come with you.'

It was ten in the morning when they started for the river.

Walking on the slushy mud road, Arif saw a handwritten poster on a defunct electric pole. It warned wayfarers about the threat of the river ghost. It said a newly married Rajput girl had committed suicide by jumping into the river and had become a pandooa, and advised against going to the river alone after dusk. There were electric poles everywhere in the village, but no electricity.

Arif and Muneer walked past the tiled houses with mud walls and thatched hutments, and then came to Shoaib Khan's bungalow. An Englishman, an indigo cultivator, had built it almost 150 years ago. While leaving India in the 1930s, he had handed the house to his only friend in the village, Shoaib Khan's father.

They climbed up the embankment of mud and sand that surrounded Jamalpura and other nearby villages. As they were climbing down, Arif looked for a suitable place to pee. As the pee hit the ground, he searched for a dry piece of earth or grit for kuluf. He brought a chunk of earth near the tip of his penis and allowed it to absorb the drops of urine and then threw it away.

'Arif, always look before you pee. See, you have pissed on ashes. Never do that again. Bones and ashes are the food of djinns. This can anger them,' Muneer remarked. Arif laughed, shaking his head slightly, but said nothing.

Despite the cold weather, they jumped into the river. They were not alone. There were four or five fishermen throwing their nets in the river and two farmers supervising their sugarcane fields on the other side of the river. They frolicked in the river for hours.

In the evening, Arif fell sick with fever and chills. He trembled and shivered continuously. Hanif the compounder, a retired army man, was called. He had experience working in military hospitals and was the best qualified doctor in the village. The shivering refused to dissipate. Arif's uncle scolded Muneer for his carelessness when he learnt about the trip to the river.

'Arif must be possessed by the river ghost,' Arif's aunt remarked. On her advice, Badke baba called the imam of the Jama Masjid. He recited from the holy book and blew his benediction on Arif with pungent onion breath.

Arif slept through the night, which went by uneventfully. But in the morning the shivering returned, and it was relentless. Two blankets and a quilt were needed to cover him. A wood fire was kept burning. Hanif was called once again and he assured everyone that in a couple of days Arif would be all right.

After taking his medicines, Arif fell asleep again and dreamt about Sumitra as a sixteen-year-old girl with braided hair, but still in a sari. Arif called out to her but she did not respond.

When he woke up, he was shivering again. Badke baba wanted to take him to the doctor in Inayat Nagar but Arif was in no position to travel in the overcrowded jeep.

Many people came to see Arif. Among the visitors were neighbours – Nagma, once a moon-faced beauty, now a bony-faced woman, married to a middle-aged widower with five children; Sahab Khan, once a child molester, now a bearded man with prayer beads in his right hand; Musa Raza, once a poor orphan, now a successful industrialist in Delhi; and Asma Begum, an old lady whom Arif called Asma dadi. Asma Begum told Saleha Begum that it was nothing but Jarwa-Jaraiya.

'Dulhan! You must call Baso nani immediately. She knows the totka and rituals to get rid of Jarwa-Jaraiya. Inshallah! He will be fine by tomorrow,' Asma Begum insisted.

Saleha Begum immediately sent Muneer to fetch Baso nani. Abdul Waheed Khan, who considered this to be an un-Islamic ritual, was not at home, otherwise he would not have allowed it.

Baso nani, a frail-looking woman with silver-white hair, was grandmother to everyone in the village. From six-year-olds to sixty-year-olds, everyone called her nani. She had been living in the village for over sixty years, having moved there to live with her daughter and son-in-law, who were long dead. There were no grandchildren. She lived alone in a thatched house at the far end of the village, surviving on the charity of the village people. Many of the villagers believed that Baso nani knew magic. A few of the village women even blamed her for indulging in witchcraft.

Baso nani entered Arif's uncle's house, walking with the help of a bamboo stick. The big mole in the middle of her forehead stood out against her white khadi sari.

After exchanging pleasantries, she asked Saleha Begum to bring Arif out in the open, since Jarwa-Jaraiya needed an open space to fly away. She got ready to start the ritual, which began with the telling of its story.

Once upon a time, a beautiful widow lived in a village with her only son. Her son was very mischievous. One day, in anger, the widow hit her son on the head with a stick. He started bleeding. Enraged by his mother's behaviour, the boy left his home for a city, where he was adopted by a rich, childless couple. Twelve years passed.

After the death of his adoptive parents, the boy inherited all their property and business. One day he was passing through the village alone on business. He thought the place seemed familiar and decided to stay in the village for a few days. One evening he saw his mother but did not recognize her. Memories fade in twelve years. He fell in love with her. The widow also fell in love with him and they got married. Soon after her marriage the widow became pregnant.

One morning while massaging her husband's head, she saw a deep gash. When she asked him, he told her that as a child, his mother had hit him with a stick and he had run away from his village when he was perhaps six or seven years old. He could not recall the name of his village or his mother's face. But the woman looked at his face and understood why this man's face resembled that of her first husband so much.

When they came to know that they were mother and son, they were so ashamed and sad that they decided to commit suicide. They prepared a pyre and jumped into it. Even in death, their souls did not find peace. The man became Jarwa and the woman became Jaraiya. Now they trouble people by possessing them, making them shiver. Whenever the story of their shameful liaison is repeated in the presence of the person they possess, they run away.

'O Jarwa and Jaraiya, if you have shame, go away from here. If you don't go away, I will repeat the story of your sinful liaison again,' Baso nani spoke in a very loud voice, looking directly into Arif's eyes. As she finished her rituals, Saleha Begum took out a two-rupee note and pressed it into her hand. A few moments later, Abdul Waheed Khan entered. He understood why Baso nani was there.

Turning to Saleha Begam, he yelled, 'Foolish woman, I've told you time and again to keep away from these ancient rituals. And how could you allow Arif to sit in the open air with his fever!'

Baso nani slowly walked out of the house. Saleha Begum was silent, her eyes downcast. Muneer had already left for his afternoon prayers.

Arif had listened to the story with great attention and, in fact, enjoyed this unusual treatment. He tried to calm his uncle down by saying, 'I am actually feeling much better now.'

~

> Thousands of Kar Sevaks and members of extremist Hindu parties have been gathering for the 'Shila Pujan'. The State Government has promised the Supreme Court that the Babri Masjid will be protected at any cost. There is palpable tension in the neighbouring districts. Many leaders of the Bharatiya Janata Party are present in Ayodhya.

Seated on a chair in front of the mosque, Muneer was reading aloud from the day's *Qaumi Mizaj*, a popular

Urdu newspaper in the state. A dozen or more people were listening attentively to him. It was the afternoon of 6 December 1992.

Arif was much better now, but still weak. Propped against the headrest of his bed, he was looking outside the window. He could see and hear the proceedings in the courtyard of the mosque. A few minutes later, Arif saw Sajjad Hussain, a stout man who ran a small provision store in the village, taking long strides towards the gathering. He let out a loud wail before announcing, 'Babri Masjid has been destroyed. The Hindus have reduced it to dust.'

'Inna lillahi wa inna ilayhi raji'un,' Badke baba recited loudly.

Anger began to well up. Arif was shocked. He had never imagined that this could happen in a secular country like India. He had heard on the radio yesterday that Kalyan Singh, the chief minister of Uttar Pradesh, had promised the Supreme Court of India to protect the Babri Masjid at any cost.

'All Hindus are Jan Sanghis. And this Congress prime minister is a BJP agent, a secret member of the Sangh Parivar,' Rahman, a tall man with a narrow moustache, roared.

The imam of the Jama Masjid gave a sermon after the evening prayer which Arif heard on the loudspeakers: 'We Muslims have left our traditions, forgotten the Holy Quran and Hadith. So, we are being humiliated everywhere. There was a time when Muslim rule extended from Turkey to Al-Andalus. As the great poet Allama Iqbal said:

Dasht toh dasht hain dariya bhi na chhode hamne
Bahr-e-zulmat mein dauda diye ghode hamne

(Deserts are just deserts, we did not spare even seas
We galloped on our horses in the ocean of darkness)

The imam continued, 'Of late, Muslims have started to behave like infidels and . . .'

Arif's thoughts wandered. He couldn't bring himself to listen to the sermon, and feared that something dreadful was going to happen in the village.

After the prayer, a meeting of Muslim men was organized in the courtyard of the mosque. Wrapped in a woollen chadar, Arif was also present, settled on a chowki with Sadaqat and Muneer.

'To avenge the martyrdom of the Babri Masjid, we will demolish the only temple in the village,' thundered Rahman.

'In our village there is no animosity between Hindus and Muslims. Why should we punish the Hindus of our village for the mistakes of somebody else in a far-off place?' Ali Ahmed Khan, Badke baba's childhood friend, spoke in a low voice.

'Ali bhai is right,' Badke baba seconded him.

'I think Ali Ahmed chacha and Waheed uncle are right,' Sadaqat said as he scratched the back of his head. A few disapproving eyes turned towards him.

'Your father, Razzaq Khalifa, is sitting here. You needn't interfere in important issues. Anyway, we don't need advice from a drunkard,' Rahman said arrogantly.

'Mind your language, Rahman chacha; I don't drink any more. And don't make me open my mouth. I know your character. It is you who are a regular visitor to our village carpenter's house to see his beautiful wife,' taunted Sadaqat.

'Shut up, you imbecile!' Razzaq Khalifa, a former wrestler who had won the title of Rustam-e-Champaran once upon a time, yelled at his son.

Sadaqat left the meeting in a huff.

'What we are planning to do is simply wrong,' Arif spoke up a bit hesitantly.

'Arif beta, you don't know these low-caste Hindus. They are pucca supporters of that Bhumihar MLA Suresh Singh. They should be taught a proper lesson,' Rahman Ali said.

At the end of the meeting that lasted two hours it was decided that the only temple in the village of Noniya Tola would be razed to the ground. Like Ali Ahmed Khan and Badke baba, a few more voices of sanity opposed the idea but the vociferous majority shot down their opposition.

Badke baba angrily walked away, refusing to participate in their ill-conceived plans.

Sleep eluded Arif. He strongly felt that he should do something to thwart the villagers. He thought of Badke baba but didn't discuss anything with him. Then, he thought of his friend Sadaqat, and left his bed, opened the door quietly and came out on to the road. The road was deserted. Arif started walking towards Sadaqat's house. A few yards away, he saw a shadowy figure near a defunct electric pole smoking a bidi.

'Arif bhai, where are you going so late?' Sadaqat asked him somewhat surprised, as he threw his bidi into an open sewer.

'I was coming to meet you. The villagers' plan to demolish the temple is not only wrong, but it is also dangerous,' Arif said, keeping his voice low.

'Arif bhai! Go and sleep. Don't worry; I have a plan to stop this,' Sadaqat replied.

'Really?'

'Yes.'

That night, two things happened. Sadaqat eloped with Chameli. And a police platoon arrived and camped in Noniya Tola near the temple. Arif was relieved that the plan to destroy the temple was foiled.

For the next ten days, the police stayed in the village. Things gradually returned to normal and the villagers' anger began to cool down. Many of them had changed their minds and by now felt that demolishing the temple would not be right. A couple of days later the police left the village.

The following Sunday, when things seemed to have settled down, news spread to every corner of the village that the Noniyas were going to march with a victory flag to celebrate the demolition of the Babri Masjid, as had been done in some of the neighbouring Hindu-dominated villages. They wouldn't dare conduct such a procession in the village. So, they had decided to do it in their mohalla. People started gathering in front of the Jama Masjid with bamboo sticks, pickaxes and spears in their hands.

Sheikh Hamid Ali, the grain merchant and erstwhile usurer, raised the first slogan, 'Nara-e-Takbir . . . Allah-o-Akbar.'

A mob of about fifty marched towards Noniya Tola, to the west of the mosque, and barely half a kilometre away.

Arif tried talking to some of the Muslim men but they pushed him aside. The man leading the mob was completely drunk. Vowing to sacrifice his life in the name of Islam, he spoke in broken syllables. After each jumbled sentence he yelled, 'Nara-e-Takbir . . .' and the men responded with 'Allah-o-Akbar' as they moved in the direction of Noniya Tola.

Helpless, Arif didn't know what to do. *If Badke baba had been here, he would have done something*, he thought. Badke baba had left for the neighbouring village with his family to attend a funeral. Arif and Farzana had been left behind in Jamalpura.

There is another person I can ask for help, Arif thought.

By the time Arif reached Noniya Tola with Ali Ahmed Khan, an argument had broken out between the Muslims and a small band of young Hindu men, mostly Noniyas. Arif noticed a small saffron flag planted near a thatched house. On the wall of the neighbouring house was a poster of MLA Suresh Kumar, smiling and palms folded in namaste: 'Vote for the Bharatiya Janata Party'.

Ali Ahmed Khan tried to intervene, but the mob was too rowdy and they would not let him speak. They might have heard him out in the mosque when sober, but not now when they had their minds set on revenge.

As the argument heated up, somebody had snuck up and set fire to a house. Seeing the fire the Hindu men got into a scuffle with the Muslim men, but they were heavily outnumbered. Many began to leave the fight to run to their families and homes as the fire spread. Many more got beaten badly. Arif heard men, women and children screaming and saw them running around trying to save a loved one or their belongings.

As the fire spread, the Muslim mob began to disperse. Ali Ahmed Khan dragged Arif away against his protestations.

'What are you going to do? You will get killed. And you cannot do anything to save them now. It's too far gone,' Ali Ahmed Khan yelled over the roar of the fire and the panic around them.

Within an hour or two, all the houses in Noniya Tola were gutted. The sky was smoky and dark.

Distressed at the barbarity he had just witnessed, Arif sat silently in a chair in his uncle's house after telling Farzana he didn't want to have dinner. He was also worried about the consequences. He knew that the police would take stringent action against the Muslims. Even he would be punished. Even Badke baba, who wasn't in the village when all this happened, wouldn't be spared. There were chances of the Hindus from the neighbouring villages attacking them the very next day.

In the morning, Arif learnt that three people had died in the fire. A senile man attempting to save his house had jumped into the fire. A man in his early twenties who had been beaten up by the mob was unconscious when the fire caught him. A partially blind woman who couldn't find the door in time was engulfed in the thick smoke and choked to death.

Initially, a few of the men responsible for the disaster boasted that they were Pathans and that they wouldn't shame the community by running away from the battlefield.

The imam of the Jama Masjid announced that nobody should leave the village.

In the evening, there was no azan at the Jama Masjid. To take stock of the situation, Arif came out to the street. There was not a soul in sight. Then, he saw Chhuttan Miyan, who worked in Badke baba's farm, walking quickly, almost running. He saw Arif and stopped.

'Arif babu, there are no Muslims left in our village. Just run away to a safer place. The Hindu mob and the police can come any time.'

So much for being Pathans and not running away, thought Arif.

Standing alone on the road, Arif looked at his wristwatch. It was almost five o'clock and Badke baba had not yet returned. Arif went back inside the house and explained the situation to Farzana as briefly as he could.

A few minutes later, they heard chants of 'Jai Shri Ram' at a distance. 'It seems like the Hindu mob is coming. We should leave the village immediately,' he told Farzana.

Farzana started crying.

'I am here. You needn't worry,' Arif reassured her and placed his hand on her head, but he was trembling within.

The sound of chanting became louder. Arif panicked, not knowing what to do. Then he rushed out of the house and locked the door from the outside and got back in through a window. Farzana and he together bolted all the windows from the inside.

He hoped that the mob would presume that they too had fled like the other villagers.

Soon, they heard the thumping of what sounded like

thousands of feet, just outside their house. A jeep came to a halt. Somebody yelled orders. With his heart beating fast, he went to the window in the corridor leading to the main door. And through the crack, he saw a hundred-odd men, many of them with pickaxes and swords in their hands, in the courtyard of the mosque. Half a dozen policemen were also there, armed with rifles and revolvers. A short, dark-complexioned man in a checked lungi carried a petromax. A white khadi-clad person was talking to a police officer, who addressed him as 'Vidhayakji'. From the poster Arif recognized him as MLA Suresh Singh.

'Teach the Pathans a lesson. For years we have tolerated their mischief. Don't spare a single katua.'

'No, no, Vidhayak ji, I will lose my job,' the police officer was pleading with him.

'Jai Shri Ram!' the crowd shouted. Their voices echoed through the empty house and fear gripped Arif.

'Farzana, we have to run away from here now. See where the torch is.'

Farzana wore her sweater. She was trembling. Arif put on his jacket and pushed his feet into his shoes, throwing the socks away. There was a knock on the door that soon turned into pounding. They were trying to break it down. Fear crawled all over his body. Despite the chill of the winter, beads of sweat appeared on his forehead.

Arif held Farzana's hand and whispered, 'Don't panic, Farzana. Just do what I say.'

He helped Farzana climb up the window that opened into the backyard of the house. As she sat on the windowsill, he went up the window as well. Arif jumped first, landing on slush. He held out his hands to Farzana and she jumped into his arms and landed softly next to him. Silently and quickly they crossed the adjacent graveyard, under the cover of trees and shrubs that bounded it.

They could see silhouettes of people on the road. Suddenly, one of them started to walk towards them and Arif and Farzana crouched low on the ground, frozen in fear. But the man stood at the edge of the road, turning towards the graveyard to pee. Arif pulled Farzana closer to him and they sat snuggled amid the dense shrubs and foliage. An insect jumped on Farzana and sensing that she was about to shriek, Arif covered her mouth tightly with his hand, stifling the sound and pulled her even closer. She clung to his chest, where he could feel her uneven breathing. They stayed in that position for what seemed like an eternity but was perhaps about half an hour. Arif finally looked up to see the road empty.

'We are going to Shamshad Nagar. A friend of Abba lives there,' Arif whispered, and Farzana nodded.

They reached the end of the village and saw men with big torches keeping vigil on the road leading to Shamshad Nagar. It was too risky to walk on the road. Arif led Farzana to the bank of river Son Bakya instead, and they walked along the riverbank, hidden by the embankment from the view of anybody on the road running parallel to the river. Farzana had by then started reciting the Ayat-ul-Kursi.

After a good hour or so, they entered the guava grove, which spread over four kilometres, and on the other side was Shamshad Nagar. As they went deeper into the dense and fragrant orchard, Arif began reciting the Quranic verses as well. Darkness had completely enveloped them and they stumbled on roots and stones often. They were almost at the end of the orchard, when a voice thundered:

'Stop!'

There were three masked men; two of them had guns slung from their shoulders.

'Who are you?' one of them thundered.

Arif could feel the words lodged in his throat.

'Maybe they are police informers,' the second masked man, holding a huge steel torch in his hand, said. He sauntered drunkenly towards them. 'I should ask this girl,' he said and held Farzana by her hand. Farzana started screaming, jerking her body in order to free her hand from his clutches.

'We . . . we . . . we are not police informers,' Arif stammered. 'Please leave my sister alone.' In a swift move, which surprised Arif himself, Arif shoved the masked man. But the drunken man was quicker than him. The steel torch landed with a clank on Arif's head and he collapsed on the sandy ground.

The torch man removed his mask, twirled his moustache and said, 'See how beautiful this girl is. We can have a good time with her.'

'No!' the other two replied in unison. 'You seem to have forgotten how Gagan Dev punished Shambhu for misbehaving with a woman during a dacoity raid in Bairagania.'

'Gagan Dev is crazy. He believes that he is an incarnation of Lord Rama. You can stay here like a eunuch; I am taking this girl with me.' He started dragging Farzana. She kicked and screamed. Arif felt dizzy. He had to do something quickly.

Then, suddenly, the man shrieked, let go of Farzana's hand and sank to the ground. Arif focused his eyes to see a new masked man. How could this be good? The new entrant kicked the second masked man.

'I don't want anyone to spoil the name of the Gagan Dev gang,' he shouted.

By then, at least two dozen masked men had gathered there.

'Bring this miscreant to our place. I will decide his fate there.'

Arif had heard countless stories about Gagan Dev, the most notorious dacoit of Motihari and the neighbouring districts. During the last five years, his gang had looted more than a hundred businessmen and rich farmers, but had never been caught. Arif had heard that Gagan Dev was a man of principles. He always distributed half of his booty among the poor and there were no stories of the gang ever troubling women. Popular legend was that he had shot dead one of his gang members who had violated the code of conduct by raping a girl.

So this was the legendary Gagan Dev.

Farzana had crawled towards Arif and was clinging to him, sobbing. Despite the situation, Arif couldn't help feeling astonished that the head of a dreaded robbers' gang was a short, thin man. He wore white trousers and a khaki jacket, and a cream-coloured muffler was wrapped around his neck. He removed his mask. His moustache was meagre, almost invisible from a distance. He spoke in Bhojpuri, asking Arif why he was in the orchard in the middle of the night, that too with a girl.

Arif narrated the incidents as quickly as he could, taking care to mention how he had wanted to stop the massacre. This was a Hindu gang lord after all.

Gagan Dev turned to Farzana, 'Don't worry, sister, you are safe.'

Farzana looked stricken and she dug her fingers into Arif's arm. Gagan Dev gave Arif directions to Shamshad Nagar. Arif thanked him, held Farzana's hand in his and began to walk as quickly as possible towards the village. Farzana could have easily been raped and he would have been powerless to stop it. He was in no position to protect her against a mob. They had to get to safety as soon as possible.

Farzana continued sobbing all the way. And Arif patted her back now and then to console her, but he didn't have any kind words to share.

~

Once they reached Shamshad Nagar, Arif pointed to a two-storey pucca house and said, 'That is Ilyas chacha's house.' As soon as they were inside the house, Farzana broke down in Ilyas's wife's arms and sobbed uncontrollably all night. Nobody in the house slept that night.

Early next morning, Ilyas's son accompanied Arif and Farzana on an old Mahindra jeep taking a longer route to Inayat Nagar, as it was unsafe to travel through the Hindu-majority villages, which was the regular route.

In Inayat Nagar, they saw Rapid Action Force personnel patrolling the desolate streets. News of the Jamalpura riots must have reached there. A uniformed man with a gun stopped them and asked them who they were and where they were coming from. Arif didn't tell him about Jamalpura, worrying he might be arrested, and instead said that they were returning from a visit to Shamshad Nagar. The man let them pass. The tightness in Arif's chest reduced just a little.

Hakim sahab was pacing around on his veranda when they arrived. Farzana's mother, who was sitting on the ground, started crying as soon as she saw them.

EIGHT

Back in Patna, Arif woke up in the morning with a heavy head and a stuffy nose after a sleepless night. Standing on the balcony, he rubbed Vicks on his forehead and nostrils. He inhaled deeply, comforted by the relief from the sting of the medicine.

The previous night, he had had more nightmares about the burning houses of the Noniyas. He also couldn't stop thinking about the dreadful night in the guava orchard. What if Gagan Dev hadn't come in time? What if the drunken bandit had had his way with Farzana?

To distract himself, he thought of his IAS interview preparations. His studies had suffered during the last few weeks, first because of his illness and then because of the riots.

The sun on the horizon was ready for its day-long journey. The road in front of his building was deserted. A beggar, frail, bearded and old, stood on the steps of the veranda.

The pot-bellied Mr Surya Pratap Singh emerged from his flat and yelled at the beggar, 'Who allowed you to enter the camp area? Go away at once, otherwise . . .'

The beggar beseeched him to give him something to eat. Mr Singh raised his hand threateningly in the air. Frightened, the beggar flinched, took a step back and tripped. He went tumbling down the stairs.

What a heartless man, Arif thought. Mr Singh was an inspector with the Bihar Military Police. His affair with his orderly's wife was a matter of gossip in the colony. Arif had also heard that his orderly had no qualms about letting his wife sleep with him.

Arif went inside his house to bring some food for the beggar, but he was gone by the time he returned. Mr Singh stood in front of the building, barking orders to two young recruits.

Arif felt like spitting on Mr Singh's face.

'Why do I hate Mr Singh?' he wondered. *Because he misbehaved with the beggar? Or because he is sleeping with someone else's wife? Am I not trying to do the same thing with Mr Ramesh Kumar's wife? How am I different from Mr Singh?*

But he hadn't even touched Sumitra. He liked her but had not committed any sin. *Well, not yet anyway.*

Once Sumitra came to his mind, he was restless. He was surprised that after everything he had endured in the last few weeks Sumitra refused to leave his thoughts. It had been ages, he felt, since he had seen her. The two months away from Patna had done nothing to temper his yearnings for her. On the contrary, he missed her terribly.

As he picked up the day's newspaper from a chair, he realized it was a Saturday. The day Sumitra worshipped the peepal tree. But not this Saturday.

The previous day, at Mritunjay's place, Arif happened

to meet Rahul, Sumitra's son. He had discreetly enquired about Sumitra and Rahul had told him that his mother had gone to Bombay to see her ailing bhabhi.

Arif returned to his study room, picked up *Civil Services Interview: How to Excel* and tried to concentrate.

~

On a cool winter morning in 1993, Arif's house had a celebratory air.

'Just in his second attempt, he overcame the second hurdle. Not a small feat. He did not attend tuitions, like most people do. I am sure my son will also clear the interview,' Arif heard Abba praising him to Mr Verma, their neighbour.

Arif was immensely pleased but Abba's belief in him frightened him. *What if I am not selected?*

Mritunjay too had cleared the mains. So they started studying together more frequently. Every Saturday they conducted mock interviews of each other.

On one such day, Arif was returning from Mritunjay's house when he saw Ramesh Kumar pulling out a big carton from the boot of his car. Clearly, it was too heavy to be carried alone.

'May I help you?' Arif said.

'Yes please, thank you.'

A girl of about seventeen or eighteen opened the door when Ramesh Kumar rang the bell to his house. Arif looked at her for a few seconds. She had a striking resemblance to Sumitra, but was younger, taller and fairer.

'Pranam bhaiyya,' she said and moved aside to allow them to enter the house.

Arif nodded in reply.

'My daughter, Kavita. She studies at Indira Gandhi Balika Vidyalaya in Hazaribagh,' Ramesh Kumar said as they placed the carton gently on the floor. There were a dozen potted chrysanthemums and roses near the balcony railing.

'That's good,' Arif said. 'Okay, uncle, I'll take your leave now.'

'Arif, stay for a cup of tea,' Ramesh Kumar said, pulling a red plastic chair for him.

Arif sat on the chair as Ramesh Kumar went inside. He emerged ten minutes later with two cups of tea and homemade potato chips in a white china plate.

The telephone rang in an adjacent room. Arif heard Kavita pick up and say, 'Hello?'

'So, how is your preparation for the interview coming along?' Ramesh Kumar had not even completed his question when they heard Kavita crying. Ramesh Kumar rushed to the room. Arif followed him. Ramesh Kumar took the phone receiver and as the person on the other end spoke, his expression turned grim. Kavita was sobbing by now.

When Ramesh Kumar hung up, Arif hesitantly asked, 'Is something wrong?'

'There are Hindu–Muslim riots in Bombay. Sumitra is there and she had gone to the market in the morning and hasn't returned. The town is under curfew with shoot-at-sight orders. No one knows where she is.'

Arif didn't know how to react. Suppressing his own emotions, he sat with Ramesh Kumar and Kavita for the next couple of hours consoling them. Then he left for his house, distraught.

That night Arif couldn't sleep. He kept pacing on his terrace and praying for Sumitra.

As soon as dawn broke, Arif visited the nearest PCO to call Ramesh Kumar.

Sumitra had returned. Ramesh Kumar explained how she had been saved by a Muslim man from being killed by a mob of rioters. He was leaving for Bombay to bring back his wife.

Arif paid the PCO owner and came out. He heaved a sigh of relief. Walking past the Shiva temple, he stopped in front of a closed provision store where a skinny beggar sat with his aluminium begging bowl. He emptied his pockets of all his money and dropped it in the bowl. The beggar blessed Arif copiously.

Arif moved away, humming an old Kishore Kumar song, overcome with relief.

Humein tum se pyaar kitna, ye hum nahin jaante
Magar jee nahin saktey, tumhare bina

(I don't know how much I love you
But, I know that I can't live without you)

Three days later when he heard from Mritunjay that Sumitra had been brought back to Patna, Arif didn't go to their house. He stopped visiting Mritunjay as well. He reminded himself that Sumitra was married.

NINE

Arif found it torturous to deprive himself of the sight of Sumitra. A few months seemed like centuries. The wait for the results of the civil services interview was also nerve-racking.

A rolled-up newspaper, tied with a small piece of jute cord, landed on his balcony with a thud. With his heart thumping, he unrolled the newspaper. Mritunjay's name was not there. With a trembling index finger, he searched through the newsprint many times. He too hadn't made it through the interview.

Arif refused to leave his bedroom for the next ten days, moping over his failure. He began to feel like he would never succeed. He would never see his name suffixed with the initials 'IAS'.

Contrary to Arif's expectations, Abba was not devastated. In fact, he behaved normally, consoling Arif and telling him not to worry about his unsuccessful attempt. On the eleventh day, Abba came to his room and dragging a chair next to him he sat down and placed his hand on Arif's head.

'I know you are unhappy with your civil services final result. But, my son, don't lose faith in yourself.'

Arif smiled while looking at his father's face. Abba smiled back and quoted a famous couplet in Urdu by Azeem Dehlvi:

Girte hain shahsavar hi maidan-e-jang mein
Vo tifl kya giregaa jo ghutnon ke bal chale

(Only knights mounting horses fall in the battlefield
How can a child crawling on its knees fall)

'You should keep on trying. Don't lose heart,' Abba said, and held out the day's newspaper. 'This year's civil services advertisement has already been published. Apply again. I am sure you will sail through this time.'

Abba's pep talk had a magical effect on him. He pushed his disappointment to the back of his mind and began planning for the next round of exams.

On a Saturday, Mritunjay came to his house early in the morning. He had a brown envelope in his hand.

'Prelims form. I went to Ashok Rajpath to buy it. I got one for you too,' Mritunjay said as he settled down on Arif's bed.

'Thanks, my friend.'

'And we'll work out some new strategies for this year's examination.'

'I too have some new ideas, especially for the general studies papers. If we concentrate more on the science and technology portion, we can . . .'

Dadi entered the room just then. Mritunjay got up and touched her feet.

'May Allah bless you, my son,' Dadi said. 'I am going to make halwa for you, Mritunja.' Dadi couldn't pronounce his full name, so she always called him Mritunja. Mritunjay loved the way she said his name.

'No, Dadi. I have to go now. Next time. My favourite chane ka halwa,' Mritunjay said, touched Dadi's feet once more and left for his house.

Arif stood on the balcony and saw Mritunjay struggle to start his scooter. A dozen kicks later, Mritunjay's Bajaj Super coughed to life, letting out a dark trail of smoke.

Returning to his room, Arif looked at the wall clock. He had to hurry if he wanted to get the bank draft for the application fee ready.

By the time he reached the service counter of the State Bank of India, a wooden CLOSED sign was already in place.

Arif looked at the man at the counter with hopeful eyes. Wrinkling his nose in disgust, the man said, 'Don't you know working hours are till 12.30 on Saturdays?'

Arif was about to leave when he saw Ramesh Kumar coming his way. He might have seen him standing at the counter.

'Have you any work in the bank?' Ramesh Kumar asked.

'Yes, uncle, I have to get a demand draft issued.'

'Srivastava' – he turned to the man behind the counter – 'prepare a demand draft in favour of . . .'

'Union Public Service Commission,' Arif said. 'Here are the details.' He extricated a piece of paper from his pocket and handed it to Ramesh Kumar.

'But the cash is already closed, sir,' Srivastava said, annoyed.

'No problem! Pass a transfer entry from my savings account. Send the draft to my cabin once it is ready,' Ramesh Kumar said and placed the piece of paper on his desk. Then he turned to Arif, 'You come with me.'

It was a small cabin of wood and glass with a black revolving chair for Ramesh Kumar and two cushioned steel chairs for visitors. Ramesh Kumar enquired after Arif's parents and siblings, till a peon came in with the demand draft ten minutes later.

As Arif was about to leave, Ramesh Kumar placed a brown jute bag on his table.

'Arif, if you don't mind, can you deliver this bag to my wife? I'm leaving for Khagaria to attend a wedding. I don't have time to go home.'

'Sure, uncle,' Arif said. He cursed himself for saying yes, but he was also excited at the prospect of meeting Sumitra after so many months.

~

Arif was about to ring the bell at Sumitra's house when he heard her angry voice.

'For Ramesh his sister comes first. I have been observing this since the day I arrived in this house. Even now his sister keeps interfering in our lives . . .'

It seemed like Sumitra was talking to someone over the telephone.

Arif waited for about twenty minutes with the bag by his side but Sumitra didn't disconnect the phone.

'But I know the bitch very well. I know how to deal with . . .' he heard her saying as he pressed the bell.

A few seconds later Sumitra opened the door, her face tense. But as soon as she saw Arif, a big smile wiped away her agitation. She was dressed in a red chiffon sari and matching sleeveless blouse. Her loose hair fell on her shoulders and she looked breathtakingly beautiful. Arif tried to keep his eyes away from her, but couldn't. His heart leaped and he began to lose control of himself.

'Ramesh uncle asked me to give you this bag,' Arif said. He had faltered before saying uncle.

How can I call a person whose wife I am coveting uncle?

'Come inside, Arif,' she said warmly. Arif fumbled to unstrap his sandals as he entered her flat. She pushed the first door on her left and ushered him into her drawing room.

'There was no need to take off your sandals,' she said. Arif smiled without saying anything.

Arif's eyes scanned three abstract oil paintings on canvas hung on the walls and blue curtains that matched the sofa. In a corner of the room, on a wooden platform, stood marble statues of Hanuman, the monkey god; Ganesha, the elephant-headed god; and Lakshmi, the goddess of wealth. Flowers lay at their feet and incense sticks had already burned to white ash. Just above the platform, there was a smiling portrait of the blue-skinned Lord Krishna. He hadn't had the time to take all this in the last time he had been here with her husband, worried about her safety.

Sumitra asked him to sit and then walked out of the room and returned carrying a tray laden with biscuits, chips, roasted peanuts, milk cake, a glass of water and two cups of tea. Placing the tray on the centre table, she pushed a cup of tea towards him.

'I have a shikwa,' Sumitra said, using the sophisticated Urdu word for complaint.

'Shikwa?'

'You didn't come to see me when I returned from Bombay. Kavita told me you had been home when my relatives called to inform my family that I was missing. I thought you would have been happy to hear that I was safe and that you would come to welcome me. I was in a dangerous situation, you know?'

'Sorry, Sumitraji. I thought . . .'

'Firstly, my name is Sumitra and not Sumitraji.'

'Okay, Sumitra,' Arif stammered. 'Just wondering how your Urdu is so good. Where did you learn it?' Arif tried to change the subject.

'I grew up in the Muslim-majority town Imdad Nagar, near Gaya, and studied in an Urdu-medium school. In those days I used to read a lot of Urdu magazines and novels.'

'Wonderful . . .'

The doorbell rang twice in quick succession.

'Sumitraji,' a woman's voice called out.

'Must be Mrs Mishra. I'll be back in ten minutes,' she said, walking out of the room. She shut the door of the drawing room from the outside. But Arif could clearly hear the discussion between her and Mrs Mishra.

'I came to tell you as soon as I heard. You know Premlata, Sumitraji? Arrey Chaubey sahab's daughter? She is carrying on with a Harijan boy. A Brahmin girl's lover is an untouchable!'

'Really. I can't believe this,' Sumitra said.

'Haan, Shrinath Singh's unmarried daughter has had an abortion. Sacchi, bhagwan kasam.'

'Mai, Father is back from office,' said a boy in Bhojpuri.

'Okay, Sumitraji! Chala tani, I am leaving now. We'll discuss this tomorrow.'

Arif heard the door shut and seconds later, Sumitra returned. She smiled at Arif, settled down on the sofa and said, 'You write nice ghazals.'

'Where did you read my poetry?'

'From the diary you left with me the day you helped me take my father to the hospital.'

'Oh! Thanks. But your poetic skills are far superior.' Arif hesitated before adding, 'Why don't you recite some of your ghazals?'

'You really want to listen to my ghazals?'

Looking at you is like reading a ghazal, Arif thought, and looked at Sumitra intently. She smiled and dimples appeared on her cheeks. Tauba tauba, he thought, and fought the urge to get up and kiss her.

'Yes, please,' he said instead.

Ye maikad-e-ishq hain, yahan jaam-e-junoon milta hain
Giriya-e-deed-e-Qaish wa qalb-e-Laila ka khoon milta hain

(This is a tavern of love, you get wine glasses of passion here
Tears from the eyes of Majnoon and blood from the heart of Laila are sold here)

Sumitra started with this couplet and the poetry session went on till five in the evening.

'Sumitraji, I have to go somewhere,' Arif said, overcoming the heartache of ending the lovely afternoon.

'Sumitra.'

'Okay, okay, Sumitra.' Arif smiled.

'Will you accompany me to a film tomorrow? My husband is out of town and my son too is at my father's place. I have been wanting to watch this movie. It might be out of the theatres before my husband comes back,' Sumitra said.

'Why not!'

What are you doing, Arif? His conscience questioned him. *Pursuing her will take you nowhere.*

Shrugging off his moral dilemma, Arif asked, 'Which movie is this, Sumitra?'

'*Saajan*,' she said.

'You'll come alone?'

'Yes.'

'Your daughter, Kavita?'

'I told you earlier that she studies at Indira Gandhi Balika Vidyalaya in Hazaribagh.'

'Yes, you did.'

Saajan, a love triangle featuring Salman Khan, Sanjay Dutt and Madhuri Dixit, was running to packed houses in

Patna. It was decided that Arif would go first and get the tickets. Sumitra would join him later.

The next day, Arif reached Mona Cinema by 10.30 in the morning and was disappointed to find a 'House Full' sign. Right next to the booking counter, two black marketeers, each with a bunch of tickets, were murmuring, 'DC for 30, Balcony for 20'. Arif bargained and bought two dress circle tickets for fifty rupees. It was a bit expensive, but he didn't want to miss the opportunity.

He was in turmoil. Was he doing anything wrong by spending time with Sumitra? Then he dismissed these thoughts. *Just watching a movie with a woman doesn't make a person an adulterer.* And he was only accompanying her so she didn't have to go to the movie alone. He waited for her at the eastern end of Gandhi Maidan, in front of Mona–Elphinstone, the twin cinema halls.

Gandhi Maidan, the huge open space in the middle of Patna where almost every public event in the city took place – from political rallies to religious congregations, from trade shows to book fairs – was often called the lungs of Patna. For years it had been a silent witness to history. From the Quit India movement to anti-Emergency protests, it had seen stalwart Indian politicians launching various movements that had changed the destiny of the country.

Standing in a corner of the Maidan, it was astonishing to see the numerous people it provided space to rest, play, protest, conduct business and, above all, survive the rigours of the heartless, lawless city. For many, the day began and ended in Gandhi Maidan.

It was a hot day. Arif sat on a concrete bench under the shadow of a peepal tree. A few steps away sat a palm reader with a customer. To Arif's left stood a dozen people with red banners that read 'Hang the culprits of Sangapura', 'Stop the killing of the poor', 'Down with capitalism', 'Down with pseudo-democracy', 'Inquilab Zindabad'.

Two women held photographs of men whose throats had been slit. Arif knew that they were supporters of the Naxalites. From the newspapers he had learnt that they had been gathering here for the last two days to protest the killing of thirty-five men from low-caste families by an outlawed private army of upper-caste landlords in Jehanabad.

The road around the circular Gandhi Maidan had very few people as the sun overhead blazed magnificently. Even the birds had taken shelter in their nests and the ice cream and cold-water sellers were swatting away flies. The seller of pornographic magazines on the adjacent footpath didn't have any customers. A couple of rickshaw pullers were relishing the humble repast of sattu balls with tangy onion and hot green chillies. It was only near the cinema hall that hundreds of people stood braving the sun.

Half an hour later, he went back to the main entrance of the hall and immediately spotted Sumitra in the crowd. She stood apart, dressed in a resplendent purple sari and blouse, waiting for him. They smiled in acknowledgement and with minimal conversation entered the hall together. Settled in their seats, Arif was a bit nervous, wary of people around him. What if an acquaintance found him with Sumitra? What if this news reached Abba? What if there was a scandal?

Arif turned to look at Sumitra and found her eyes on him, a smile on her lips. And that eased his discomfort.

As the song '*Dekha hain pehli baar saajan ki ankhon mein pyaar*' played on the screen, people went berserk. The hall reverberated with sounds of raucous whistling. Arif felt the warmth of Sumitra's touch on his hand. A chill ran through his body, making him perspire. He breathed in deeply and the sweet smell of her perfume filled his nostrils, reminding him of crisp winter air and snow-capped mountains, though he didn't know why. He barely registered the scenes on the screen, breathing in Sumitra's smell and planning the next 'accidental' grazing of their hands.

After the movie, they were coming downstairs from the dress circle when the pallu of Sumitra's sari slipped down, revealing her ample cleavage through the low-necked blouse.

Arif saw some ogling eyes and heard a few giggling voices.

Turning to Sumitra, Arif whispered angrily to her, 'I don't think you should wear sleeveless blouses.'

Sumitra looked at Arif with surprise but didn't say anything. She smiled, biting her lip. It was afternoon by the time they walked out of the theatre and the sun was hot.

'Did Sumitra touch my hand intentionally?' The question popped up in his mind and he felt a tingling sensation tugging at his heart.

They were walking in the direction of the autorickshaw stand.

'Sumitra, I am in love with a married lady,' Arif said. He couldn't understand what had come over him. The proximity to Sumitra in that dark theatre had driven him mad. He couldn't control himself any more.

'Really?' There was no element of surprise in Sumitra's voice.

'And her name is Sumitra.'

Sumitra turned to look at him with sad, unblinking eyes. 'Let's get an autorickshaw. I want to go home immediately.'

She started walking briskly. Arif followed her.

A beggar appeared from nowhere and blocked Sumitra's way.

The woman was in a dirty petticoat, her blouse was torn and hair matted with mud. The cheekbones of her unwashed face were prominent, her eyes gaunt and sunken. She came closer to Sumitra and looked at her in a bizarre way. Then, she started laughing. *She is definitely mad*, Arif thought.

'Go away, you pagli!' A middle-aged man selling cucumbers tried to shoo her away.

'Gimme money, gimme money,' said the woman in between her cackling.

'Maya! Maya! What happened to you?' Sumitra cried.

Sumitra knew the woman! She took out a hundred-rupee note from her purse and offered it to her. In a swift move, the woman snatched it from her hand and ran away, disappearing into a nearby alley.

Arif reserved an autorickshaw and asked Sumitra to go home.

Tears were streaming down Sumitra's face.

~

On a Thursday afternoon, Arif was alone in his room. Propped against two pillows, he was going through the editorial of *The Hindu*, required reading for all civil services aspirants, with a pink marker in his hand.

When he looked up, he saw Sumitra at the door, dressed in an embroidered dark green sari and a full-sleeved blouse with a round neck.

When he had dropped her home the other day, she had tearfully said goodbye and ran into the house, without inviting him in. He had gone through that day's events over and over again but couldn't make sense of it. Who was that woman Maya and how did Sumitra know her? But even more than that strange incident, he recalled every touch of Sumitra's, the smell of her perfume, her lovely purple sari.

Arif was about to greet her with a namaste when she gestured him to be silent. She came close to him. Arif rose from his bed. Looking directly into his eyes, she held his right hand and placed an envelope on his palm. Then, she placed a quick kiss on his cheek and left the room without a word.

Arif's knees went weak and he felt a flutter in his stomach. He walked out and went to his study. Shutting the door, he settled in his chair, tore open the envelope with shaking hands and began to read the letter.

Dear Arif,

I am wonderstruck how easily you opened your heart that day. I was too shocked to respond then. Later, I thought I should ignore whatever you said at Gandhi

Maidan and stop meeting you forever. But my restless heart forced me to write this letter.

You must be wondering who the madwoman was you saw at the autorickshaw stand. And how I knew her and why I was crying for her. Let me start with Maya's story first.

Six years ago, I met Maya Banerjee in Jamshedpur. I can still remember her effervescent smile. Her kohl-lined eyes. Her Bangla-flavoured Hindi. We became good friends. She lived in the same locality in Jamshedpur where we had rented a house. As Ramesh was always busy with work, I often went out with Maya. We shopped, watched movies together. It was Maya who introduced me to Satyajit Ray's movies. It was she who recommended I read novels by Anne Tyler and Edna O'Brien. She was a fabulous cook and the divine taste of her fish in mustard paste still lingers in my memories.

Almost a year after I met her, I overheard two neighbourhood women whispering. I didn't believe them and asked Maya directly. Denying the allegations, Maya said that they were just jealous of her. I believed her but only to discover the next day that Maya had lied to me.

Maya had been cheating on her husband for many months. Her husband was a medical representative in a renowned pharma company and travelled a lot outside Jamshedpur. During his absence, a young man visited her.

That evening I had gone over to her house to return her book, and I caught her with the young man. I returned home without saying anything. What a cheap woman, I thought.

I couldn't stop thinking about her actions. She was dear to me after all; I couldn't dismiss her like that. There must be some solid reason for Maya to stray from what we are told is the sacred boundary of marriage. She was a reasonable woman. I wanted to ask her about this. But I couldn't. Two days later when I arrived at her place I found her house locked. Her landlord said they had left the place. Nobody had any idea where Maya and her family had gone. For months I worried about her and waited for her to return, but she didn't.

How could a married woman in her mid-thirties fall for a boy who was only a little older than her own son? I had wondered through the years. And now I am about to tread the same path on which Maya once walked.

To come to our story, it began the day we met in Nehru Park. I can vividly remember that afternoon.

Babuji had just arrived from Katihar and was feeling uncomfortable. I mentioned this to Ramesh but he trivialized Babuji's illness by calling it exhaustion and old age. I insisted on taking him to a doctor, but Ramesh refused. Instead, he went to drop his sister at the railway station in his car and didn't return for the next hour. I was angry and decided to take my father to the hospital in an autorickshaw. I didn't get one on the road and had to make him walk to the main gate of Nehru Park, where I expected to find an auto or a cycle rickshaw. But there were none. Babuji asked me to take him inside the park. He thought fresh air would make him feel better. You know what happened after that.

Initially, it was gratitude for you that dominated my

thoughts. I was thankful to you for saving my father's life. Three days after Babuji was discharged from the hospital, I took out the blue diary and the poetry book you had left behind. I started reading *Diwan-e-Momin* and finished it in two hours and then, out of curiosity, opened your diary. On the first page was a black-and-white photograph of you, dressed in a denim jacket, your Amitabh-style long hair covering half of your ears. You looked endearing.

On the following pages were couplets by Zauq, Ghalib, Momin, Mir, Dagh and Shad Azimabadi. I admire all these Urdu poets.

On the next few pages there were some descriptions of a girl called Simran. I guessed she was your childhood crush. Your poems about Simran were interesting and I liked them. But at the same time, I discovered I was jealous of Simran.

The following afternoon I opened your diary again and read a couplet by Shad Azimabadi.

Khamoshi se musibat aur bhi sangeen hoti hain
Tadap aye dil tadapne se zara taskin hoti hain

(Silence and quietness will only aggravate your
sufferings
By torturing yourself, oh my heart, you will get
some peace)

These lines by Shad triggered some sort of emotional upheaval inside me. I suspected I had begun to like you.

For the next few weeks I didn't touch your diary. I feared if I kept reading it I would fall in love with you.

That Sunday, Neeta, my only sister-in-law, came to my house quite early and an argument broke out between us over a trifle. As expected, Ramesh sided with his sister. Angry and humiliated, I retired to my room and shut the door. I came out an hour later; no one was home. I took some Disprin for my throbbing head, returned to my bedroom and drifted into a deep slumber. I woke up two hours later; the headache had vanished. I sat down with a cup of adrak chai and your diary in my hands. I had automatically gravitated towards it in a moment of heartache.

There were short write-ups on contemporary social issues. Your views on women, religion, culture and the nation impressed me. In one of the essays you said, 'To respect a woman you need no excuses. Her being a woman is strong enough reason to adore, love and respect her.'

There were free verses on love, relationships and human values. Those poems touched my heart and made me happy.

My liking for you became admiration for you.

I had often seen you in Nehru Park with Mritunjay. I have wanted to come over to you and talk to you, thank you for your help and tell you how much I have enjoyed your writing, but I couldn't. Instead, I hid behind the shrubs whenever you walked past me.

For the next six months I kept reading and rereading

your diary till I realized that admiration had given way to love. I was afraid of meeting you.

I came face-to-face with you almost two years later. A week after moving to a new rented house in Bank Colony, I saw you looking at me from Mritunjay's room window. And after that I began to lose control of myself.

I was dreading the day you would utter those words. But at the same time I waited for that very moment.

Now, I must confess that I love you too. But I have my limitations. I can't go beyond the moral boundaries I have drawn for myself. So, please don't ask anything from me that is rightfully my husband's.

Please promise that you'll keep our love sacred. That you will never taint our relationship with the tar of lust.

Lovingly yours,

Sumitra

TEN

The summer vacation for schools and colleges had begun. Arif's family was to leave for Jamalpura, which was by then back to normal. Arif had excused himself saying he didn't want to waste even a single day. He had begun preparations for the next set of exams.

The day his family left for their native village, Mritunjay visited Arif and told him that he was also alone at home for the next two days and was renting a VCR to watch movies.

'We need to recharge ourselves with some wholesome entertainment,' Mritunjay told Arif.

In the evening, Mritunjay's distant cousin Anand brought the VCR and set it up on the table next to their colour television.

'Have you shut the door properly?' Mritunjay enquired. 'If anybody learns that we have rented a VCR, our room will become a fish market. No one will miss an opportunity to watch movies for free. How did you bring the VCR? The neighbours might have seen it. If any of them comes knocking, our evening will be spoiled.'

'Arrey bhai, you needn't worry. I packed the VCR in a

travel bag. Nobody would have guessed.' Anand pointed to a brown travel bag lying on the floor.

'Great,' Mritunjay said, 'have you brought sattu?' Mritunjay asked.

'Yes!' Anand replied, tossing a packet of Shree Kamal Brand sattu on the sofa near Mritunjay.

Mritunjay had already burnt the cow dung cakes in the balcony. The spices and herbs were ready. The flour was already kneaded into a dough. In a big bowl, Mritunjay emptied one of the sattu packets and mixed it with spices, herbs, salt and mustard oil. He filled the small hollow doughs of wheat flour with sattu mix and made them into balls. Then he placed the balls of dough into the hot ashes. Mritunjay kept the litti turning with a small iron rod in the hot ashes to avoid burning them. In the kitchen, Anand roasted eggplants and tomatoes on the gas stove. The littis were taken out and wiped with a piece of cloth to get rid of the traces of ash and then smeared with ghee. The tomatoes and eggplants were peeled, crushed and mixed with chopped garlic, green chillies and salt.

There was no dish as delicious as litti-chokha, thought Arif, when he saw the bowlful of ghee-drenched brown litties placed on the centre table in the drawing room. His mouth began to water. Since Arif hadn't helped with the cooking, he washed the plates and glasses and filled water in a mug from the Zero-B tap.

They wiped the bowl clean in twenty minutes. Anand burped heartily and settled on a cushioned chair.

'After a hot and spicy meal, we need a hot and spicy film,' he said as he pressed a button on the TV.

The title flashed on the screen. Hungry Girls.

Three gorgeous white girls with large breasts and round bottoms appeared on the screen and got rid of their clothes quickly. Then, a well-endowed naked guy with brown hair started to make love to the girls one by one.

It was a transcendental moment for Arif. Of course, Arif had heard about blue films but hadn't realized that such films left nothing to the imagination. His throat was parched, his body smouldered. He observed that Mritunjay's eyes were fixed on the TV screen, and beads of perspiration were appearing on his forehead. Anand had a beatific expression on his face.

Barely ten minutes had passed when the guy and the girls changed positions and began to work assiduously with their mouths.

'What is this?' Arif enquired involuntarily.

'This is called 69, friend.' Mritunjay giggled.

But the scene appalled Arif. He felt like he was going to throw up. He ran to the bathroom. The litti-chokha came out in two instalments. He gargled, washed his face and cleaned up the vomit.

Arif told Mritunjay he was going home, and before Mritunjay could say anything he unbolted the door and got out of the flat. He heard the door being shut behind him.

'Tauba Astaghfar! Tauba Astaghfar!' Arif said softly and sought forgiveness from God as he walked back home.

That night he had a dream. He saw Sumitra lying naked on the bed next to him and he did with her what he had seen in the movie that evening.

In the morning, he found his lungi drenched in semen

and felt guilty for his dirty dream. He had a severe headache and a stuffy nose. Arif put water in a saucepan on the stove. Then he boiled tea with ginger and drank it. He needed to inhale Vicks VapoRub.

It was five minutes to eleven. The sun outside was blazing. The ceiling fan dispersed warm air. On the table the book on public administration lay open. Arif was attempting to read a chapter on Abraham Maslow's 'Hierarchy of Needs: Physiological Needs, Security Needs, Belonging and Love Needs, Esteem Needs and the Need for Self-Actualization'.

Why have I suddenly developed a craving for Sumitra's body? His desire for Sumitra fell in the category of physiological needs, he had thought. Arif felt distracted and closed the book.

He reached out for his tiny black radio set and switched it on. The song being played by Vividh Bharti was a classic by Lata Mangeshkar, '*Dil ki girah khol do chup na baitho, koi geet gao*' (Untie the knots of your heart and don't be silent, sing a song). He adjusted the volume of the radio. The next song was a sensual number from the film *Aradhana*.

Roop tera mastana
Pyaar mera deewana
Bhool koi humse na ho jaaye

(Your form is intoxicating
I am crazy with love for you
I am afraid of committing a sin with you)

Arif conjured the scene from the movie. He could see the passionate Rajesh Khanna embracing the coy, semi-naked

Sharmila Tagore. Sharmila's images swapped with Sumitra's and Arif could see her scantily dressed, walking towards him.

He switched off the radio and picked up the novel he had been reading for the last ten days – *Love in the Time of Cholera*. Two pages in, he stopped to reread a passage:

> She took off the taffeta blouse with the beaded embroidery and threw it across the room. On the easy chair in the corner, she tossed her bodice over her shoulder to the other side of the bed. With one pull she removed her long ruffled skirt, her satin garter belt and funeral stockings and she threw everything on the floor until the room was carpeted with the last remnants of her mourning. She did it with so much joy and with such well-measured pauses, that each of her gestures seemed to be saluted by the cannon of the attacking troops, which shook the city down to its foundations. Florentino Ariza tried to help her unfasten her stays, but she anticipated him with deft manoeuvre, for in five years of matrimonial devotion she learned to depend on herself in all phases of love, even the preliminary stages, with no help from anyone. Then she removed her lace panties, sliding them down her legs with rapid movements of a swimmer, and at last she was naked.

As he read through the passage, a feverish desire began to choke him. He replaced Florentino Ariza with himself and the widow Nazareth with Sumitra.

He reread the paragraph: Sumitra took off her sari and threw it across the room on to the wooden chair in a corner; she tossed her sleeveless blouse over her shoulder to the other side of the bed. With one pull she removed her petticoat. Arif tried to help her unstrap her bra . . . Then she removed her black cotton panties, sliding them down her legs with the rapid movements of a swimmer, and at last she was naked.

The fantasy derived from Marquez's novel made a volcano of desire erupt inside him, and the lava coursed through his veins. A sudden breathlessness took hold of Arif and he grabbed the glass of water and gulped it down in one go.

An hour later, Arif was in front of Sumitra's house. He pressed the bell. Sumitra opened the door, looking fresh and smelling of bathing soap. The lemony fragrance of Liril soap tickled Arif's senses.

'Are you alone?' Arif asked.

'Yes,' she replied with a smile.

Before she could say anything further, Arif pushed his way into Sumitra's flat, bolted the door and asked her to come inside the room. Once in her room, Arif held her hand and said, 'I love you,' and then in a swift move, he grabbed her by her shoulder and kissed her cheek.

'No,' she said, trying to free herself.

Ignoring Sumitra's weak resistance, he held her tight, pushing her on to the bed. This is a sin, Arif. Arif's conscience was sedated by the intoxicating smell of her body. Soon, Sumitra stopped pretending to resist and began to enjoy being held by Arif. She closed her eyes and lay still. He pressed his body against hers. He had never been in such close proximity to a woman. Within a minute or two, he came in his pyjamas.

His grip loosened. He stood up and left the place at once, without saying anything to Sumitra. He didn't have the courage to look at her face.

He heard the azan as he pedalled his cycle furiously. It was a Friday.

He panicked. 'Ya Allah! I have chosen this pious day to commit such a sin.' A few minutes later, Arif stopped his bicycle in front of his building and ran upstairs.

He needed to have a bath and change his clothes before going to the mosque for the prayer.

~

Before the Friday prayer, at the gate of the mosque, one of his father's colleagues, Taimur Ali, asked Arif where Zakir was. He told him his brother was not in Patna.

'Zakir never comes for the weekly prayers. I have never seen him in the mosque,' he said. 'I heard he has joined some drama group. For Muslims, drama, film and music is unlawful. He has gone astray. Doesn't your father stop him from doing all these un-Islamic things? Being his elder brother, you should also teach him the difference between sin and virtue.'

Arif said nothing. He was not in a mood to argue, though he did not like Taimur Ali criticizing his brother. He knew that his brother had not gone astray. Zakir was neither a sinner nor an atheist. He was just convinced of the futility of rituals. But he did not reject every ritual. At funeral prayers, he was always the first to arrive.

It is me who is going astray, thought Arif, as he performed

the ritual ablution at the mosque. First, I fell in love with a mother of two, claiming that it was sacred love. Now I have crossed all moral boundaries.

He despised himself. The sacred surroundings of the mosque filled him with a sense of righteousness. A few minutes later, the imam's sermon instilled a sense of divine fear in him, the fear of being burnt in hell, the fear of that eternal fire. The imam continued with his discourse.

'About Nafs-e-Ammarah, the holy book says: the mind of man is ever ready to incite evil but, they who obey the Nafs-e-Ammarah, the natural self, will find their abode in hell. Think! The lightest of hell's punishment is many times more severe than the most severe punishment on this earth.' Then he talked about zina, the sin of fornication; the deepest abyss in the hell is reserved for a fornicator. 'The deadliest of snakes will await you there.'

Descriptions of hell and punishment frightened Arif. He felt like he was being roasted in hell's fire, heat searing his skin. Arif regretted his inappropriate behaviour and resolved not to repeat it. So far, he had been justifying his relationship with Sumitra because the involvement was at an emotional level. But that barrier had been broken now. What kind of filthy degenerate had he become? Arif thought.

How could he face Sumitra now?

He was thankful that he hadn't gone through with the actual act.

~

During the next three weeks, Arif locked himself up in his room and tried to concentrate on his studies. He had ignored them for the last few months; there was a lot to catch up on. Sticking to his weekly routine, he finished the entire book on public administration by Awasthi and Awasthi. He hadn't visited Mritunjay's house fearing an accidental meeting with Sumitra.

Unable to keep away from his friend's place, he decided to visit Mritunjay in the night. Arif walked to the pebbled main road of Bank Colony and was about to turn into the lane leading to Mritunjay's house, when he saw Rahul coming towards him.

As soon as he saw Arif, Rahul began to cry, 'Bhaiyya! Mummy is very ill. And Papa is not home. He has gone to Ranchi,' he said.

'Is Mritunjay home?' he asked.

'Everybody in the colony has gone to attend Sharma uncle's daughter's wedding at Hotel Chanakya.'

'Don't cry, come with me,' Arif said reassuringly.

He thought hard and came up with a phone number. Though he knew that Dr Devashish Ganguly did not make home calls, he dialled his number. He requested, beseeched, pleaded with him. Exasperated, Dr Ganguly agreed.

Spending the night at Sumitra's place was not a good idea. If somebody heard of it, there would be a scandal. But there was no way out. The doctor had advised him to stay with her till morning. He couldn't leave her alone. If something happened to her, he would never forgive himself.

At last, he decided to stay. 'Come what may, I am staying

here,' he said to himself. Sumitra was much more important to him than his reputation. He called his neighbour to connect with his mother and let her know that one of his friends from college was in the hospital and he was going to stay with him during the night.

Arif prepared toast and omelette for Rahul and asked him to go to bed after dinner. Sitting on the edge of her bed where she was sleeping, he felt her forehead with the back of his right palm. It was still hot. As instructed by the doctor, he kept wiping her face and forehead with a piece of cloth soaked in cold water. The doctor had also told him to take a reading of her body temperature from time to time; if the temperature showed a rising trend, she was to be admitted to the hospital immediately.

She was not fully conscious. It was not safe to put the thermometer into her mouth; there was a chance of her snapping it with her teeth. To insert the thermometer in her armpit, Arif would have to insert his hand into her blouse. After what happened on Friday, he did not trust himself. He feared that an accidental touch of her bosom might arouse him. He thought of waking up Rahul but didn't.

He recited some verses in Arabic:

> He who purifies his soul of earthly passion shall be saved and shall not suffer ruin but he who is overcome by his earthly passions should despair of life.

He then recited the Surah Al-Fatiha from the Holy Quran:

> I seek refuge in Allah from the outcast Satan. In the name of Allah, the Most Beneficent, the Most Merciful Praise be to Allah, Lord of the Worlds, the Beneficent, the Merciful. Owner of the Day of Judgement. Thee (alone) we worship; Thee (alone) we ask for help. Show us the straight path, the path of those whom Thou hast favoured; Not (the path) of those who earn Thine anger nor of those who go astray. Amen.

Turning his eyes away, Arif undid two buttons of Sumitra's blouse. With the thermometer in his hand, he moved swiftly, brushing the edge of her bra as he placed the thermometer in her armpit. Her temperature was down to 100.

It was half past two and Arif was dozing by her bed, when Sumitra stirred and muttered something.

'Sumitra,' Arif said softly, overcome with emotion. There was no response and she was fast asleep.

As dawn peeped into the room, Arif woke up and found himself sleeping beside Sumitra, sharing her blanket. Her arms were on his chest. Her hair partly covered his face. He could feel its fragrance. Moving away from her gently, without disturbing her sleep, Arif touched her forehead and was relieved to see that she wasn't warm any more. She was sweating, another indication that the fever had broken. In the kitchen, he washed his face and made himself a cup of tea and a couple of slices of toast for Rahul. Then he called the doctor.

'There is nothing to worry about. Keep giving her the medicine regularly and meet me after three days at my clinic,' the doctor said.

Arif hung up and went back to Sumitra. Despite her pale face, she looked beautiful as ever. Unable to control a sudden impulse, he bent and kissed her on her forehead. She didn't move.

Later, he instructed Rahul to sit by his mother and give her the medicines on time.

'Make sure she eats some biscuits or bread before taking the medicine,' he added. 'When is your father coming back from Ranchi?'

'Today at noon.'

'I am going home now,' Arif said, and wrote down his neighbour's number for Rahul in case Arif needed to be reached. 'Haan, don't tell anybody, not even your father, about my staying at your flat at night.'

'Why?' the boy asked innocently.

'Just don't tell him, that's all. Promise me.'

'Theek hain, I will do as you say, Arif bhaiyya,' he replied.

When Arif came out on the road, it was desolate. Then he saw a stout middle-aged man having a bath beside a handpump by the road.

'Bam Bam Bhole . . .' the man recited loudly and poured water from a jug on his head.

ELEVEN

Arif was in his study and was reading another letter by Sumitra. She had delivered it the same way she had the last time, except she didn't kiss him this time. The letter was shorter and scribbled on a sheet of ruled paper. She had thanked him for his help and also expressed the desire to meet him more frequently.

As Arif read the letter, a blend of happiness and restlessness began to seize his entire body. Self-doubt engulfed him again. He didn't know what he wanted from her. She would never agree to leave her husband and children for him. Even if she did, would he go against his family to marry her? He knew he couldn't.

'Why am I pursuing Sumitra then?' he asked himself.

The sound of footsteps approaching his room alerted Arif. He folded the letter and pushed it under a book on his table.

'Hi Arif.' Mritunjay walked into the room, a tennis racket slung over his shoulder.

Mritunjay had come to invite him to play a tennis match at the New Patna Club. Arif readily accepted the invitation.

He hadn't touched a tennis racket in years. He felt as excited as one feels when going to meet a long-forgotten old flame. There was a time when he had been passionate about the game. One of Mritunjay's former schoolmates, Ajit, who had been recently selected for the IAS, would also be playing. He would ask Ajit to give him some tips for cracking the interview, Arif thought.

Arif paired with Mritunjay against two of Mritunjay's former school friends. Arif found it difficult to control his strokes and served many double faults. Many of his returns went into the net. The volleys he hit landed outside the lines. And his lobs were killed forthright. Even Mritunjay became impatient with Arif's performance and yelled twice during the match. They lost the match in straight sets.

Settling on an iron bench adjacent to the tennis court, Arif looked dejected. Ajit, one of the opponents, said, 'Arif, it was just a friendly match. Don't take it so seriously.'

Arif smiled. 'No, no, Ajitji! I am not upset.'

Mritunjay and Ajit's cousin joined them.

'What is the best way to prepare for the mains and the interview?' Mritunjay asked Ajit.

'See, preparation for the civil services examinations is like playing tennis. Either your service should be very strong, or your return should be perfect. If your backhand is not very good, your forehand should be exceptional. Similarly, you should have one optional subject in which you can excel and are capable of scoring 65 to 70 per cent,' Ajit said.

'That's an interesting analogy,' Arif and Mritunjay said in unison.

'And what about the interview?' Arif asked.

'Collect information about your home state, home district and think about your hobbies, etc. The rest is sheer luck,' Ajit said.

'I'm planning to move to Delhi,' Mritunjay said. 'The coaching classes in Patna are not good.'

'That's a wise decision,' Ajit said.

Arif felt disappointed. He knew Abba couldn't afford to send him to Delhi.

On a grass court, at the far end of the club, Arif saw Ramesh Kumar playing tennis with a middle-aged man.

Soon after, Ajit left in an Ambassador car with his cousin.

'Ajit's father is also an IAS officer,' Mritunjay told Arif.

'Excellent!' Arif was impressed.

Mritunjay had to go to Postal Park to meet somebody, so he started his scooter and went on his way.

Arif stood alone on the footpath outside the New Patna Club, waiting for an autorickshaw.

Ramesh Kumar pulled up in his car next to Arif and offered him a lift, which Arif politely refused. He felt awkward interacting with the man whose wife he was having an affair with. But Ramesh Kumar wouldn't take no for an answer and persuaded Arif to get in.

'During my college days, I used to be a great fan of Rod Laver and John Newcombe, and, of course, our own Vijay Amritraj. It's become very difficult to find time to play after work nowadays, though occasionally I do get together with my friends,' Ramesh Kumar said.

'That's good.'

'Sumitra was telling me the other day that your maths

and English are very good. And that you have agreed to give tuitions to Rahul?' Ramesh Kumar asked. They had crossed Raja Bazaar and were about to reach Ashiana Mor.

Sumitra hadn't talked to Arif about this. But he could guess why she had said this to her husband. Don't say yes Arif; you are only stepping closer to the fire.

'What are you thinking about, Arif?'

'Nothing, uncle!' Arif said, rubbing the back of his neck.

'So, when are you going to start teaching Rahul?'

'From . . . next Monday,' he stammered, feeling overwhelmed at the prospect of meeting Sumitra almost daily.

'Great!'

As Ramesh Kumar dropped Arif near the main gate of his colony, Arif saw a police sub-inspector sitting on a red plastic chair under a mango tree, barely ten yards from the gate. Four constables stood at the gate with sturdy sticks in their hands.

From the colour of their caps, Arif knew that the officer and the constables were from the District Police, a wing of the police force distinct from the Bihar Military Police where Abba worked. The former were perceived to be more powerful as they were responsible for maintaining day-to-day law and order in the state, and were in a better position to intimidate civilians and extract bribes from them. The latter were more of a reserve force.

The officer languidly raised a hand with a cigarette, gesturing at Arif not to enter.

'What's the issue, sir?' Arif asked the officer.

'There is a meeting of VIPs going on at the police

auditorium. This road has been closed for security reasons,' the officer said haughtily.

'But I live inside this colony. My father is an inspector here,' Arif argued.

'Go from gate no. 2.'

'But my house is right here. Why should I walk two more miles?' Arif's tone had become aggressive, too.

He started walking towards the gate but the officer grabbed him by his collar and said, 'Rangdari karta hain; don't try to act clever.'

Arif, too, turned and grabbed the sub-inspector's collar.

'How dare you touch my brother?' Zakir suddenly appeared out of nowhere and slapped the officer. Zakir easily overpowered the sub-inspector who was short and plump. Seeing their officer scuffling with two boys, the constables at the main gate ran towards them.

As Arif tried to separate Zakir from the sub-inspector, he felt a sharp pain on his shoulder, and before he could react, a constable took hold of him. Arif watched in horror as one of the constables raised his thick stick to hit Zakir. Arif screamed as his brother collapsed to the ground, his long hair wet with blood. Unthinking, Arif jumped over the policemen with red caps, pulling one of them to the ground. From the corner of his eye he saw four or five policemen in green caps rushing towards them.

'Arrey! They are Khan sahab's sons. Call the jeep immediately. Fuck these bastards from the District Police. How dare they hit our children on our campus?' Arif heard them saying.

The fight had now turned into Bihar Military Police

versus Bihar District Police. Their contempt for each other was well known. Something hit Arif on the head and everything became blurry.

Arif opened his eyes and found himself in a hospital bed. His bandaged head throbbed with pain. Abba stood next to his bed, worry lines criss-crossing his face.

'How is Zakir?' Arif asked.

'Zakir is in the ICU. The doctor said there might be internal injuries.'

Pangs of guilt coupled with pain hit Arif. He wished he had not gotten into a fight with the sub-inspector. God forbid, if anything happens to Zakir, I'll not forgive myself.

Years ago in Jamalpura, when Zakir was just five, he had slapped a teacher of the local madrasa because he had twisted Arif's ears for not completing his homework. 'Saala maulvi, why did he hurt my brother? I will kill him,' Zakir had fumed as Arif pulled him away from the teacher.

'Baua!' It was Amma, her face stained with tears.

'I am fine, Amma. Please pray for our Zakir,' Arif said.

Dadi was also there, quietly reciting holy verses.

He saw Rabiya, Nazneen and Huma enter the general ward. Their faces were pale and they didn't say anything.

Closing his eyes, Arif dozed off as images from the past flashed in his mind. He had turned into a six-year-old boy again. He saw Zakir playing hide-and-seek with him in the courtyard of the mosque in Jamalpura. Suddenly, Zakir began to run away and Arif called out to him.

'What are you mumbling?' Arif heard a familiar voice.

He woke up with a start and realized it was already morning.

'How is Zakir, Abba?'

'The doctor says he is better now.'

'Shukr Allah!'

'Did you find out who the police officer was, Abba?'

'I filed an FIR at Shastri Nagar police station. Once Zakir is out of hospital, I'll try to find out more. I'll certainly teach the bastard a lesson for daring to touch my sons,' Abba said, his eyes blazing.

Half an hour later, Abba, Amma and Arif's sisters went to see Zakir. Dadi was offering namaz. Suddenly, Arif heard sounds of wailing from the adjoining waiting room.

Were his mother and sisters crying?

Arif panicked and jumped out of his bed, stumbling to the waiting hall.

Two women were howling over a dead body on a stretcher, covered with a white sheet. A ward boy stood near them, almost expressionless. Arif heaved a sigh of relief but felt sorry for the women. Turning away, he saw Abba on the phone at the reception. And he also noticed Sumitra talking to his sisters in the waiting area.

Abba saw Arif and came running to him.

'You shouldn't be getting out of bed,' Abba said.

'I want to see Zakir, Abba.'

'I will take you to him as soon as he is moved to the general ward,' Abba said, and helped him back to his bed.

Sumitra followed them in with his sisters a few minutes later. She too had been crying. Her reassuring presence worked as an anodyne on his restless soul.

A few minutes later, Mritunjay's father, Prem Prakash Pandey, came to see him. He was a short, plump man with a French-cut beard. He sat on the chair next to Arif's bed and enquired about his health. He also informed Arif that Mritunjay had left for Delhi to attend coaching classes and would call Arif once he was out of the hospital.

~

A month later, on a cool afternoon, Zakir sat on his bed at home, his head still bandaged. Arif had recovered completely and sat next to his brother. Dadi sat on a bamboo ottoman near the bed.

'Dadi, tell me a story,' Zakir said. This had been his routine since he had been discharged from the hospital. Arif smiled.

Dadi cleared her throat and recited Bismillah before narrating her story.

'During the reign of Mughal ruler Akbar the Great, a strapping young Pathan called Bakhtiyar from Afghanistan arrived in Delhi. As soon as he reached the city, he visited the dargah of the great Sufi saint Hazrat Nizamuddin Auliya to offer his prayers. Walking back from the shrine, he saw an old man with a long white beard being mercilessly beaten up by two sturdy-looking masked men. Bakhtiyar instantly caught hold of the masked men and threw them to the ground. He was a Pathan in the real sense, strong and brave. He beat the two attackers with much relish. Finally, they took flight and disappeared into the narrow alleys of Nizamuddin.

'The old man was wounded. So Bakhtiyar sought help from a passer-by and took the old man to a hakim. Once the treatment was over, Bakhtiyar dropped the old man off at his home in a hired horse cart. The old man had a palatial house in the heart of the city. Bakhtiyar later discovered that the old man was an emperor's officer-in-charge for the Delhi administration.

'Impressed by Bakhtiyar's valour, the old man not only helped him acquire a senior position in Akbar's army, but also offered him his only daughter's hand in marriage.

'Soon a son was born to Bakhtiyar. He was named Jamaluddin Khan. Bakhtiyar wanted his son to rise to the post of army chief, and to become as powerful as Bairam Khan, the then army chief. But Jamaluddin was more interested in spirituality and Sufism and didn't have worldly aspirations. He became a disciple of a well-known Sufi saint of Delhi and spent most of his time in his master's company, either in prayer or serving the poor. Despite his parents' constant pestering, he refused to get married. He was forty-two when his father died in a ferry accident. A few weeks later, incapable of overcoming the grief of losing her husband, his mother was found dead in her sleep.

'Devastated, Jamaluddin sought refuge in prayer. One night he fell asleep after the midnight prayer and dreamt about a saint with a glowing face. The mysterious saint asked him to go to the east and spread the message of Islam.

'The very next day he set out on a journey.

'After months of travelling, he reached Motihari in the suba of Bihar. Another dream directed him to go further. He didn't know his destination, but he was being guided by some unseen force. So he kept walking and reached a desolate place where there was an old, dilapidated palace.

Deciding to spend the night there, he cleaned the veranda of the building, and placed his meagre belongings – a lota, a prayer mat, a sheet and some dried dates – in a niche in the veranda wall. Then he unrolled a straw mat on the dusty stone-paved floor and lay down. That night the same saint appeared in his dream and told him to stay on and spend the rest of his life in that uninhabited palace. In the morning, he woke up and found himself surrounded by the men of the nearby villages.

'The villagers were surprised to find a stranger with a resplendent halo sleeping in the veranda of a haunted palace. The spirits had infested that palace, supposedly to protect the treasure of an ancient king. Anyone who had gone to the palace at night had died mysteriously. Fifty years earlier, the local king had sent twenty armed soldiers to search for the so-called treasure. All the soldiers had been found dead the very next day. After that nobody had dared to step inside the palace.

'Only a holy man could have spent a night unharmed in the haunted building, believed the villagers. From his beard and skullcap, they could guess that he was a Muslim saint, a Sufi. So, they started calling him Pir sahab. In a short span of time, men and women from faraway places began to visit Pir sahab for his blessings.

'Pir sahab's fame also travelled to the Rajput feudal lord of the area, Zamindar sahab, and he came to see him. The zamindar, a tall handsome man with a thick moustache, was so impressed by Pir sahab that he became his devout follower. Later, he and his entire family converted to Islam.

His only daughter was so fascinated by Hazrat Jamaluddin's spiritual beauty that she vowed to marry no one but him. When the zamindar came to the saint offering his daughter's hand in marriage, Pir sahab reluctantly accepted his proposal. Pir sahab built himself a hut of mud and straw in front of the old palace. As time went by, the couple had three sons. From these sons, their descendants multiplied. Around the hut grew the village of Jamalpura.

'After his death, the saint was buried in his hut and it became his mausoleum. It came to be known as the Hazrat Jamaluddin Rahmatullah Alaih's shrine. Years later one of Pir sahab's descendants rebuilt the shrine into a huge sandstone structure with four minarets and a big green dome, which exists even today.

'Hazrat Jamaluddin Pir is not only the patron saint of our village but also our ancestor. We and all our extended family have descended from him. Our village is named after him,' Dadi concluded the story.

Arif had heard the story before but he enjoyed this new revelation of a family history. Dadi had the knack to turn a simple narrative into something intriguing and magical.

Dadi looked at the wall clock, and then rose from her place. As she walked out of the room, she said, 'Time for namaz-e-asar.' Zakir stretched out on his bed to get some sleep. Arif picked up a yellow silk Bhagalpuri chadar from the clothes line and covered Zakir.

It took three more months before Zakir recovered fully and was able to attend classes in his college. And this was when Arif began tutoring Rahul.

On the first day, Kavita opened the door for Arif. Sumitra was sitting on a red plastic chair in the balcony and shelling peas.

As he entered, Sumitra got up, pulled up a centre table and two wooden chairs from a corner of the balcony and then called her son. 'Rahul, Arif bhaiyya has come to teach you.'

On his next visit, Arif didn't see Kavita.

'Where is Kavita?' he asked.

'At school in Hazaribagh. She'll come back to Patna only after her exams are over,' Sumitra replied.

Arif would tutor Rahul six days a week in the afternoons. After the lessons, Rahul would leave to play cricket with the neighbourhood boys.

Left alone, Sumitra and Arif would sit together in her drawing room reciting their favourite poets' couplets to each other. On many occasions they recited the poems they had written for each other. At times, Arif would hold Sumitra's hands and gently kiss them. And, at times, Sumitra would close her eyes and permit him to plant a soft kiss on her cheeks.

On some days, they would discuss a particular book which they had read recently.

On one such afternoon, Arif had asked Sumitra a question about the benefits of falling in love.

Sumitra had replied with a famous couplet:

Poochhte ho ishq se kya fayeda?
Pehle yeh batao fayeda se kya fayeda?

(You ask me, what is the benefit of being in love?
I ask you, what is the benefit of being benefited?)

Nobody does a cost–benefit analysis before falling in love, Arif thought and smiled. Once or twice a month, Ramesh would be home and he would invite Arif for a game of chess over a cup of coffee, which Arif sometimes reluctantly accepted and when possible excused himself under some pretext or the other. Arif felt uncomfortable, pretending indifference towards Sumitra in her husband's presence, never looking at her face.

TWELVE

Arif was intrigued when Zakir asked him to come to the terrace to discuss something. He was even more surprised to find Rabiya and Nazneen waiting for them.

'What is the issue, Zakir?' he asked.

'Rabiya wants to tell you something,' Zakir said.

'Bhaiyya . . . Nazneen . . . you tell,' Rabiya said, fumbling with her words.

'Don't hesitate. Please tell me,' Arif said.

'One of my friends in Bank Colony said that someone told her you are having an affair with Sumitra aunty. She also told me that she is a woman of shady character. And–'

'Who told you this?' Arif's face turned white.

'Sorry, bhaiyya, I can't name her. We are sure you can't do anything like that. We also don't believe Sumitra aunty is that kind of woman. I am personally very fond of her. You are our brother, so it is our duty to inform you.'

'Don't be sorry for telling me. In fact, you should have told me earlier.'

'I did, bhaiyya. I hinted to you discreetly on many occasions. You should stop visiting her house immediately.

Think of our family's reputation. Think of her reputation, too,' Rabiya said.

'Are Abba and Amma aware of this rumour?'

'Fortunately, no.'

'Anyway, I'll immediately stop teaching Rahul. So, no more visits to her house,' Arif said. But his voice lacked conviction.

'Rabiya! Nazneen! Where are you? Are you upstairs?' It was Amma.

'Okay, bhaiyya. Amma is calling us.'

Once their sisters were gone, Zakir looked intently at Arif. 'Can you tell me the truth?'

'What truth?'

'Is Sumitra aunty the woman you told me about a few years ago?'

'Yes.'

'Oh my God, I can't believe it. I thought you had forgotten her. I didn't bring up the topic fearing it would revive your obsession.'

'Yes, I tried to do that. But–'

'What next?'

'Nothing. I haven't done anything. It's just an emotional attachment. I promise you I will get out of this relationship very soon.'

'I know, bhaiyya. You can't do anything wrong. But if this news leaks out to our relatives, it will be very difficult to find a suitable match for our sisters. And Abba and Amma! They'll die of shock.'

'I understand, Zakir . . . let's drop this subject. I promise I will snap all ties with her. Let's talk about something else.'

Arif was struggling to recover from the shock that people had noticed, and worst of all, now his little sisters knew.

'Okay. What happened to the Golden Coaching Centre job?' Zakir asked.

'They have promised to call me soon. But don't tell Abba that I am planning to start teaching,' Arif said.

'I won't.'

'Arrey Zakir, I forgot to tell you something important. Gulshan Kumar has launched a talent hunt competition to find actors for his new film.'

'Really?'

'I have a copy of this month's *Priya* magazine. The application form is attached with the magazine. If selected, Gulshan Kumar will launch you as a hero.'

'It is a good opportunity.' Zakir looked visibly excited.

'Come downstairs, I'll give you the application form.'

Their worries forgotten, the brothers went downstairs together.

~

Sumitra's daughter had returned to Patna and joined Patna Women's College after graduating from school. Meeting Sumitra at her house was out of the question.

In a city like Patna, lovers have to risk their reputations and, at times, their lives to meet each other. At the Sanjay Gandhi Biological Park, popularly known as the Zoo, on Bailey Road, one can find couples behind bushes, under trees and inside the rose garden, struggling unsuccessfully to steal a few private moments with each other. Even a soft kiss or a hug can invite disapproving stares, vulgar comments and, occasionally, police interventions. Then, there's the courtyard of the Patna Museum, with few visitors, and a lush green stretch of lawn. But all the autorickshaws from Bailey Road to Gandhi Maidan take the route adjacent to the museum, and there are chances that someone known to you will find you with your lover, and there will be a scandal – in Patna you just need to be seen with a girl for a scandal. Kumrahar is another place where lovers meet in the shadows of the ruins of ancient Pataliputra built by Emperor Ashoka. But on the behest of the archaeological department, policemen move around to save the cultural heritage from 'defacement' by people. So, all the three possible locations were out of bounds for Sumitra and Arif.

They talked to each other through love letters written in Urdu, under the pretext of exchanging magazines and books. Once or twice a month when Ramesh Kumar was out of Patna, Sumitra met Arif near the Patna junction. From there they would take an autorickshaw to go to the other side of the Ganga to the neighbouring town of Hajipur. In the corner of the dingy Ganesh Chitra Mandir theatre, they would talk in whispers, sharing a bottle of cold drink and hot samosas, occasionally touching each other's oil-stained hands.

'I get great comfort in your company, Sumitra. I feel like I'm in heaven. I don't have any worries when I am with you,' Arif often said.

Sumitra would reply, 'I too feel serene and peaceful when I am in your arms or when I rest my head on your shoulder.'

THIRTEEN

Heavy rain slapped Arif's face as he stood on his balcony, bent over the railing, his hands outstretched, his palms feeling the full force of the raindrops. Soaked in the cold rainwater, he felt great. The downpour was so thick and dense that it cut the visibility down to a couple of metres. The sidewalks of the roads facing his building were flooded. On the road, he saw a man with an umbrella rushing in the direction of his apartment building. When he came closer, Arif realized it was Zakir.

As soon as Zakir entered their flat, he threw the umbrella on the floor with a flourish and pulled Arif in a tight hug.

'I have been shortlisted for the screen test for Gulshan Kumar's next film,' Zakir said, beaming. He pulled out an envelope from the inner pocket of his windcheater. Grabbing a bath towel from a chair on the balcony, Arif dried his hair, face and hands. It was only then that he took the envelope from Zakir and read aloud the letter, his voice brimming with excitement. His brother had made it to the top twenty out of 40,000 applicants, no easy feat.

Dear Zakir Khan,

You are among the top twenty out of forty thousand applications received. You are invited for the screen test in Bombay.

Date: 12 August 1995. Time: 11.30 a.m.
Venue: Mehboob Studios, Hill Road, Bandra West
Bombay, Maharashtra – 400050
For Super Cassettes Industries
Ritika Oberoi

'Would Abba allow me to take the screen test?' Zakir was apprehensive.

'Don't worry, I'll talk to Abba. I'll convince him to let you go.'

'No, bhaiyya! Please don't say anything to Abba. I've made up my mind. On Friday evening, I'm leaving for Bombay. I've already asked a colleague from the theatre to book a ticket. You tell Abba after I leave for Bombay.'

'As you wish, my brother.' But Arif was worried. He didn't know how Abba would react. 'But you need money to survive in that big city.'

'I have two thousand rupees from the prize I won in the inter-university drama festival last month. I will manage with that for a while. In the meantime, I'll find a part-time job. But this is only if I'm not selected for the movie.' Zakir's voice was full of confidence.

On Friday morning, Arif pressed two thousand rupees in Zakir's hands.

'Bhaiyya, how did you arrange this money?' Zakir enquired.

'Arrey, why do you worry about that?' Arif tried to avoid the question.

'Phir bhi,' Zakir insisted.

'You seem to have forgotten that I have started teaching at Golden Coaching.'

'Oh yes. But you need money to pay for your Hindi literature tuition.'

'I'll manage. Anyway, the current batch of Balram Tiwari is full. I'll start only early next year. By that time you'll be a big star and then you can help me.'

'Inshallah!' Zakir smiled.

'Where are you going to stay in Bombay?'

'One of my friends from my theatre group is already there. He'll arrange for my stay as a paying guest with a Maharashtrian family.'

'When you reach there, call me on Mritunjay's phone. I'll be there in the evening around seven.'

'Theek hain, bhaiyya.'

Zakir didn't return home that night, Amma was worried and asked Arif. Hesitantly, Arif told Amma where Zakir was. Amma was shocked but she managed to pass on the news to Abba. To everybody's surprise, Abba didn't get angry. Instead, he asked for Zakir's address in Bombay so he could send him a money order.

Grief

FOURTEEN

Getting down from a minibus at Naya Mor, Arif looked around for a cycle rickshaw, but there were none.

It was a summer afternoon in 1996. The wind felt as if it was blowing from a blast furnace. Dust rose in tiny whirlwinds. Pieces of paper, polythene bags and dry leaves moved in circles, rising up a little before falling back to the earth to wait for the next whirlwind to lift them. All the shops were closed and there was not a soul in sight. The desolate road leading to gate no. 2 of Police Colony sizzled under unrelenting heat.

The colony was at least a thirty-minute walk from there. Arif decided to take refuge under a huge peepal tree and wait for a rickshaw. He unfolded the Hindi newspaper *Hindustan* and settled on a cemented platform under the tree. The front page had a photograph of Atal Bihari Vajpayee taking the oath as the new Indian prime minister.

Suddenly, Arif heard a girl shriek and turned to look in the direction of the sound. Barely twenty yards from him, he saw a man trying to pull a girl towards him. As Arif rose from his place, the girl shrieked again and Arif saw her face clearly.

It was Kavita.

'Abey saale!' Arif yelled, as he bent and picked up a half-broken brick from the footpath and started running towards them.

'Arif bhaiyya,' Kavita shouted in relief and anguish when she saw him.

By the time Arif reached her, the man had gotten on to his black Yamaha parked nearby and sped away. Arif hurled the piece of brick in his direction but it missed him.

Arif turned to Kavita and found her convulsing in sobs.

'Don't cry, Kavita. You are safe now.' He felt a surge of affection for her, almost in a fatherly sort of way.

Kavita was still sobbing when Arif spotted a rickshaw and hailed it.

~

'What happened?' Sumitra asked in a panic-stricken voice. She looked at Kavita intently and then turned to Arif. Kavita remained silent for a few seconds and then she grabbed her mother and started crying.

Arif described the incident briefly.

'Hey bhagwan!' she said, and hugged Kavita even tighter. 'Thank God for sending Arif in time.'

~

Three or four days after the Naya Mor incident, one morning Arif was surprised to find Kavita sitting with his sisters in their makeshift drawing-cum-bedroom. She had the *Fundamentals of Organic Chemistry* in her hands. She was dressed in a long sand-brown skirt and a cream-coloured top.

'I am here to learn chemistry from you,' Kavita said, smiling as she brushed her hair away from her face.

Arif smiled back. 'Okay. Come with me to my study room.'

Why had she come suddenly?

Amma, who was chopping vegetables in the same room, turned her disapproving gaze towards them. The expression on Rabiya's face had suddenly changed. Maybe she was trying to decipher the meaning of Kavita's sudden arrival at their flat.

'I think my study room is very small. Better to sit in the balcony.'

From that day, Kavita's visits became frequent.

Amma suspects something is cooking between Kavita and me, Arif thought. Though she hadn't said anything, Arif could sense it. Arif was sure that Sumitra too was suspicious. She even hinted at it a couple of times. But Arif didn't know how to convey this to Kavita. And he wasn't sure himself why the girl was there, but he didn't have the heart to turn her away.

A few months later, on the day of Raksha Bandhan, Kavita visited Arif's flat to tie a rakhi on Arif's wrist, proclaiming him her brother.

From that day, Amma's behaviour towards Kavita changed and she started to call her 'beti'. Rabiya too began to treat Kavita differently. There was no room for suspicion any more.

It sounded awkward to Arif when Kavita called him brother. How could a daughter of the woman he was courting be his sister? Arif felt like he was a character in a Greek play.

Many months had passed since Kavita had started visiting Arif regularly. They had grown closer and Kavita began to share details of her personal life with him.

One day, she hesitantly told him that she was in love with a Muslim boy called Manzar Ali and showed him a photograph of a fair, plump man dressed in a black suit. She wanted Arif to meet him. Arif wondered how he would react if one of his sisters told him she wanted to marry a Hindu boy.

Manzar's name seemed familiar and so did the man in the picture. But where had he seen him?

That night as Arif lay in bed, he suddenly recalled that a 'Manzar Ali' had been in the newspapers last year and his photo had been on the front page. He had had an affair with the daughter of a prominent Marwari business family of Patna. When she had become pregnant, he had abandoned her. The girl had committed suicide. The local media had picked up the incident and an FIR had been lodged against him. But Manzar's father had the right political connections and deep pockets, and Manzar had come out unscathed. Arif was sure that he was the same Manzar Ali. Beset by a strange foreboding, Arif decided to meet him immediately.

They decided to meet at Mayur restaurant inside the Sanjay Gandhi Biological Park. Manzar came dressed in white. Even his white patent leather shoes matched his safari suit. He was a man of medium height, with puffed-up cheeks, and was fair, almost like an Englishman.

'Assalam alaikum, bhaijaan,' he greeted Arif. There was extra warmth in his voice.

Arif didn't like him at all. There was something devious about him.

'Please wait for us here,' Arif said to Kavita.

'Okay, bhaiyya,' she said, settling on an iron chair in the restaurant.

Arif and Manzar came out and started walking together.

'When Kavita told me that her brother was coming to meet me, I was worried. Then she told me about you. I was happy.' Manzar grinned. 'See, it will be a work of great virtue for you if you help me marry Kavita. You'll discharge your duty as a brother . . . and you'll earn the merit – sawab – for converting a non-believer to Islam.'

'Who told you that I'll allow you to marry Kavita?' Arif said.

'Kyun? What's wrong with me?'

'Everybody is aware of your reputation in Patna. Need I say more?' Arif replied.

'Arif sahab, people make up stories. I've also heard a lot about you and Kavita's mom,' he said, combing his long hair with his fingers. 'By the way, one of my friends lives in Bank Colony.'

Manzar stopped and looked directly into Arif's eyes. The grin was back on Manzar's face. 'I haven't told Kavita about this. Because I don't react on the basis of hearsay and rumours,' Manzar said quietly.

Arif felt as if a cauldron of boiling oil had been poured on him. *How dare he talk to me like this?*

'I don't want to talk to you. Go away and do what you please,' Arif said as anger coursed through his veins. Arif quickly walked away from Manzar.

'What happened, bhaiyya?' Kavita was right behind him.

Arif hoped Kavita had not overheard the conversation. Then he said in a stern voice, 'Let's go home. I have to share something about Manzar.'

They walked in grim silence for some time.

'Bhaiyya, please don't tell Papa or Mummy about Manzar.' The poor thing looked terrified.

'On one condition,' Arif said.

'Condition?' Kavita was surprised.

'You won't meet this rascal again.'

'Why, bhaiyya?'

'Manzar is a complete scoundrel. He has ruined the lives of many girls.'

'I don't believe . . .'

'If you're ready to ruin your life, go marry him.' Arif hailed a cycle rickshaw for himself and left the place.

~

The same evening, Arif told Sumitra about Kavita's affair with Manzar. There was an expression of horror on her face.

'I can't believe that my daughter is having an affair with a Muslim boy. And one with such a bad reputation. Is she just meeting him? Or has she done anything else?' Sumitra said, holding her head in her hands.

Arif understood what she meant by 'anything else'.

'And why not? If I can have an affair at thirty-nine, why can't she?' she continued talking to herself. 'I must talk to Ramesh immediately.'

She went inside her house and Arif heard her agitated voice as she spoke to her husband on the telephone.

'What are you going to do now? Are you going to talk to Manzar Ali?' Arif asked cautiously.

'What should I say to that guy? And what is left to say to Kavita? She has tainted the name of our family by having an affair with a Muslim. These Muslims are all alike. First they'll seduce a Hindu girl into a relationship and then they will force her to convert.'

'How can you talk like this? All Muslims aren't bad,' Arif said.

'But why is it always that a Hindu girl elopes with a Muslim boy and not the other way round?'

'Well, Muslim girls also elope with Hindus all the time. Probably you think our love affair is also a conspiracy. And that I'm a jihadi who has come here to defile a Hindu woman,' Arif said.

'Who knows,' Sumitra replied instantly.

Arif felt as if somebody had hit him with a hot iron rod. He still couldn't believe that Sumitra had actually said what she had. Arif was silent and hurt and trying hard to find appropriate words to respond to her sarcastic barb.

He couldn't.

He simply walked out of the room.

~

It had been a month since the encounter with Sumitra, but her words still bit him like scorpions. How can she think about me like that? Arif wallowed in self-pity. His love story with Sumitra was over. Or was he going to see her again?

Arif was waiting for his turn at the Young Bihar Cyber Café, the only internet café in the entire Raja Bazaar area, when his thoughts invariably went back to his brother, as they had often in the last two months, for Zakir had neither called nor sent a message in the last three months. It had been over a year since Zakir had left for Bombay. Arif had called Zakir's landlady and she had told him that Zakir had moved to some other place and she had not seen him since. He had not left any address or number with her. Everybody was worried. Arif decided that he would go to Bombay if Zakir didn't call him in the next ten days.

It was Zakir's habit to go incommunicado whenever he travelled out of Patna. But three months was too long a period, even by Zakir's standards.

Since there was no phone in their home and Zakir had to call on their neighbour's number, Zakir preferred letters to telephone calls.

'Why disturb the Verma family unnecessarily?' Zakir wrote to Arif.

His first letter had arrived a month after he reached Bombay. He had not been selected in the screen test. An assistant director had mocked his pronunciation and called him suitable for acting only in nautanki performances.

Zakir had initially written letters to Arif detailing his daily struggles to make his mark as an actor and to survive in the megacity. In between, he had telephoned him four times, but those had been brief conversations and had been limited to 'How are you? And how is everyone in the family?'

A year later, an internet café had opened at Raja Bazaar, and his letters had been replaced by emails. Internet was a new thing in Patna and it cost a fortune to use it. So Arif visited the café only once in two weeks, mostly on Saturday afternoons. For just fifteen minutes, he had to pay twenty rupees. That was how much his week's travel around the city cost him.

Today there was no new email in his inbox, except unsolicited promotional mail offers to buy a designer purse, bestselling books, cures for impotency, etc. He began to reread Zakir's earlier emails.

From: zakirkhan_actor@hotmail.com
Date: 21 June 1997
To: Arif Khan <arif1970@rediffmail.com>
Dear bhaiyya,

Assalam alaikum,

I hope everything is fine in Patna. I have got a chance to work with a model coordinator called Malkani. He has promised to get me a role in one of Yash Chopra's films. I am very excited about meeting Yash Chopra in person. What a great filmmaker he is!

More in the next email.

Give my regards to Dadi, Abba and Amma. Love to Rabiya, Nazneen and Huma.

Your brother,

Zakir

Date: 11 July 1997

Dear bhaiyya,

Assalam alaikum,

You will be disappointed to know that the meeting with Yash Chopra didn't happen. Malkani is a fraud. In fact, he has taken money from many aspiring actors and then disappeared. Next time I will be careful.

Give my regards to Dadi, Abba and Amma. Love to Rabiya, Nazneen and Huma.

Your brother,

Zakir

Date: 2 February 1998

Dear bhaiyya,

Assalam alaikum,

As suggested by my actor friends, I have started to visit Prithvi Theatre regularly. You know, this theatre is owned by the famous Kapoor family. Everybody says this is the place where well-known directors and producers come and the best way to get noticed is to be seen here.

Let's see what happens next.

Your brother,

Zakir

The next and last email was sent on 24 February, in which Zakir mentioned starting part-time work for a company and that there was no need to send him money.

As he was reading through the emails, Arif received a new email from Rajeeb Mohanty, one of Zakir's new friends in Bombay. Arif had recovered the email ID from the last mass email Zakir had sent out, an inspirational quote on how to succeed in life. Zakir sometimes shared these with his friends and Arif. Not having heard from his brother, Arif had written to the three email IDs in Zakir's forwarded mails. One of them had finally replied. Arif opened the email with both fear and enthusiasm.

From: rajeeb.mohanty@yahoo.com
Date: 23 April 1998
Subject: Zakir
To: Arif Khan <arif1970@rediffmail.com>
Dear Arif bhai,

Salaam,

The first time I met Zakir was when he came to live with the Tirodkar family as a paying guest. I was also a paying guest there. I'm a budding screenplay writer from Orissa.

Zakir worked part-time at a gift shop and was paid two thousand rupees for a month's work. But that isn't enough to survive in this city. After paying our landlady, he wasn't left with enough to pay for travel to the studios and offices of film producers. He told me that he didn't want to be a burden on his family, so he lied to you that he was getting small ad films and he could support himself financially. Malkani had duped him out of ten thousand rupees. He regretted that loss greatly. He had borrowed that money from three of our actor friends and he had to pay them back as well.

Two months back he lost the part-time job at the gift shop when it shut down. He desperately needed work. He paid the landlady what he got from the gift shop as his last salary and vacated the place.

Zakir's dream of acting in a film is still alive and kicking. He often spoke of his life in Patna with you. From his stories, it seemed like you were friends rather than brothers. He was also worried about you and thought of you often.

The last time I met him, he was with Aslam bhai who is an office-bearer at the Junior Artists' Association. Zakir was almost in tears when he told me that he had to do tiny roles in movies. He had come here to be a Dilip Kumar or an Amitabh Bachchan or a Shah Rukh Khan and had instead ended up playing small roles of beggars, lepers or a goon's sidekick and was often part of a crowd in some inconspicuous scene. They pay him between two hundred and five hundred rupees for an eight-hour shift.

I felt sorry for him. But what could I do? I too am struggling to make ends meet in this city of dreams. The city that beguiles many like us with the promise of a great fortune, but assigns most of us to the dustbin of history. For the last one and a half months, I haven't seen Zakir. If I meet him somewhere, I'll ask him to call you.

If he talks to you, please ask him to return to Patna. I have also promised my father that if nothing happens in the next three months, I will return home.

Hope my letter has given you some solace.

Regards,

Rajeeb

FIFTEEN

On a breezy summer morning in 1998, Arif was lying on the old sofa in the balcony and going through the sports pages of the *Times of India* when there was a knock on the door. Abba, who was sitting on a chair studying an official file, opened the door before Arif could get to it. A dark-skinned man with paan-stained teeth and dressed in white khadi clothes stood at the door. The man greeted Abba with folded hands and then whispered something, pointing a finger in the direction of the road.

'Come downstairs with four or five glasses of Rooh Afza sherbet,' Abba told Arif and accompanied the khadi-clad man.

Arif looked out at the road in front of his apartment building. There were three vehicles, one white Tata Sumo, a blue Mahindra Commander jeep and a white Maruti 800 car. Abba was standing near the Sumo and was talking to someone inside the vehicle.

Arif went downstairs with the sherbet and offered it to the men inside the car. A plump man with a double chin and a thick gold chain around his neck sat on the back seat. He was wearing a pair of green-framed Ray-Ban sunglasses. The man lifted a glass and sipped slowly as he talked to Abba.

'See Khan sahab! Because of the Muslim–Yadav factor you are untouched so far but if you continue with your arbitrary ways, you may find yourself in big trouble. Dadan Roy is not only my friend but he also has direct connections with the chief minister.' He scratched his head in a leisurely fashion as he talked. His tone had an element of threat.

Abba looked worried. He had been posted in the police headquarters for the last ten years and had been looking after an important department called NGO or 'Not Going Out'. His responsibilities included keeping track of intelligence reports on anti-national activities in the state, looking into allegations against senior IPS officers and arranging for transfers of officers. Handling transfers was lucrative for those who had no qualms about accepting money for recommending a transfer of an officer to a place where the officer could make good money through bribes. A deputy superintendent of police seeking a transfer near the coal mines of south Bihar would easily pay fifty thousand rupees because he knew that he could recover twice that amount in fifteen days' time.

Abba, being the head of his department, didn't permit bribes. He was particular that every transfer and posting be decided according to government guidelines. Many of his juniors resented him for preventing them from getting some 'upar ki kamaai'. So far his boss, the head of Bihar Police, had been of the same orientation. But with the arrival of the new director general of police, things had changed. He had brought in Dadan Roy as a sub-inspector to the police headquarters on the recommendations of a senior cabinet minister in the state. Dadan, from day one, disliked Abba's style of functioning. He knew that making some quick money was impossible. Dadan wanted to get rid of Abba. Abba, too, kept a close watch on him.

The men left and although Abba remained concerned, he was stubborn. He would never give up on his principles.

The following Thursday Abba was transferred from the police head office to the fifth battalion of the Bihar Military Police at Patna. Dadan Roy replaced him as the head of the NGO department. The same evening Abba reported to his new boss. Three days later Abba got a letter of deputation for a police picket in a Naxalite-infested area near Jehanabad.

About a month back, Maoists had attacked a police picket in the district. Hours later reinforcements arrived and found five constables with their throats slit. They never found the bodies of the rest of the policemen. That incident was fresh in everyone's minds. Amma begged Abba to refuse the posting and if it didn't work, maybe even go into voluntary retirement.

Abba wasn't in the mood to listen. 'Hamida, I am a Pathan and I can't run away from my duty like a coward,' Abba said. 'Thousands of policemen are performing their duties in the Naxalite areas. Anyway, life and death are in Allah's hands,' Abba added philosophically. Behind the facade of a philosopher and a Pathan was a man worried about feeding his family, even at the cost of his life.

A few weeks after Abba had left for his new posting, Arif saw Amma pacing in the corridor with prayer beads in her right hand. In the morning, she had seen a crow perched on the windowsill of her room, cawing incessantly. It was a bad omen, she told Arif. 'Ya Allah, please save our family from evil eyes,' Arif heard Amma murmuring as she unrolled her prayer mat.

Zakir hadn't called or emailed yet. Though his friend Rajeeb had again confirmed in an email that he was all right, Arif was still worried. *Why is Zakir not getting in touch? This time when Abba comes home on leave, I'll seek his permission to go to Bombay.* As he thought of Abba, he was concerned about the difficult life he must be leading in the heart of the rebel-controlled zone.

Amma hadn't slept well since Abba had left. Perpetually worried, she had also started to offer tahajjud, the midnight prayer, along with Dadi. One night, Arif was in his room studying when he saw Amma and Dadi praying. In the distance, the bell at the magazine was hammered twelve times, breaking the silence of the night.

Abba has to risk his life because both his sons are good for nothing. If we could earn a living for our family, Abba would have certainly retired from this awful job. Even after putting in eight hours every day, what I earn from the coaching classes is a pittance. I have to try even harder this time and clear the civil services, at any cost. For Abba and Amma, Arif thought as he pulled out a book called *Administrative Thinkers* from the shelves. He had to finish a chapter titled 'Decision-Making' by Herbert Simon that day.

He walked to the kitchen to make a cup of tea for himself. He checked the pot and found that the milk had gone bad. In this heat, it was really difficult to preserve milk for long without a refrigerator. But what could Amma do. She boiled the milk at least three to four times through the day. They couldn't afford a refrigerator.

He spotted a sliced piece of lemon on the counter. He decided to manage with a cup of lemon tea.

By the time he finished his tea, Dadi was done with her prayer and had retired to her room. Amma was still on the prayer mat, her eyes closed.

As soon as Arif returned to his room, the calling bell rang twice in quick succession.

Who could it be at this time? Arif wondered. He rushed to the door and found Amma talking to a constable. There had been a Maoist attack in Jehanabad on Abba's platoon. There was no further news about the number of policemen killed or injured in that encounter. The constable spoke in a matter-of-fact way, his sentences punctuated with yawns. He was trying very hard to keep himself awake. Amma remained silent till the constable went away. Then, she shrieked. The entire house woke up. Dadi, Rabiya, Nazneen and Huma joined her and they all wept.

Arif was stunned. He couldn't speak at all for a while and then tears began to run down his cheeks. The neighbours began to pour in. From other houses, too, he heard the inconsolable wails of women.

'Amma, please don't cry. Abba will be all right. I'm going to the police headquarters to get the latest update,' Arif said and then turned to Dadi, who was whimpering. 'Dadi, please pray to Allah. Your son will return safely.'

On the road inside Police Colony, many men and women were discussing the attack in fearful whispers. Two of his neighbours were leaving for the police headquarters in a jeep and he joined them. Arif had comforted his family, but his stomach was in knots. He thought he might throw up. 'Ya Allah, please let Abba be okay,' he prayed silently.

Two hours later, Arif returned with the news that Abba was one of the five survivors, but a bullet had scraped his shoulder. They were bringing him to the Patna Medical College and Hospital for treatment. Amma immediately fell in sajda, thanking Allah for sparing her husband's life. Dadi and his sisters too unrolled their prayer mats to offer nafil namaz.

Although Arif was relieved about Abba's narrow escape, the continuous wailing sound coming from neighbouring houses disturbed him greatly.

Tomorrow, he would have to witness too many funerals.

'Beta, when can we go to the hospital? And inform Zakir,' Amma said.

~

Abba reached the hospital the next day and Arif got busy travelling between hospital and home. It was only after three days that he was able to write to Zakir. He checked his email the very next day and was relieved to see Zakir's reply. He would be in Patna that Sunday.

A couple of months back, Arif had seen his brother in a Shah Rukh Khan movie. Zakir had played a beggar, dirty and dressed in rags. He was barely there for a minute onscreen. Arif saw another movie later, after Mritunjay told him about it, where Zakir was the villain's sidekick – his screen time was barely five minutes. So Rajeeb Mohanty was right. Zakir had become an extra, a junior artist, the kind of actor who was counted as the lowest in the hierarchy of the acting fraternity. The more he thought about this, the sadder Arif felt.

How awful Zakir must be feeling right now. Arif imagined himself as a peon in a collectorate cleaning the cabin of an IAS officer. That was why he had stopped calling; perhaps he was ashamed of his inability to succeed in Bombay and did not want to return to Patna empty-handed.

On Sunday, Arif reached the station on time but the train was late.

After a two-hour delay the train finally arrived. Arif couldn't recognize his brother immediately. Zakir had grown thinner and his eyes looked sunken.

Arif hugged his brother and did not ask him anything.

After a week in the hospital, Abba was discharged. But he continued to have shoulder pains, which the doctor said would take time to heal.

Arif was sure that after this incident Abba wouldn't be sent to a Naxalite-infested area again. But the day the doctor issued a certificate declaring him fit to rejoin, Abba got his orders to go to a police post in Palamu district, another stronghold of the Maoists. On Amma's pleading, he went to talk to the commandant of the battalion about being posted somewhere else. Arif accompanied him.

'Rashid, I didn't want to send you to the Naxalite area again. But this is the order of our new DIG, Mr Shehzad Ali. You need to talk to DIG sahab.'

'Okay sir,' he said.

Arif knew why Shehzad Ali was after his father.

A few years ago, Shehzad, then the superintendent of police at Hazaribagh, had been accused in a sexual harassment case. He had come to Abba for help because Abba was handling his case file. Abba had refused outright knowing what kind of man he was.

Shehzad Ali was settling old scores with Abba.

Abba applied for voluntary retirement. He didn't want to, but Amma and Dadi forced him to.

Abba was tormented by the fact that he was making a mistake in taking voluntary retirement. His salary had not been enough to fulfil the bare necessities of his family; now how would he manage with half the amount? For a man in his mid-fifties to find another decent job was next to impossible.

'It would have been better to die at the hands of Maoist guerrillas than to see my family starve,' he told Arif one day.

Not knowing what to say, Arif remained silent. He didn't want Abba to rejoin the police and go to Palamu. Abba wanted to withdraw his application for retirement, but it had already been forwarded and was approved by Shehzad Ali in no time.

~

Amma was leaning against the parapet of the balcony, looking tense.

'Why are you so worried, Amma?' Arif asked.

'I don't know how to run the household on your father's pension. Nazneen wants to do an MA. Having a BA is enough for a girl . . .' Amma paused. 'Rabiya is already twenty-five. And wedding expenses . . . Ya Allah! And then we have to vacate this government quarter in two or three months. That means very soon we will also have to rent a house.'

'Don't worry, Amma. I'll start taking more coaching classes. Zakir is also trying to get a job.'

'But that will disturb your IAS preparation. You are already spending half your day in coaching classes.'

'Both things can be done simultaneously,' Arif said, knowing that his part-time job with Golden Coaching Centre was already taking a huge toll on his preparations.

It was his fourth and final attempt at the exam, rather at fulfilling his family's dreams, and this year, at any cost, he had to clear the final hurdle. Inshallah!

But what if he failed this time as well?

A boy in the neighbourhood colony had jumped into the Ganga after failing to clear the civil services exam. His bloated dead body had been fished out three days later.

Was Arif heading towards the same fate?

He was lost in his thoughts when Amma asked, 'What are you thinking, baua?'

'Nothing, Amma.' Arif shrugged, dismissing the idea of committing suicide as he looked at Amma. Dadi was also there but she was not involved in Arif and Amma's discussion. Settled on the sofa, she was reading a book in Urdu about the companions of Prophet Muhammad, peace be upon him, her spectales perched on her beautiful tiny nose. A few minutes later, Dadi closed her book and went inside.

The doorbell rang.

'Is Abdul Rashid at home?' Arif recognized the voice. It was Shamimullah Khan, Amma's second cousin. A retired senior accountant in the Bihar government, he lived in Samanpura.

'Come in, bhaisahab!' Amma said, drawing the pallu of her sari to cover her head.

'Where is Abdul Rashid?' Shamimullah Khan asked.

'Arif's Abba has gone to Raja Bazaar.'

Shamimullah Khan settled down on the old brown sofa in the balcony.

'Bhaijaan, would you like to have lemon tea?'

'No, sister. No tea; diabetes has started troubling me again and I hate to drink tea without sugar. So don't trouble yourself,' he said, and fumbled with a yellow envelope. There was a postcard-size photograph of a young man.

'Who is this handsome boy?' Amma asked.

'Azad Khan. My friend Qasim Khan's only son. Azad is a probationary officer in SBI. Azad's mother saw Rabiya last month at my daughter's marriage. She wants Rabiya to be her daughter-in-law,' Shamimullah Khan said.

'Ya Allah, you're so merciful,' Arif heard Amma murmuring.

'And dowry?' Amma asked.

'No, sister. They are god-fearing people. They will accept whatever you give them.'

Arif smiled and looked at his Amma's radiant face.

This unexpected piece of good news brought great happiness to the house after a long time.

Abba proudly announced that he was going to organize a big wedding feast befitting the position of his to-be son-in-law. There was a perpetual smile on Amma's face. Dadi couldn't stop smiling all the time either. Rabiya walked around dreamy-eyed, secretly holding the photograph of the boy, as Nazneen and Huma teased her.

As the date of the nikah inched closer, Arif's relatives began to pour in. The flat was crammed. A two-storey house just outside Police Colony was also rented for a week to accommodate many more relatives.

Four days before the wedding ceremony, Arif was in the balcony with Abba and Zakir discussing the banquet menu, when a middle-aged man came to meet Abba with a letter from the groom's father. Handing over a white envelope to Abba, he left immediately, though Abba insisted he stay for lunch.

As Abba ripped open the envelope and unfolded the letter, his face was horror-struck.

It was a long dowry list, which also included a car.

The singing stopped. The women rubbing turmeric and sandalwood paste on Rabiya's body looked confused and they started talking in whispers. Amma was in tears. Dadi didn't know how to react.

Enraged, Abba announced in front of the relatives and guests that he had made up his mind to break off the engagement.

'If I succumb to their demands, I'll end up spending my entire life's savings. I've two more daughters to marry off. Moreover, I don't want to have these greedy people as my relatives,' Abba thundered.

Amma didn't say anything. She looked at Dadi, silently requesting her to intervene.

'Abba, breaking off the engagement at this juncture is not the right thing to do. Think of the bad name it will bring to our family, and it'll be very difficult to find another suitable match for Rabiya,' Arif argued.

Zakir seconded his brother.

'But . . .' Abba hesitated.

Zakir said, 'Trust your sons, Abba. We'll manage to do something for our other sisters. In the worst-case scenario, we will have to sell all our land and ancestral house.'

'Yes, Rashid. Arif and Zakir are right. It's a question of Rabiya's future,' Dadi said.

Amma wiped off her tears, smiling, when Abba agreed not to break off the engagement.

'Allah is great, if He has given us three daughters, then He must have made provisions for all three,' Dadi added.

Abba had no choice but to agree.

Things settled down, and Amma went to offer a special prayer to thank Allah.

~

Ten days after Rabiya's wedding, Arif, settled comfortably in a deckchair, was reading a book on Muktibodh's *Chand ka Munh Tedha Hain* when he heard Nazneen's laughter. He turned to see Nazneen sitting on the bed, laughing. Amma and Huma sat next to her, confused. Her laughter grew louder as if she had gone crazy. Then, she started wailing.

Amma grabbed Nazneen by the shoulders and shook her. 'Nazneen beti! Beti!'

'What happened, baji?' Huma panicked.

Nazneen continued to wail.

Dropping his book on the floor, Arif rushed into the room.

'What has happened?' Arif tapped his sister's cheeks softly.

Nazneen kept crying.

'Arif, go and fetch a doctor,' Amma said.

By the time Arif returned with a doctor from the Police Hospital, Nazneen had stopped crying. She was lying on the bed, unconscious, breathing heavily. Amma was fanning her with a magazine. Dadi was reciting from the Quran and was blowing benediction on her.

The doctor held her wrist, observing her pulse, and checked her heartbeat with a stethoscope.

'She seems fine. Nothing to worry about. She must have been troubled by something,' said the doctor. He picked up a glass from the side table and sprinkled some water on Nazneen's face.

Nazneen opened her eyes.

'What happened, Amma?' Nazneen asked, confused, as she tried to read the faces around her.

Amma said, 'Nothing, beti. You must have fainted from the heat.'

The doctor rose to leave. Amma and Arif followed him to the main door. The doctor advised Amma to consult a psychiatrist.

She asked Arif what the doctor meant by 'sychaist'.

When Arif explained, Amma lost her temper.

'How dare he say that my daughter is mad,' she fumed.

'This is happening quite frequently, Hamida,' Dadi intervened. 'The last time Nazneen had a similar kind of fit, your brother, Hakim sahab, was here and he had told me that she was suffering from something called . . .'

'Hysteria,' Arif remembered.

'A girl who is not able to fulfil her physiological needs succumbs to this disease. And the only treatment is to get her married,' his uncle had said. But Arif knew hysteria was no longer recognized as a disease by doctors.

'It's better to consult a Unani doctor than a doctor who treats crazy people,' Dadi suggested.

Amma added she was sure her sweet-tempered daughter wasn't mentally ill and whatever ailed her could be treated by Hakim sahab.

Two days later, when Hakim sahab visited Patna, his diagnosis was the same and he reiterated that marriage was the only solution. Amma immediately agreed with her brother, but Abba had doubts. Shouldn't they consult a psychiatrist first?

'No!' Amma said emphatically. 'Do what Hakim sahab says. Anyway, Nazneen is already twenty-three.'

'Hamida apa is right. Inshallah, she will be perfectly all right after marriage. For the time being, use this medicine,' Hakim sahab said as he took out a jar from his black leather bag. Arif could read its name in Urdu: Khamira gaozaban ambari jadwar ud saleeb.

'I have spent almost my entire savings on Rabiya's marriage. I need time to arrange a dowry for Nazneen,' Abba said, scratching his cheek with his fingernails.

'See, Arif's abba, we can't afford a marriage ceremony like Rabiya's. We have to be practical and just find a decent boy from a decent family.'

Abba nodded, but Arif could see anxiety creasing his face.

Arif knew that dowry was going to be the biggest issue in finding a suitable groom for Nazneen. Arif hated himself for not being able to help.

~

Despite all his hard work that year, he didn't get through the civil services exam. Abba had been sure that his son would succeed in his final attempt.

Amma, Nazneen and Huma conveyed their disappointment in silence.

'It is all written in our fate,' Dadi said, comforting Arif. 'Allah does everything for a reason.'

Zakir consoled him, 'I know how it feels when you have to bury your dreams, bhaiyya.'

Arif couldn't bring himself to go teach coaching classes. He just moped around the house, spending most of his time lying in his room or sitting alone in the balcony, staring blankly at the sky. Nothing worthwhile was left in his life, he thought.

Why did he not pass the civil services exam? This year he had done all the papers reasonably well. Even his interview was quite good. He suspected some foul play. Maybe because I am a Muslim.

The pain got aggravated when he saw his friend Mritunjay's photo on the front page of the *Times of India*.

His friend was ranked seventh and would definitely become an IAS officer.

He called Mritunjay in the evening to congratulate him and had a long chat. Mritunjay suggested that Arif give the Bihar Public Service Commission a try.

'Through the provincial civil service route, you can also get into the IAS cadre in seven to ten years,' Mritunjay told Arif.

Arif remembered the days when he used to help Mritunjay with his preparation, especially in public administration, Mritunjay's weak area. He felt miserable.

~

A couple of months later, one Friday, on the way to the mosque for the weekly prayer, Abba told Arif, 'Don't lose heart, my son. Cracking the civil services is very tough. Out of a thousand only one gets selected. Despite your limited resources, you have done well. Life doesn't end with the IAS. You have many avenues to make your career.'

Arif looked at Abba with affection but didn't say anything. He knew he did not have any energy left to try anything new.

But for the sake of my family, I will certainly try for the state civil services, Arif consoled himself.

SIXTEEN

A list of biodatas and photographs of boys for Nazneen were requested from a marriage bureau run exclusively for Muslims in Patna. Three of them were shortlisted by Abba. The first one was a bank cashier from Muzaffarpur. But his father demanded too much dowry.

'We can't afford this match. Whatever I received from the provident fund and gratuity was spent on Rabiya's marriage. Even if I decide to sell my ancestral house at Jamalpura, I can't fulfil their demands. These Darbhangia and Muzaffarpurias are avaricious people. Their rate of dowry is very high. For his cashier son, he's demanding five lakh in cash. We didn't spend that much even for Rabiya's wedding,' Abba said, and kept the photograph aside.

The second one was a boy from Gaya, plump but good-looking. He was an assistant in the irrigation department. The groom's father wasn't demanding much. But there was a catch here. Though the groom's father was a Pathan, his mother wasn't. She was from a lower caste. The grapevine had it that she was a julaha, of the weaver caste.

'Who cares about all these things in today's world, Abba.

I think it's a good marriage proposal. Accept it,' Zakir argued. Arif seconded his brother.

'I have to live in this society. So I have to follow its rules. I have one more daughter to marry off,' snapped Abba.

Amma stayed out of it.

The third one was a pure Pathan. His father was a Yusufzai from Siwan district and his mother was a Sherwani from Darbhanga. Abba knew the groom's maternal grandfather. He was related to the royal family of Darbhangi Khan of Darbhanga. With an LLB from the Bihar Institute of Law, he assisted a famous criminal lawyer at the Patna High Court.

'He is a bit dark,' said Amma tentatively, fearing she might offend Abba by questioning his choice.

'It's okay for boys to be wheatish.' Abba spoke with authority, leaving no room for further discussion.

Arif took a look at the photograph and he was aghast. The man was ugly. With a receding hairline, dark complexion, thick moustache and potbelly, he was in his late thirties or possibly early forties.

The photograph of the boy was passed on to Zakir and he burst out, 'Instead of marrying Nazneen to this boy, why don't you push her into the Ganga?'

'You aren't the guardian of this family. Are you in a position to contribute a single penny towards the dowry for your sister? What have you done so far other than waste time in frivolous pursuits? You are saying that I don't know what is best for my daughter. I know my limitations. Unlike you, I'm not a daydreamer,' Abba shot back.

Zakir was rendered speechless. Arif never thought

Abba could be that angry. Zakir got up and left the room. Suddenly, Abba started coughing. Amma called out to Huma to bring water. She patted his back and made him have a sip or two of water. Nazneen came running from the adjacent room. She must have overheard these discussions.

Arif thought it was better not to say anything.

'Nobody has the right to question Abba's decision. I know he will do his best for me and whatever he decides is acceptable to me,' Nazneen said, teary-eyed.

Arif went looking for Zakir and found him in his study room, leaning against the windowsill, looking outside. Arif patted him gently on his shoulder.

'Everything will be all right, bhai,' Arif said.

'Abba is right, bhaiyya. We are responsible for what is happening to Nazneen,' Zakir said in a choked voice.

Arif hugged Zakir. Something was gnawing at him and he wanted to scream. His failure in his career was going to be followed by his failure as a brother.

~

Within a week, Arif and Zakir had accepted the eventuality of Nazneen's marriage. They began helping their father with the preparations. Years ago, when Nagma, the most beautiful girl in Jamalpura, was being married to a middle-aged widower because her family couldn't afford to pay dowry, Arif had remarked, 'Shame on the brothers; how are they allowing their sister to be married to a man twice her age? If I were her brother I'd never have allowed this to happen.' But now, Nazneen was faced with the prospect of an even worse groom. And Arif was a mute spectator. His own words returned to haunt him.

Three days before Nazneen's nikah with the bald advocate, a notice arrived from the office of the commandant, Bihar Military Police-5, Patna. It was the final notice to vacate the government quarters. Abba had retired more than a year ago. As per regulations, a retired person could live in the official residence for six months. They had received a few notices.

Many flouted this rule, but most of them were well connected. Babban Yadav, a retired sub-inspector, had been living in the government quarter despite his retirement three years earlier. But that was because of his connections in the chief minister's house. Rajnath Singh had remained in the official residence for the last one and a half years despite his transfer to Munger. But he was a Rajput, as was the commandant.

Abba neither had connections in the CM's house nor was he a Rajput. So, he had to go to the commandant's office to request him to allow them more time to vacate the house. Arif went with him.

The commandant was at his acrid best. 'Every time you receive a notice, you come up with an excuse. First it was your wife's illness, then your daughter's marriage. Now, you are telling me that you will hand over the flat after the marriage of your second daughter. Mr Abdul Rashid Khan, there is a system, rules and regulations that everybody has to follow. I have decided that no further time will be allowed. And if you don't vacate the house within two days, I'll have to employ force to get the flat vacated.'

This was the same person who used to call his father bhai. And when charges of corruption were levelled against him, he had come running to Abba for help. The commandant had known that Abba was in the good books of the director general of police and that his opinion carried a lot of weight.

'Sir, please give me a week. I'll move out immediately after my daughter's marriage. Please, sir,' Abba pleaded.

Arif's heart felt as though it was being slashed into small pieces seeing Abba imploring the commandant.

'Rules are rules,' the commandant said tersely.

Disappointed, Abba turned to go.

'Stop, Abdul Rashid!' It was the commandant again.

'I will give you three months. But please don't compel me to send you another notice,' the commandant finally said.

'Thank you, sir,' Abba said. 'Three months is more than enough time. I'll leave the flat long before that.'

Abba thanked him repeatedly as he walked out of the cabin. As Arif walked out he noticed the red-and-blue sign at the door of the commandant's cabin: R.P. Singh, IPS. A twinge of regret pierced his heart. If he were an IPS or an IAS officer, the commandant wouldn't have dared speak like that to his father. He began to rub his palms furiously.

On the ground, about fifty yards away, the passing-out parade of the newly recruited constables was going on; hundreds of pairs of boots thumped the earth in unison at regular intervals. The chorus of 'left-right-left' echoed in the air. The raucous babbling of thousands of birds on the trees surrounding the parade ground annoyed Arif. As

Abba was stopped by some old acquaintance, Arif walked away briskly towards the officers' quarters.

~

As expected, the wedding was not as lavish as Rabiya's. Abba had sold off half their ancestral land. Arif had managed to borrow twenty thousand from the coaching institute where he was teaching as an advance on his salary. Abba invited only close relatives for the wedding. Rabiya arrived just two days before the nikah with her husband. Her husband, Azad, offered to help but Abba refused out of pride.

Mritunjay also attended the wedding, with a Banarasi sari as a gift. Most people of Police Colony attending Nazneen's wedding knew about Mritunjay's selection in the IAS and were trying to congratulate him or say hello. Eager to get tips for success, many IAS aspirants surrounded him. Arif also saw Abba hugging Mritunjay and thanking him for coming. When Abba turned to Arif, he could clearly see the face of a defeated father. He knew that Mritunjay's presence had once again reminded him of his son's failure.

Immediately after the nikah, Mritunjay left.

'Next month, there is a party at the Maurya Hotel for IAS officers of the Bihar cadre. Everyone is allowed to invite one of their friends. Please do come. I'll let you know the exact date and time,' Mritunjay said to Arif as he was getting into his car.

'Sure.'

~

In his dreams, Arif flew like a bird. But, strangely, he didn't have wings. He saw the moon glowing like a huge bulb and the stars twinkling as if they were fairy lights embedded in the ceiling of an eternally big dome. Suddenly, a weird panic gripped him. He became breathless and started falling like a skydiver, but no parachute was attached to his back. As he got closer to the ground, he frantically tried to stay afloat in the air but couldn't. He fell with a loud thud on a hard surface.

He woke up with a start, sweating profusely. The room was dark except for the light from the street lamp finding its way through the skylight. He switched on the light and looked in the mirror. His eyes were bloodshot as if he was drunk. Walking up to the window, he drank water from a jug. Insects whirred around the street lamp.

He exhaled and then breathed in deeply. What had they done to Nazneen? They had married her off to an ugly man at least fifteen years older than her. He had read the story 'Beauty and the Beast' in his class ten English reader, where when Beauty kissed the Beast he transformed into a handsome prince. That wasn't going to happen with his sister. His father's pale face came to his mind. Abba's anxiety was because of his financial inability to carry out his responsibilities as the head of the family. And that anxiety had gifted him many diseases ranging from blood pressure to gastritis.

Instead of single-mindedly pursuing the civil services, if I had tried something else, I would have been in a position to help my father, Arif thought regretfully.

On the table lay photographs from Nazneen's wedding.

He looked through them. A photo of Nazneen and her husband, shot just before her bidaai. Her husband looked happy, his teeth flashing between swollen, dark lips. He felt nauseated when he thought that his sister had to spend her entire life with this man. Then another photograph: Rabiya and her husband, Azad. They were a perfect couple. In a cream-coloured tailored suit, Azad looked like a movie star.

Arif felt awful.

In another photo was Mritunjay sitting next to Zakir, confidence, or was it pride, on his face and in his posture.

Allah has punished me for my sins. Especially for coveting a married woman.

~

The next day, Arif went to see Sumitra. They hadn't met properly since the day they had argued over Kavita's affair with a Muslim boy. Two months ago, he'd heard about Kavita's marriage to a groom based in the US. She had sent an invitation through Mritunjay, but Arif didn't attend the wedding.

On the day of Nazneen's nikah, he had seen Sumitra in the crowd and then she had appeared for a split second by his side to give him a piece of paper on which she had written a big 'SORRY'.

He couldn't but forgive her.

Arif was still carrying the huge guilt of allowing his sister's marriage to the dark and balding advocate. He felt Sumitra's company would cheer him up. *I hold my passion for Sumitra somewhat responsible for my failures, and at the same time I'm seeking refuge in her company*, he thought. *How ironic! What a shame!*

The fragrance of her body, the silkiness of her long hair, the warmth and sweetness of her gentle touch. He imagined himself in bed with Sumitra, cuddling and kissing.

No! No! It was not Sumitra's fault. She has always inspired me to work hard for success. She has always showered me with unconditional love. I have always found solace in her company.

Arif sped along on his bicycle, a smile slowly appearing on his face.

As he reached Bank Colony, one of the tyres of his bicycle got punctured. He pushed his cycle to the nearest repair shop. The cycle mechanic was busy and asked him to wait. Arif sat in the adjacent teashop, picked up a Hindi newspaper and ordered a cup of tea.

'She is a chalu-type auntie.'

The words caught his attention. He stole a glance to his left. On the bench sat three teenage boys, gossiping.

'Really,' responded a plump boy with thick glasses, chuckling.

'A Muslim boy used to visit her regularly,' a curly-haired boy said. 'But I haven't seen him in the last few months.'

'She might have taken a new lover. Do you also want to try your luck?'

They all broke into laughter.

'Bechara, her poor husband. What is his name? Yes, Ramesh Kumar. He is totally unaware of his wife's extracurricular activities when he is away from home.'

Arif felt like throwing the hot glass of tea on their faces.

How dare they talk about Sumitra in such a way? He fumed silently, smothering the anger welling up inside him.

The boys continued with their gossip.

'Haan, I've also seen her with some other men. Even today I saw a man going into her flat.'

'Must be her new lover.' All three laughed together.

'Arrey, let's go. India's innings must have started.'

As they walked past him, Arif covered his face with the newspaper.

Arif's temper was rising with each and every word. But then his thoughts meandered somewhere else: if they know so much about his discreet affair with Sumitra, they might be right about her affair with other men. Was Sumitra such a slut? If a woman could betray such a caring husband, she could also betray her lover.

Arif recalled something he had overheard a few months ago, from a conversation between Mritunjay's mother and a neighbourhood woman he didn't know. 'Behenji, I was Sumitra's neighbour in Jamshedpur. Maya used to be a frequent visitor at Sumitra's house. Everyone in the neighbourhood knew that Maya wasn't a good woman. I also warned Sumitra about Maya's reputation but that made no difference to her. Later, I realized that she was also the same kind of lady.'

But Sumitra had already told him about Maya.

Wavering between his complete faith in Sumitra and suspicion about her possible affairs with other men, he left the teashop. His bicycle was ready by then.

He was in front of Sumitra's house in five minutes. The door was ajar.

Pushing it open, he looked inside. On a chair was a pink envelope, a diary and a helmet.

That means somebody is inside. As Arif tiptoed into the hall, he heard a man's laughter from the adjacent room. And it was not Ramesh's. Turning his face, he concentrated on the glass pane of the window. He saw Sumitra hugging a man. Everything the boys had been discussing at the teashop reverberated in his mind. So, this is the man Sumitra is seeing nowadays. Arif's face was red with rage as he came out of the flat. He waited on the road for the man to come out. The road was deserted because of the World Cup match between India and Australia. The sound of people cheering erupted from the houses. India must have hit a four or a six.

Minutes later, a forty-something man with a thick moustache and curly hair emerged from her house. He was tall and fair. Arif heard him humming a Bollywood song as he hurried past him to get to his scooter parked under a mango tree by the road.

Pangs of jealousy and anger drove Arif crazy. There wasn't an iota of doubt in Arif's mind that Sumitra was a whore and that he was just one of her many lovers. He must talk to her right now. As he turned to go towards her flat, two women entered Sumitra's house. He paced on the road waiting for the women to come out, but they didn't for a long time. Finally, he left the place.

On his way back home, he stopped his bicycle at a phone booth. The booth owner was busy watching the match on a black-and-white portable TV. Azhar was facing McGrath. It was a short rising ball, Azhar went half forward and edged the ball towards point, and Steve Waugh caught it quite comfortably.

'Fuck!' Arif said involuntarily.

The Indian score read 17/4.

'No chance in this match,' the booth owner said with a heavy sigh as he switched off the TV.

'Local call,' Arif said.

The booth owner pointed towards a small glass cabin.

Arif dialled Sumitra's number.

'Hello!' Her sweet voice almost made him forget his anger.

Then he recalled everything he had heard and seen during the last couple of hours. And that renewed his rage. Everything he said to her was something of a surprise even for him. He hurled his choicest expletives at her. He neither asked her who the man was nor did he explain the reason for his anger.

Initially, Sumitra had responded in whys and whats which were soon replaced by sobs. But her weeping didn't deter Arif. He had heard from many elders that a woman's ultimate weapon was tears, which, for centuries, they had used to defeat, fool, win over and tame men. 'Whore!' he said before hanging up the phone.

He clenched his jaw as he felt a sudden sensation of pain at the back of his throat. He rode his bicycle as darkness enveloped the city. He stopped near the peepal tree, looking accusingly at it as if the tree had been complicit in this game of betrayal. He searched his pocket for his wallet, found it, pulled out two photographs of Sumitra from its inner pocket, tore them to pieces and threw them into the pond nearby.

SEVENTEEN

Arif returned home late from his job at the coaching class on a pleasant Friday evening in 2000 and was surprised to hear Nazneen's laughter. Arif had presumed that after her marriage with the balding advocate, his sister would be perpetually sad. When he entered the room, he was welcomed by a beaming Nazneen. He hugged his sister and planted a soft kiss on her forehead.

'How is my sister?'

'All well, bhaiyya.'

'There are two pieces of good news, bhaiyya,' Huma said as she entered the room with a box of laddoos.

'Achcha?'

'Soon you are going to be a mamu. Nazneen baji is in the family way,' Huma said.

Nazneen blushed.

'And jiju has been selected for the Bihar judicial services. So now Nazneen baji is the wife of a judge,' Huma said, beaming.

'Mashallah! Mashallah!' Arif hugged Nazneen again. He wiped his tears with the back of his palm and added, 'Come to my study room, Nazneen. We'll chat.'

The brother and sister walked into the room to catch up in private.

'I know you feel guilty about my marriage to Shafique because you think he's not a suitable match for me. Looks are not that important, bhaiyya. He is a good man,' Nazneen said, 'and my in-laws treat me like their own daughter. My father-in-law never takes any important decisions without consulting me. And Rafique, my brother-in-law is . . .'

By the time Nazneen finished, Arif's guilt had melted away. A sudden lightness seeped through his entire body.

'Assalam alaikum, bhaijaan.' His brother-in-law appeared at the door. He looked thinner than he had been on his wedding day. He had also shaved off his moustache and looked much younger.

'Walaikum assalam, Walaikum assalam. Many many congratulations,' Arif said and then stood up and hugged him. 'Thank you very much for making my sister happy.'

Then, surprised to see a mobile phone in Huma's hand, Arif asked, 'Whose phone is this?'

'Jiju has brought it for us from Bangalore.'

It was a Nokia 3515.

'Shafique babu, there was no need to buy such an expensive gadget,' Arif said.

'Arrey bhaijaan, it is not expensive at all,' Shafique replied.

'Anyway, thanks.' Arif smiled as he held the blue-and-silver cell phone in his hands. He thought of calling his friend Mritunjay but didn't.

~

His failure in the civil services and Sumitra's betrayal had been the two most painful events of Arif's life. But fate had more sinister plans lined up for him. Zakir's visit to Delhi was to bring his family more misery.

Soon after Nazneen's marriage, Zakir had announced that he was going to Delhi in search of a job. One of his childhood friends from Jamalpura lived there. Abba approved. Arif saw it as a good sign that after the setbacks in Bombay, Zakir was trying to start afresh. He also knew that his brother had never been a bright student and to push him towards an academic career wouldn't bear any fruit.

Arif had moved to teach at another coaching institute where he got paid better, but the hours were longer. As the eldest son in the family, wasn't it his duty to share more of Abba's financial burden? His childhood dream of joining the IAS was dead. At thirty-one, he was not sure about other employment prospects.

'Bhaiyya! I think the diploma in computer applications I have earned here will help me find a decent job. I want to help Abba with Huma's marriage,' Zakir said. 'But you shouldn't invest so much time in coaching classes. Instead, concentrate on the Bihar civil services. I have a gut feeling that you will pull it off this time.'

Two months after Zakir's departure for the capital, there were a series of bomb blasts in Delhi. In Karol Bagh's Gaffar Market a scooter exploded, ripping through a dozen or more shops, claiming more than fifty lives. Explosives were kept in a car outside New Delhi railway station. The casualties numbered twenty-five. At Nehru Place the blast killed twenty-one people. Delhi Police's anti-bomb squad defused two bombs, one at India Gate and the other at Palika Bazaar.

Arif's family was worried for Zakir's safety. Abba tried to reach Zakir's friend on the phone but the sudden rush of millions of calls from relatives and well-wishers to people in Delhi jammed the network.

Later in the night, when connections were restored, Zakir called them. 'I'm at my flat, Abba. Nothing to worry about.'

It was half past midnight when the mobile started ringing again. Arif woke up and reached for the phone. It was Zakir.

'Bhaiyya, the police have picked me up with my friends and other roommates. They say we are behind the bomb blasts in the city. We are being kept in a farmhouse somewhere in the Mehrauli area. They'll kill us, bhaiyya. Ask Abba to come to Delhi and save us.'

Arif heard Zakir screaming, followed by a coarse voice with a heavy Haryanvi accent, 'Abey Dahiya! Did you conduct a body search of these guys or not? Madarchod, you'll get all of us in big trouble. See, this boy was talking on a mobile.' Then Arif heard a sharp sound and the phone went silent.

Arif stood as if he had had a sudden attack of paralysis, the mobile still stuck to his ear. Abba, who had been waiting for Arif to say something, shook him out of his stupor. Between hiccups and sobs, Arif managed to repeat Zakir's story. By then, everyone in his family had woken up. Abba didn't say anything for hours.

How could somebody as gentle as Zakir be accused of terrorism? He was someone who abhorred violence and religious extremism.

But in India a Muslim youth didn't have to do much to be branded a terrorist. Whenever a terrorist attack happened, many Muslim youths were picked up by the police. Some of them simply disappeared and the majority of them were exonerated after a tedious battle in court.

Zakir must have become a victim of the police's prejudice against Muslims, Arif thought.

The next morning Abba and Arif left for Delhi by the Shramjeevi Express on waitlisted tickets.

Inside the crowded train, Abba unfolded a bed sheet to spread on the floor of the passage leading to the toilet. During the sixteen hours of an anxiety-ridden and torturous train journey, both of them mostly remained silent.

After arriving in Delhi, Arif and Abba went straight to the address in Shaheen Bagh where Zakir used to stay. The house was a three-storeyed building inside a narrow alley which was flanked by open sewers on both sides and littered with household garbage.

The landlord of the building lived on the ground floor. He was not home, but his wife was. She seated them in her tiny drawing room on a sofa when Abba told her who they were. She told them that two days earlier, around midnight, she had heard the sound of a vehicle stopping near her house and had woken up. She had seen the police taking away the four boys living in their first floor apartment in a white car.

'I was all alone at home that night with my daughters. I didn't come out of my room,' the lady said as she stood behind a door curtain. 'Yes, I saw the face of one of the police officers. He had a scar on his cheek.'

'To which police station have they taken them?' Abba asked.

'I don't know, but I overheard them mentioning Jamia Nagar thana,' she said. 'Zakir is a very nice boy. There must be some confusion. I hope they release him after asking a few questions. Inshallah.'

Her assurances didn't relieve Abba or Arif. Abba had been in the police for almost thirty-five years and he knew what these policemen could get up to. Arif had heard from Abba how fake encounters and killings of innocent tribal youths for alleged involvement in Naxalite activities were staged just to get gallantry awards or promotions.

'Can I talk to your husband?' Abba asked.

'My husband will return tonight; you can talk to him tomorrow morning,' she said.

'Can you show me Zakir's room?' Abba asked.

'Sure,' she said.

She went into her bedroom and came out with a bunch of keys. She led them up a flight of narrow stairs to an open terrace and a small room, and opened the door. It was a ten by fifteen room with four narrow wooden cots. Things in the room were in their usual place. There was no sign of struggle. In the far corner, on a side table near a bed, there were framed photographs of Aamir Khan and Salman Khan from the film *Andaz Apna Apna*. Arif knew that it was Zakir's bed. Abba sat on the bed and tried to look at the things lying on the side table. But they didn't reveal anything.

On the walls near the other beds were posters with Arabic inscriptions. One of them said 'Nasrum Minallaahi

Wa Fathun Qareeb' (Help and victory from Allah is imminent).

'Bhaisahab, please stay for breakfast,' the landlady said as Abba rose from the bed.

'Thanks, sister, but we have to leave now,' Abba said.

Twenty minutes later, they arrived at the Jamia Nagar police station. The station house officer (SHO) had a menacing look. And a scar on his left cheek. He acted in an odd manner when Abba enquired about the arrest of Zakir two days back. Abba told him that he was a retired police officer and showed his police department identity card, but it made no difference to the officer. Finally, he also mentioned his discussion with the landlady and her statement about a police officer with a scar. The SHO's hand involuntarily moved to cover the scar.

'You just get out of here,' the SHO screamed.

'I have to get help from Jain sahab,' Abba said to Arif as they came out of the police station.

They hailed an autorickshaw and went to Noida to see the former director general of police of Bihar. Abba had worked with him for almost five years.

Abba and Arif returned to the police station with Mr Jain by their side. Mr Jain introduced himself to the SHO, who spoke cordially but still denied that the police had anything to do with Zakir's disappearance. He even accompanied Abba, Arif and Mr Jain to the flat where Zakir used to live. The landlord had returned from his tour. A diminutive man with a closely cropped beard, he refused to accept that either he or his wife had seen Zakir or anybody else being taken away by the police.

When Abba insisted that he had talked to his wife, the landlord retorted, 'Bhaisahab, there is some misunderstanding. My wife is a purdanasheen lady and she never talks to strangers.'

'Why are you not telling the truth? Be afraid of God and not of the police.' Abba began to cry and Arif held him by his shoulders.

The SHO turned to Mr Jain and said, 'I knew it was nothing like that, but I have come here for your satisfaction, sir.' He went on to add, 'Mr Khan, my sympathies are with you. If your son is missing, register an FIR. We will try to find him.' Then the SHO left.

'Abdul Rashid, I have to leave now. I'll try to talk to the police commissioner. I'm a retired police officer. I hope you understand my limitations,' Mr Jain said, and then gestured to his driver, who had parked his car across the road.

Abba and Arif spent the following four days visiting the police commissioner's office, media houses, the Minority Rights Commission and NGOs. But they couldn't convince anybody that the police were inolved in Zakir's disappearance.

On the fourth day, Arif was woken up early by a call from the muezzin of the Jama Masjid, followed by azans from other mosques. He saw Abba performing wuzu.

'Would you like to come for the prayer?' Abba asked, wiping his eyes with a red-and-blue gamchha.

'Yes Abba,' Arif replied in a choked voice, biting his lip.

They climbed down the steep stairs of the Al Madina Lodge, where they had been staying for fifty rupees a day. The historic Jama Masjid was walking distance and every day Abba went there for his day's first prayer. While returning, Arif saw minced buffalo meat being fried. He pulled a handkerchief from his kurta pocket and covered his nostrils.

Abba stopped at a news stand and picked up a Hindi newspaper. As he looked at the front page, his eyes grew wide with fear. Three dead bodies had been found in three different localities of Delhi. The cause of the murder was yet to be ascertained, but the victims' names were: Altaf, Kamil and Abdul Wahab. Zakir's three flatmates.

'Has Zakir also been killed?' Abba cried out, sitting down on his haunches in the middle of the road and weeping. Arif felt like his world was coming apart. Tearing the newspaper into pieces and throwing it on the road, he grabbed Abba by his arms. Father and son wept bitterly holding each other. Passers-by looked sympathetically before moving on.

In the evening, they went to the Jamia Nagar police station again and confronted the SHO. Abba threatened to go to the media about the fake encounter.

The SHO lost his temper and said, 'See, Mr Khan. You should worry about the safety of your other son. Do you know the implications of getting into an unnecessary conflict with the police?' He paused for a while and then added, 'Sorry, I forgot that you are a retired police officer and know the repercussions better than me.'

Abba didn't say anything further and came out of the police station.

'Abba, what should we do now? I am sure this SHO is hiding something from us.'

'I should call Shafique babu,' Abba said and walked to a nearby telephone booth. Arif waited outside.

Abba came out in ten minutes and said, 'Shafique babu is not in Patna. Nazneen asked a lot of questions about Zakir's disappearance. I evaded her questions and told her that Zakir would be back home in a couple of days,' Abba said.

'Then?'

'I talked to an advocate I know at the Patna High Court. He advised me to contact some Mahtab Alam of the National Legal Forum for Human Rights and gave me the address.'

They caught an auto to the address, which turned out to be a tiny office in one of the dilapidated buildings in South Delhi. Mahtab turned out to be a fellow Bihari. In his late thirties, he had a closely cropped beard and a perpetual intense expression. He listened to Abba and Arif, carefully noting down every detail. When they were done, Mahtab assured them that he would do his best to find out about Zakir and walked out with them to see them off.

In the evening, Mahtab called them at their lodge. He told Abba that he had been to the police station and had had a heated exchange of words with the SHO. He suspected that the SHO was involved in Zakir's disappearance. He wanted to discuss the next course of action with his colleagues.

Arif left the hotel to get something to eat for both of them. He had barely walked ten yards on the main road when a car stopped close to him and someone called out his name. Surprised, he turned to find a tall man with sunglasses. The last thing he remembered was being dragged inside the car and then something being pressed against his mouth.

When Arif opened his eyes again, he found himself in a tiny room with an attached bathroom. There was a wooden bed with a bed sheet and a pillow. The only door of the room was locked from the outside. He panicked and started knocking on the door frantically, but there was no response. He noticed a small window in the room. He unbolted it and pushed it with all his might but it didn't open. Defeated, he lay on the floor crying. And hour later, the door opened and a stainless steel plate was pushed inside. It had three tandoori rotis and fried aloo–gobhi.

Days passed in this manner and Arif began to lose his sanity in the solitary confinement of the room. He couldn't tell the time of the day and didn't know whether he had been there for a week or a month.

One day the door opened wider than it usually did for the steel plate and tumbler, and two masked men entered the room. Arif got up from his bed and was about to lash out and scream when they rushed forward and pressed a handkerchief soaked in some awful-smelling liquid against his face. Instantly, everything went blank.

~

When Arif woke up he found himself on the footpath of a road. It was night and there was hardly anybody around. His head was heavy. Things looked hazy. There was a terrible smell that lingered in his nose. He was finally able to focus on the signboard of a closed wine shop. This couldn't be.

Its address line read, 'Fraser Road, Patna 800 001'

Noticing a public water tap a few yards away, Arif pushed himself up on to his weak legs and stumbled towards it. He splashed water on his face, gargled and washed the inside of his nostrils. How did he get here? Where was Abba? What had happened to Zakir? It hurt to think. As he looked around confused, wanting to cry, he spotted a cycle rickshaw.

The rickshaw puller was asleep and Arif had to shake him violently to wake him up. The rickshaw puller refused to go anywhere but when Arif promised him a hundred rupees, he agreed to go to Raja Bazaar.

Arif was in front of his flat in Police Colony when the muezzin at the Veterinary College mosque started calling the faithful for the morning prayer. The rickshaw puller followed him up the stairs to get his money. As soon as Arif knocked on the door, someone pulled it open immediately from the other side, as if they had been waiting for him. It was Abba.

As soon as Abba saw Arif, he grabbed him in his arms and began to cry loudly. Soon, Amma, Dadi and Huma emerged from the room and hugged him.

The rickshaw puller stood mutely for a while, allowing the family reunion. Then he tapped on the door and asked for his money. Arif asked Abba to give the man a hundred rupees. When Abba handed over the money to the rickshaw puller, he only took half of it and wished them better days before leaving. The rickshaw puller's parting words made the whole family break into uncontrollable sobbing.

After a while they stopped and settled on the bed. Amma ran into the kitchen telling him she would get him something to eat. Arif refused but she wouldn't have any of it. Abba sat quietly, looking intently at Arif, his hands trembling. Dadi sat near him, crying and fondling his hair. Huma stood in front of him, holding his hand, her silent tears dropping on it.

'Did they beat you? Did they hurt you in any way?' Abba finally asked.

'Who, Abba? How do you . . .' Arif struggled with the words.

'I know,' Abba said quietly. 'But tell me, they didn't harm you in any way?'

'No, Abba. Someone took me away in a car as soon as I walked out of the hotel. They used some drug to make me unconscious. When I came to my senses, I found myself in a locked room. They slid food through a small gap in the door, but I never saw anybody. And that's where I remained for . . . How many days has it been?'

'Fifteen days,' Abba said, now looking away from Arif.

'You knew who took me, Abba? What is going on? Where is Zakir? When did you come back to Patna? Where is Zakir?'

Abba had tears in his eyes now. He beat his chest and his forehead and wailed loudly. Dadi and Huma too broke down, but tried to pacify Abba. Amma came running out of the kitchen. The whole family wept again. Arif too cried but he was confused and he wanted to know where his brother was. He held his father by his shoulders till he calmed down.

'Tell me what happened, Abba.'

'Fifteen minutes after you went downstairs, I received a call in our hotel room. The man on the other side told me that you were in his custody and threatened me with dire consequences if I pursued Zakir. He warned me not to seek help from Mahtab. He promised to let you go if I didn't pursue the case and instead went back to Patna immediately.'

'Then?'

'I didn't know what to do. Both my sons were missing and I was in a new city and I didn't know anybody. I was hesitant to go to the police. I called Mahtab. He advised me to file an FIR with the nearest police station immediately. After filing the FIR, I didn't know what to do next. So I came back to the hotel. At least Mahtab could reach me there. As soon as I entered the room I got another call from the same stranger. He threatened to kill you if I sought any help from the police. They were watching me. After they called me, Mahtab called back. I told him I would get in touch with him and hung up the phone. I didn't want to lose my other son as well. I went back to the station and lied that you had returned and withdrew the FIR.

'I left for Patna immediately. As the days went by we were worried we had lost our other son too. I thought of calling Mahtab. I didn't know what to do. I wondered if I shouldn't have withdrawn my FIR. What have they done to my boys? What have they done to my Zakir?'

'Abba, I am here now. It's okay. Where is Zakir? Did that person on the phone tell you anything about him?'

'I think we have already lost him. I don't want to lose you now,' Abba said amid sobs, his body shaking. Moving closer to him, Arif wrapped his arm around Abba's shoulders, as he tried unsuccessfully to contain his own tears. Amma, the food forgotten, came closer and hugged both Arif and Abba.

'Hamida,' Abba said, trying to hold back his tears, his voice quivering, 'we've lost our son forever. The police have killed him. There is no justice in our country. They even deprived us of his last deedar. We can't do anything. Thanks to Allah at least they spared Arif.'

Amma held Abba in her arms, her lips pressed hard, but her eyes were dry.

Dadi by now was sitting on the wooden bed, a little away from them, reciting from the Quran, her tears bathing the pages of the holy book.

Huma sat on the floor crying to herself, hugging her knees.

Arif felt bile rising in his throat. His stomach churned. He rushed to the bathroom and vomited smelly yellow liquid.

For the next one month, relatives kept pouring in. Somebody suggested a prayer and funeral service to be conducted for Zakir. Amma shrieked and wailed till Arif and Abba had to carry her away into a room. The subject was never brought up again. They were by now sure Zakir was dead, but they did not want to acknowledge it with a funeral. They also couldn't mourn his loss fully, get any kind of closure.

Shafique suggested they file a case against Delhi Police. But Abba was not interested. He knew very well that only their time, energy and money would be wasted.

~

One day a notice arrived from the commandant's office:

Dear Mr Khan,

We are pleased to inform you that we have extended the allotment of your flat by twelve months. You have to pay a token amount of Rs 100 per month as rent. You are advised to vacate the flat before 30 April 2001.

Sincerely yours,

R.P. Singh,

Dated: 11.04.2000

EIGHTEEN

Weeks, then months, passed sluggishly, but Zakir's absence hung over Arif's house like a cloud of doom.

In November 2000, Bihar was bifurcated. To celebrate the formation of the new state of Jharkhand, people danced on the streets of its proposed capital, Ranchi. Wrapped in a blanket, Arif watched the events unfold on their black-and-white television and thought of Zakir, who had had strong views against the division of Bihar.

Arif also thought of the chilly winter mornings of his childhood in Jamalpura, when he and Zakir snuck away from their house to the outskirts of his village and looked at the majestic Everest shining in the predawn light in the north. The mountain was far away from his village, but in the winter mornings, one could see its silhouetted magnificence kissing the sky.

'How big is this mountain, bhaiyya?' Zakir would ask. And before Arif could answer he would add, 'Allah must be bigger than Everest because He created it.'

Arif also remembered the day Zakir almost got himself

killed by fighting with the police sub-inspector. For Arif, Zakir was more than a brother, more than a friend.

Arif searched the drawer of his table and found a strip of tiny tablets. He took out one and swallowed it. He often took the pill to sleep through the night.

Dadi sought refuge in prayer and the holy book. She continued to recite from the Quran, accompanied by unabated crying. She barely spoke, ate frugally and, at times, even skipped her meals.

Arif had started praying five times a day. His regular visits to the mosque provided him some comfort.

On a Friday, the imam delivered a moving sermon about the mortality of human lives and the futility of sorrows one carried after losing dear ones. 'Kullo nafsin zaikatul maut.' (Every living being has to taste mortality.)

Returning from the mosque, Arif lay in bed and thought, *Zakir is gone forever. But mourning his loss won't make things better. I must think about Abba. I must think of Huma. She is of marriageable age. We'll need money for dowry. I need to get a good job. I'll apply for the state civil services as well as for other jobs.*

Satisfied with his new resolution, he lifted an old issue of *Competition Success Review* with Amir Subhani on the cover. It was Amir Subhani who, by scoring the first rank in the civil services exam in 1986, had inspired hundreds of Bihari Muslim boys like Arif to dream bigger.

Abba used to say, 'Amir Subhani too was from an ordinary family, but he achieved extraordinary success because he worked for it.' Arif would never get his photograph on the cover of *Competition Success Review*. He became desperate and wished he could travel back in time and have another opportunity to try for the civil services. But then he thought of his brother and he was filled with the pain of loss. 'Ya Allah,' he prayed, 'I don't want anything in life, but please give my brother back.' Arif turned to the wall near his study table on which a famous couplet of Allama Iqbal, the great philosopher and poet, was pasted. Arif used to recite it whenever he felt discouraged. Today, once again, he read it loudly:

Khudi ko kar buland itna ki, har taqdeer se pehle
Khuda bande se khud poochhe, bata teri raza kya hain?

(Exalt thyself so high that before issuing the decree of your fate
God may ask, what is your desire?)

It didn't inspire him. Arif started talking to himself. 'Forget all your sorrows. Forget all your losses. Forget all your dreams. You have to live and you have to struggle for the sake of your family.'

Forcing himself to sit at his study table, he opened the book on general studies. Inside the book was a white handkerchief with dark brown checks gifted by Sumitra. His mood swung, his brow wrinkled with bitterness. He stood up and threw the handkerchief out of the window. But can I throw Sumitra out of my mind? He desperately longed to see Sumitra. He desperately wanted to place his head on her shoulder and cry.

Through the window he saw the two former chief ministers of Bihar, Lalu Prasad Yadav and Jagannath Mishra, strolling in the lawns of the police guest house. They had been arrested for their alleged involvement in the 950 crore fodder scam and had been detained in the guest house.

Before returning to his study table, he closed the door. He intended to study till evening without any interruption. He also wanted to shut Sumitra out of his memories. As he was flipping through the book, he heard a frenzied knock on the door followed by Huma's voice, 'Bhaiyya, open the door. Dadi is behaving strangely.' Then he heard Amma scream.

Arif panicked, opened the door and rushed to Dadi's room. Dadi was on the bed, motionless. Amma was shaking her frantically. She held Dadi's wrist, trying to feel her pulse.

'Ammaji, ho Ammaji! Why did you leave us?' Amma screamed. Huma joined her. Arif felt a searing pain in his heart.

Abba, who had returned from Raja Bazaar, grabbed Dadi's feet and sat next to her on his knees. Amma consoled him, her hands wrapped around his shoulders.

People from Police Colony gathered at Arif's house through the day. A group of Hindu women offered their respects to Dadi with folded hands. He searched for Sumitra in the crowd. *Despite what had happened between him and Sumitra, she would certainly come if she had heard about Dadi's death*, Arif thought.

She didn't.

Brushing aside his thoughts about Sumitra, he looked at Dadi's face. She looked serene, as if she was sleeping. Then a sudden shrill cry of a woman drew his attention. A distant niece of Dadi had arrived from Khajpura.

Arif wasn't sure any more whether it was the same day or the next. Calls had been made, relatives had been pouring in, offering their condolences.

Abba's colleague Jameel Khan, who lived in Samanpura, approached Abba and whispered, 'Abdul Rashid bhai, I have talked to my folks and taken permission from them to bury Chachijaan at the Veterinary College kabristan.' Abba nodded without a word.

Amma intercepted Jameel Khan, her voice tinged with anger.

'As per the wishes of Ammaji, we'll take her to Jamalpura. According to her wishes, she should be buried in the graveyard of her village, next to her father and forefathers.'

'Okay, bhabhijaan, then I should arrange a vehicle to take Ammaji to Jamalpura,' Jameel Khan said.

In the evening, a police pickup truck, a five-tonner, arrived. Dadi was put on a big slab of ice on the floor at the back of the truck; there was an olive-green canopy overhead. Arif and his family, along with three distant relatives and two former colleagues of Abba, sat near Dadi. In the front seat, by the driver, sat Abba's junior colleague Mangani Mandal. The vehicle moved smoothly to Hajipur, after which the condition of the road began to worsen. Arif and Huma supported Dadi from both sides with their hands. Besides the physical discomfort, Arif found despair and pain gnawing at him from inside.

Zakir's disappearance had snatched Dadi from us. And why did Zakir have to go to Delhi to find a job? Despite being the eldest son of the family, I never shouldered responsibilities as I should have.

By then, they had crossed Muzaffarpur; the road to Motihari was relatively better. Resting his head against the bench seat, he fell asleep. During that short spell of slumber, Arif saw Dadi sitting near him, telling him stories of holy prophets, folk tales and her favourite stories from their family history.

A sudden halt jolted all the passengers in the truck. Arif also woke up from his dream. His eyes began to well up again. Resting her chin on her knees, Huma was still sobbing. Just ahead, the road was closed for vehicles because of repairs to a small road bridge. The driver went to enquire and returned with the news that the road would open at 4 a.m.

Dadi's life had been full of struggles. She was the second wife of his grandfather, who had married her after the death of his first wife. Dadi had lost her husband just after Partition, when she was barely twenty-one. Abba was her only son. With the meagre produce from the land that remained in her control, scheming relatives having usurped the remaining property, she had brought up Abba and her stepson, Badke baba, single-handedly. Many of her relatives, including her only brother, had left for the newly created Pakistan. Arif felt bad for not fulfilling her wish to see him married in her lifetime. Oh Dadi! Arif spent the entire night talking to Huma about Dadi's life.

The next morning, they reached Jamalpura at around eleven thirty.

Almost the entire village was waiting for them. Badke

baba came running when he saw them approach. He hugged Abba and broke into a loud wail. Though Dadi was his stepmother, she hadn't let him feel so at any point of time in her entire life. Even as a child she had given him preference over her own son. Badke baba's wife held Amma and Huma and the three of them wept together. Behind them a dozen or more sobbed. Muneer stood beside Arif, his eyes moist.

The last rites began only after Nazneen came with her husband. Rabiya's husband was in Bangalore and they would be arriving after a day or so.

Dadi was bathed, covered and placed on a cot. Arif, Muneer, Abba and Badke baba lifted the cot to take her on her last journey. Women started screaming. The namaz-e-janaza, the funeral prayer, was to be performed in front of the Jama Masjid. Almost all relations from the nearby villages had arrived. The imam asked everyone to line up.

'No! No! The number of rows should not be in even numbers. It must be in odd numbers. Please make seven lines instead of six,' Hakim sahab said at the top of his voice.

The imam explained the method of the funeral prayer. Then he started the prayer with 'Allah ho Akbar, God is great'.

At the graveyard, two men lifted Dadi.

Inside the grave, Hakim sahab and Badke baba held Dadi and placed her on the floor. Hakim sahab gently pulled the top end of the shroud to uncover Dadi's face for the last deedar. And then, a few seconds later, her face was covered again. Abba broke down. Arif began to sob. The men around consoled them.

Badke baba and Hakim sahab came out of the grave as

the imam ordered the splinters of bamboo to be brought to cover the grave. Two mats of palm date leaves were unrolled to prevent the soil from falling inside the grave. Rose water was sprinkled. The imam asked Abba to drop three handfuls of gravel on the grave thrice. Being her son, it was his right to do so. He lifted a handful of soil, releasing it slowly. Badke baba, Arif and Muneer followed Abba.

The others started sprinkling earth on the grave. Then the gravedigger took over, covering up the grave with sand, sprinkling water and patting the grave with his shovel to settle it. Branches of the babool tree with prickles were also placed on the grave to prevent jackals from digging it up.

Arif couldn't sleep that night. Propped against a pillar, he sat in the arched veranda of his ancestral house. Under the moonlight, he could see the silhouette of the dome of Hazrat Jamaluddin Khan Rahmatullah Alaih's shrine, whom Dadi used to refer to as Pir sahab. 'Arif, Pir sahab was not only an Auliya but he was also our forefather.' Dadi had never gone inside and always prayed in the courtyard. 'It is forbidden for women to go inside a shrine where saints are resting,' she used to say. Holding Zakir's hand, Arif would go inside the tomb and imitate the rituals performed by the elders, and Zakir in turn imitated him. Zakir's memory sent a wave of sharp pain through Arif. Closing his eyes, he squeezed the tears gathering inside. Slapping his forehead, he looked at the sky, complaining to Allah for what He had done to him. 'First you took my brother away, and now Dadi is also gone,' he moaned.

He walked out of the house and towards the shrine. It was three in the morning and the sky was lit with stars.

Arif sat down on the steps of the shrine and recalled his last visit with Zakir and Dadi. His heart ached from the old memories. He could hear his grandma telling her favourite story of the origin of the shrine. Remembering his grandmother and brother, he closed his eyes and drifted off to sleep.

'I have been looking for you for the past two hours. Come home and eat something. You haven't eaten anything for the last two days,' Abba said as he blew his nose into a handkerchief. He smiled at Arif. Arif smiled back, a smile brimming with grief. He stood up and they walked back home together.

~

After returning from Dadi's funeral, Arif's family moved to a rented house in Samanpura. The flat at Police Colony was airy with its two huge balconies shaded by the trees on the campus. On summer mornings, a soft wind swept through the rooms. In winter, the sunlight streamed into the house quite early in the morning. Sitting on a chair in the balcony, Arif had luxuriated under the golden sun. During the rainy season, Arif had many a times stood in the veranda, allowing the raindrops to drench his face.

In Samanpura, the rented house had only two rooms, each just enough to accommodate two cots, and a small veranda, which had been curtained off to be used as a drawing room. The alley from the flat to the main road was lined on both sides with overflowing open sewage. Sometimes, the stench from the nullah was strong enough to cause passers-by to become nauseous. The landlord of the house had another entrance, which opened on the other side, to the main road. On the right side of the ground-floor house was a three-storey building that blocked the sunlight during the day. Fresh air could not reach the house. Amma complained that the rooms were small and cramped.

'For 1800 rupees, you can only get rooms like this. Not a bungalow,' Abba said in exasperation.

Despite its small size, the flat seemed to be only partly occupied, awaiting more people. Zakir's and Dadi's absence filled the house. Abba lost his temper over trifles. To get over their personal pains, Amma and Huma resorted to silence. Huma didn't ask Arif any more what he wanted to eat in the evening. Abba didn't yell at Arif for ignoring his studies.

Arif started spending more and more time teaching at the coaching institute in Raja Bazaar.

NINETEEN

In 2001, the holy month of Ramzan ended on 16 December with the sighting of the crescent in the evening. The next day, Eid-ul-Fitr was celebrated with traditional fervour and gaiety across the country but in Arif's house Eid was bereft of festivities.

Arif wore an old white kurta and a loose pyjama with a half-sleeved woollen sweater. Abba was dressed in a kurta pyjama which he had bought many years ago; in fact, Zakir had bought the set from Sabzi Bagh. Amma and Huma were yet to change.

It was their first Eid without Dadi and Zakir. Though Arif wished everyone in his family Eid Mubarak, his words lacked enthusiasm. His Amma's eyes were red and swollen. She must have wept for long hours over her missing son.

'Eid Mubarak, beta.' Abba said in a low voice. He took out a tiny bottle of Majmua 96, put a drop of fragrant liquid on his index finger and rubbed it on the inside of Arif's wrists. Then, he dabbed another drop of ittar behind Arif's ears. Allergic to strong smells, Arif didn't like to apply perfume, but today was Eid and he didn't want to stop Abba. If Zakir were here, he would have soaked himself in cologne, not Majmua 96, but some fancy brand. Amma had often warned him that spray perfumes might have alcohol in them. But Zakir had never listened to her.

Arif felt as if Zakir would step out of the bathroom, a towel wrapped around his waist, and shout, 'Amma, give me my kurta pyjama. Just half an hour left for namaz. We will not get seats inside the Eidgah if we are late.' Zakir had always been the last to get ready for the Eid prayers. Remembering his brother, Arif smiled as teardrops gathered inside his eyes. 'Zakir, Eid Mubarak,' he said silently and wiped the tears with the back of his palm.

'Let's go, beta.' Abba turned to Arif and handed him a white skullcap.

After returning from the mosque with Abba, Arif and his family sat down to eat a meal of homemade sewaiyan in sugary syrup, chicken curry and pulao. Ignoring the invitations from the neighbourhood families, Arif lay down on his bed after the meal. Abba sat on the veranda with the day's newspaper in his hands.

Arif fell asleep and had a dream that Zakir had returned home and Amma, Abba and his sisters were hugging him one by one. Arif was standing away from them in one corner of a room. Then his father called out his name. He woke up with a start and realized that Abba was actually calling him. Rubbing his eyes, he got out of bed, found his slippers and went out to the veranda.

Arif saw Abba talking to Janardan Gupta, one of his

former colleagues from the police department. Mr Gupta was fair and pot-bellied. There was an empty china bowl with a stainless steel spoon and half a glass of water on a plastic table in front of Mr Gupta.

'Pranam, uncle,' Arif greeted Mr Gupta by joining his palms.

'Be happy, my son,' Mr Gupta said.

'How are your studies?'

'Fine.'

'Are you appearing for the Bihar civil services this year?'

'Yes, uncle.'

'Good, good. My son is also making his first attempt at BPSC.'

'Achcha,' Arif replied as he scratched the back of his head.

'So Khan sahab, I should take your leave now.' Mr Gupta shook hands with Abba and walked away.

When he left, Abba asked Arif to sit on a chair next to him and placed a light blue inland letter on the table.

'See what this letter is. I have misplaced my glasses,' Abba said.

Arif ripped open the letter and read aloud:

Dear Khan sahab,

Your son Zakir is safe. By the grace of the Almighty, he will return home in the next six–seven months. I can't tell you why he suddenly disappeared. Please don't share the contents of this letter with anyone outside your family.

Your well-wisher

The letter was not dated. The post office stamp was smudged, but Arif could tell it was sent from Hauz Khas in Delhi. The letter looked like it had been posted a few months ago.

Abba shrieked with joy and called out to Amma and Huma.

Arif was expressionless, not knowing how to react. He rubbed his nose and scratched his forehead. He was suspicious of the letter. *Maybe someone has played a prank on us. Why on earth would anyone do so? Who has sent this letter? How does he know that Zakir will return?* But he couldn't resist the sense of hope the letter filled him with.

Amma and Huma were puzzled by Abba's uncontrollable laughter. Arif came out of his daze to tell them about the contents of the letter.

Finally, Arif smiled and looked at Amma, Huma and Abba. They were also smiling, their eyes moist. The sound of footsteps made Arif turn around to the road. A bearded man in his sixties with a dirty bag swinging from his shoulder had entered the narrow alley leading to his flat.

'Allah will fulfil all your wishes. Allah will fill your house with happiness,' the old beggar shouted. Arif searched his pocket and fished out three five-rupee coins. He placed them in the beggar's aluminium bowl. The coins made a clinking sound before settling in the bowl.

'Wait,' Amma said as the beggar turned to go. She went inside and returned with pulao and chicken in a stainless steel plate and water in a steel tumbler. The beggar settled down on the floor of the veranda, wiped off the food in ten minutes and said 'Allah' as he burped. He prayed aloud for the prosperity of Arif's family before leaving.

Arif hoped that the beggar's prayers would be answered by the Almighty.

Turning to his mother, Arif smiled. She smiled back, teardrops shining in her eyes. This letter from some unknown source had given Arif's family a reason to smile after many months. It had lit a tiny candle of hope inside the temple of Arif's heart.

From that day, he waited for his brother to return. Everyone else in his family waited too.

Destiny

TWENTY

Four more years passed but Zakir didn't return. Arif and his family stopped believing that he would ever come back. Arif was sure that the letter was a hoax.

During the past four years, Arif and his family had learned to live with this mammoth grief. They had learned to smile even when they felt like crying. They had learned to tuck their sorrow away in the farthest corners of their hearts.

'Time is a great healer.' Arif had heard this proverb many times. And he was surprised that it really worked. The pain of losing Zakir wasn't going to vanish and he couldn't forget Dadi either, but during the past couple of years, the sadness over the sudden loss of his brother and grandmother had been partly replaced by the yearning for a decent job to become the breadwinner for his family.

After unsuccessfully trying for the Bihar civil services examination thrice, he was to appear once again for the same exam, his last chance to redeem himself. Though he had neither the zeal nor the stamina to study for long hours, he still forced himself to do so.

Since he was well past thirty, he was not eligible to

apply for most government jobs. Arif earned five thousand rupees a month by teaching at the coaching institute in Raja Bazaar in the morning and by giving private tuitions to four neighbourhood boys in the afternoon. The money together with Abba's pension was enough to meet the basic necessities of a lower-middle-class family in Patna.

But there were other expenses, too. Huma had to discontinue her studies because they couldn't afford it any more. And when Amma had fallen sick two years ago, they had had to sell her remaining ornaments to get her treated in a private hospital. Then there was the question of Huma's marriage. They needed at least three to four lakh rupees to conduct a decent marriage ceremony.

I have to do something to arrange the dowry for Huma's marriage, Arif thought as he was going through a bunch of application forms for various jobs at Rahul Magazine Centre on Jagdeo Path on a hot May evening in 2005.

Arif stopped flipping through the forms as he saw the vacancies for account clerks at the Patna Collectorate. The upper age limit for the application was thirty-five. The openings were for five posts only. Arif paid two rupees to buy an application form. The next day, he sent in his application.

'I don't think you have any chance, beta. I enquired from an old acquaintance who runs a recruitment agency; he said one needed to either have a minister's recommendation or cough up two to three lakhs as bribe,' Abba said in a weary tone.

Arif had just gotten back from his job at the coaching class. He had a copy of the *Hindustan* newspaper in his hands.

'We can try, Abba. Let's hope for the best,' Arif said as he handed over the newspaper to his father, just as the ceiling fan slowed down to a stop.

'Load-shedding again, uff!' Arif said as he unbuttoned his shirt and hung it on the clothes line.

'Read this news, Arif,' Abba said in an excited voice.

Arif grabbed the newspaper. Arif's friend Mritunjay, who until the previous month had been district magistrate of Arrah, had been transferred to Patna.

'He is an old friend of yours. Go and meet him. He'll certainly help you,' Abba said.

Arif didn't respond. Should he go to meet Mritunjay? What would he tell Mritunjay if he asked him what he was doing? How would Mritunjay introduce him to his wife? Would he say, 'Meet my friend Arif, who does nothing?'

The last time he had seen Mritunjay was almost five years ago, when he had gone to the party at Maurya Hotel. He remembered that evening vividly. It had ended in huge embarrassment.

Dressed in a pair of jeans and a formal shirt, he had reached the hotel on time. Inside the party hall, he found that Mritunjay had not arrived at the venue. Nervously, he surveyed the party scene and saw men in smart formals and the women in expensive saris, chatting, laughing and drinking wine. Arif stood out in his faded jeans, cheap checked shirt and Rexine sandals.

The drinks and snacks were being served by waiters wearing white shirts and black waistcoats. He picked up a glass of orange juice. Suddenly, there was a commotion in the far corner. Two gatecrashers had been caught with glasses of whisky in their hands. They were abused and slapped by the party manager and were thrown out of the hotel. Arif observed a man next to him looking suspiciously at him and then whispering something to a waiter.

Soon, two men came to him and asked politely, 'Which batch, sir?'

'Batch?' Arif fumbled.

'Are you not an IAS officer?' the other man asked sternly.

'No.'

'Look at his clothes. Certainly, he is also a freeloader. Throw him out!' The voice was of a sturdy-looking man dressed in a blue suit.

Two waiters immediately held him by his shoulders.

'I was invited by Mr Mritunjay Pandey,' Arif said and applied all his strength to free himself from the clutches of the waiters. One of them lost his balance and fell on the floor.

The sturdy one looked at Arif menacingly, when someone pulled the waiter by the collar and pushed him to the floor.

'How dare you touch my friend!' Mritunjay thundered and advanced towards the sturdy man. Two men held him back.

'Mritunjay, there was some confusion. The waiter didn't know he was your friend,' an elderly man in a brown suit said.

The sturdy man rose from the floor and came to apologize to Arif. But Arif did not wish to stay any longer and left the hotel immediately.

The next morning, Mritunjay visited Arif, asking him to forget the previous night's incident. He also told him that he was posted in Hazaribagh and gave Arif his office phone number.

Three months later Mritunjay was transferred to Ranchi.

A year later, a wedding card arrived in the post at his father's old office address. Mritunjay's marriage was fixed with the daughter of a senior IAS officer from Lucknow. The ceremony was to take place in Delhi. Arif tried to convince himself to attend his friend's wedding but could not bring himself to do so. He didn't have money to buy a gift befitting an IAS officer. He was not sure that Mritunjay's wife would welcome him. How would he interact with Mritunjay's colleagues; most of them must be IAS, IFS or IPS officers.

After that, Mritunjay didn't try to contact him.

Arif had not informed Mritunjay when his family had moved to a rented house in Samanpura.

After so many years, he didn't know if Mritunjay was still his friend or if, after walking in the corridors of power, he had changed.

'If you don't feel comfortable, there is no need to meet Mritunjay,' Abba said, looking at Arif intently.

'I will go to meet my friend,' Arif said, resolving to place his family's well-being above his ego.

~

Arif got down from an autorickshaw near Shri Krishna Science Centre and walked towards Biscomaun Tower. Barely a hundred metres from the tower, the tallest building of Patna, and to the west of the majestic Gandhi Maidan, adjacent to St Xavier's High School, was the residence of the district magistrate or DM. It was a huge bungalow with a long driveway. Near the huge iron gate stood a sentry, a tall thin man with a Rajinikant moustache. Arif told him he wanted to meet the DM. He stammered while talking to the sentry. Arif felt he shouldn't have gone there.

'Today DM sahab is in a bad mood. He has instructed me that he won't be meeting anyone this evening,' the sentry said.

'But I'm his friend,' he said.

The sentry looked at him with disbelief.

'I mean he knows me,' Arif immediately modified his sentence. *How can a dishevelled-looking poor man be the friend of an IAS officer?* Arif thought, trying to conjure up an image of himself standing in front of a mirror. He took out a piece of paper and a pen from his pocket and scribbled his name.

'Can you pass this note to DM sahab?' he asked the sentry.

The sentry refused. 'Go to the collectorate if you want to give him some application.'

'Please inform him. He'll know who I am,' Arif made a final attempt to convince him. The sentry remained adamant.

A car honked at the gate. The sentry ran to open it. A white Ambassador came into view. Arif looked at the car hoping that Mritunjay might notice him.

'Move aside, DM sahab's car is coming,' the sentry shouted, but Arif didn't move. In fact, he hadn't even heard the sentry's voice. His eyes were fixed on the gate. The sentry raised his hand and pushed him away. Arif couldn't maintain his balance and fell to the pebbled ground.

The sentry pulled the gate open. As the car crossed him, he gave a salute. Then, the car suddenly stopped near them. Arif was sure that Mritunjay had recognized him and had asked his driver to stop. Why should he not recognize me? He is an old buddy of mine. We spent so many years together. Arif imagined Mritunjay pushing the door open, running to Arif and offering his hands to help him rise, then hugging him, the sentry looking at him in disbelief.

Arif stood up, rubbed his palms to get rid of the dirt and looked towards Mritunjay's car, some sort of hope smiling in his eyes.

But Mritunjay had not noticed him. He didn't even look outside the car. He was in the back seat, reading a book. A beautiful woman with shoulder-length hair sat next to him. She looked upset. Arif felt like calling out Mritunjay's name, but no sound came out of his mouth.

Arif mused on the past. If, like Mritunjay, he had moved to Delhi, if, like Mritunjay, he had joined coaching classes for civil services exams, he would have also passed them. He would have also had a bungalow like this. He would have also been saluted by a sentry at the gate of his house. Arif talked to himself again and again and smiled. A smile soaked with sadness. Unlike Mritunjay's father, Abba couldn't have afforded to get him admitted to a good coaching institute in Delhi.

The sentry asked him to go away. This time his voice was harsh, bordering on insolence.

Walking slowly to Gandhi Maidan, Arif bought a coneful of roasted gram for three rupees and sat on a cement bench nearby and thought of a song from *Umrao Jaan.*

Tamaam umra ka hisaab maangti hain zindagi
Yeh mera dil kahe to kya, yeh khud se sharmsaar hain

(Life asks me for an account of all my years
What will this heart of mine say? It is ashamed of itself)

Arif looked at his wristwatch and stood up, stretched and yawned. His left hand moved swiftly to cover his wide-open mouth.

'Tauba Astaghfar! Tauba Astaghfar! Tauba Astaghfar!' he said. A sad smile passed his lips as Dadi's warning flashed in his mind, 'Cover your mouth with your left hand and say Tauba Astaghfar thrice whenever you yawn. Otherwise, the devil will piss into your mouth.'

Later at the autorickshaw stand, Arif was startled by a sudden pat on his shoulder. He turned to find Ramesh Kumar standing there, smiling. He had grown older and there were signs of grey in his hair.

'Pranam, uncle!' Arif greeted him with a smile.

'Arif, how are you?' he said.

'I am fine, uncle.'

'And what are you doing right now?'

'Teaching at a coaching institute and preparing for the BPSC examinations,' he said with a sad smile. He had emphasized BPSC to add some respectability to his answer.

'What happened to your IAS exam?' Ramesh asked.

'Got stuck at the interview level.'

'Don't worry, keep trying. I think bank exams are relatively easier.'

'I am already thirty-five. I can't appear for the bank exams.'

'I forgot that. We are meeting after such a long time, but it feels like yesterday.'

'Yes, uncle.' Arif suppressed the urge to ask about Sumitra.

'Heard about your brother Zakir. I'm really sorry.'

'Everything is in Allah's hands,' Arif said and couldn't control the tears. Ramesh Kumar noticed this and changed the topic.

'I'm posted in Begusarai right now. I hope that I'll be back in Patna by next month. Let's meet then.' He took out his wallet and extracted a visiting card and wrote something on the back of it. 'This is my card with my mobile number and Sumitra's. Call me sometime and we'll chat. If it's after office hours, call me on Sumitra's number. I keep my official mobile switched off in the evening.'

The mention of Sumitra's name caused a twinge in Arif's heart.

'How are Rahul and Kavita?'

'Kavita is in New Jersey. She had a son last year. Rahul is studying mechanical engineering at IIT Kharagpur.'

'Good! Happy to hear that,' Arif said.

As Arif was pocketing the card, he saw a man approaching them.

'Let's go, Ramesh,' the man said, patting Ramesh's back.

He was the same man Arif had seen hugging Sumitra many years ago. He couldn't forget the moustache.

What the hell is he doing here with Ramesh? Does Ramesh know what this man is up to? Arif thought to himself.

Ramesh introduced the man to Arif. 'Meet my brother-in-law Gyan Prakash, Sumitra's elder brother.'

~

Long after Ramesh and his brother-in-law had left the place, Arif stood there trying to figure out the chain of events of the day he had severed all ties with Sumitra.

It was Sumitra's brother I had seen hugging her and in a fit of jealousy I had thought something else.

Arif was remorseful for the way he had humiliated Sumitra years ago. He desperately wanted to talk to her. Would she ever forgive him for calling her a whore? Would it be a wise decision to talk to Sumitra? Should he revive his relationship with her? Would their reunion do any good for them?

~

In the following week, he went to the public telephone booth thrice, but his courage gave way as soon as he lifted the receiver. 'Don't go near Sumitra again. Don't complicate your life, which is already a mess,' he told himself.

On the eighth day, he finally dialled her number. Sumitra's sleepy voice came through. He barely managed to utter 'It is Arif' and then became silent, waiting for Sumitra to respond. The line was disconnected. He tried again but found the phone switched off.

Two days later, he tried her number again and this time Sumitra answered, 'What do you want from me?'

Without asking for her forgiveness, he told her everything. About the boys he had heard gossiping at the teashop. About his visit to her house where he had seen her hugging her brother.

Arif added a formal 'I am extremely sorry' at the end. Then he asked, 'Can we meet again?' *You are walking into a trap. Leave Sumitra alone. Don't ruin her happy family. Don't spoil your life.*

After a long silence, she replied, 'Let me think about it.'

The next time he talked to her, he apologized again. Sumitra listened to him and mostly replied in 'yes' or 'no'. It was only on his twelfth or thirteenth call that Sumitra responded properly. In fact, she spoke as if nothing had ever happened between them. Sumitra told him that she was in Katihar at her parents' house. When Arif informed her that he would be in Katihar next Sunday for his BPSC exam, she agreed to meet him there.

Arif had a gut feeling that he was going to perform well in this exam. For the last six months he had been working with renewed zeal, almost in the same way he had prepared for the IAS exam.

If he couldn't crack the IAS exam, he should clear this exam and become a deputy superintendent of police or a circle officer. That would be cathartic for him. It would be some sort of redemption.

The examination was slated to take place on Sunday, 22 May 2005 at D.S. College, Katihar.

He was going to see Sumitra after so many years. Closing his eyes, he conjured his lady love, beautiful, elegant and with a voice that was as sweet as honey.

~

On Saturday evening, Arif looked into his wallet. It contained three hundred and thirty rupees. He calculated that it was enough for him to go to Katihar and come back if he travelled in general class. Anyway, he was going to travel without a ticket. No ticket checker dared to venture inside a bogie packed with students. The students sat down wherever they wanted; even people with reserved tickets were sometimes forced to travel standing. In fact, passengers who knew about the examination postponed their journeys. Earlier Arif used to insist on purchasing tickets but the heydays of his idealism were now over and he had become more practical. He was aware that whatever he saved would add to the family's income.

Arif reached the station on a smoke-belching monstrous Vikram autorickshaw. The station was crowded like a fair-ground. Students were everywhere, and finding a place to stand on the platform was difficult. Passengers with valid tickets were either lining up at the counter to get their ticket cancelled or stood among the flood of provincial civil service aspirants, with worried faces, unsure of being able to board the train.

An hour later, the train chugged in. There was a mad

rush to get on it. Arif struggled to get into the general compartment and found a seat on an upper berth with two more boys.

Inside the compartment, some of the boys tried to climb on to the upper berth where Arif sat. But a young man (somewhat tough-looking with a closely cropped beard) sitting next to him stared at them threateningly. They moved away. One boy argued that on other berths four boys were sitting but the bearded young man's intimidating look and a few expletives in Magahi discouraged him, and he, too, found a place elsewhere.

Many in Bihar, from the hoi polloi to the elite, had mastered this art of issuing threats and used it in their daily lives. But Arif had always been deficient in this skill.

On the lower berth, two boys fought with each other to claim the seat. On that hot and humid evening in May, Arif's throat was scorched. He pulled out a bottle from his travel bag, which he had filled with cold water at the Patna junction. It was soothing.

'Brother, can I have some water?' the boy with the closely cropped beard asked.

'Sure!' Arif handed him the bottle.

The boy took a few sips first and then gulped down all of it.

'I'll get it filled at the next station,' he said apologetically.

'It's okay,' Arif said and smiled reassuringly.

The boy introduced himself as Unaib Khan.

'Assalam alaikum, I'm Arif Khan,' Arif responded warmly and shook hands with him.

They talked about possible trends in that year's state civil services examination. Unaib, coincidentally, also had public administration as an optional subject. They discussed it until Unaib fell asleep. Arif fell in and out of sleep as he sat hugging his knees. The fans whirred relentlessly, dispersing hot air over them. The sweat made his shirt stick to his back. He thought of his proposed meeting with Sumitra, and that lifted his spirits, though he wasn't sure if his decision to meet her was correct.

He was dozing when a ruckus on the train woke him up. A group of boys were arguing over something. It was five in the morning and they were about to reach Katihar. The morning breeze had made the inside of the train cool.

The train stopped with a long whistle at the outer signal of the Katihar junction. Hundreds of boys got down from the train; most of them unzipped their trousers and started urinating. A hundred or more narrow streams of water irrigated the edge of the rail track. Arif, too, got down from the upper berth as he felt the pressure on his bladder. On the floor between the two lower berths, a plump boy was sleeping, using newspapers as a bed sheet. Arif searched for his sandals on the floor of the train and found one of them. The other sandal was stuck under the weight of a huge travel bag. Using all his might, he managed to pull it out. The train started moving. The boys pissing en masse near the rail track streamed back into the train. They crowded the aisles, clogging the passage to the toilet. Arif decided to defer his visit to the urinal for a few more minutes.

At the junction, Arif and Unaib decided to catch a few hours of sleep before the examination. On the platform, they spread bed sheets and used their travel bags as pillows.

They woke up at 8 a.m. and found a long queue at the public toilet outside the Katihar junction. Unlike other parts of India, in Bihar you could find public toilets in almost every city.

In our state people don't have much to eat, but at least they have Sulabh Shauchalayas to shit comfortably for just one rupee, Arif thought. He stood in the queue and waited for his turn.

The examination went well and Arif couldn't help smiling as he came out of the centre. Spotting a public telephone booth attached to a teashop, he called Sumitra. After two rings, a male voice responded. Must be Sumitra's father, he thought and immediately disconnected the phone.

After an hour, he went back to the public telephone booth and dialled her number again. This time Sumitra was on the line.

'Sumi, this is Arif.'

'How was your exam?' was the first thing she asked.

'It was very good,' Arif replied.

'That's great,' Sumitra said.

'When are we meeting?' Arif asked.

'Tomorrow, I'll be travelling alone to Begusarai by the Katihar Patna Express at 2.30 p.m. My father will come to see me off. Buy a general ticket and come to the AC two-tier compartment, A2, seat no. 35. I will get your ticket converted to an AC ticket. There are always empty seats on this train.'

'Achha!' Arif nodded as if she was in front of him.

'Where are you staying?' she asked.

'In a hotel near the junction,' he lied. If he told her he didn't have enough money to rent a room in a hotel, she would be sad.

He disconnected the phone and came out of the telephone booth smiling.

On the pavement just outside the booth, a vendor was frying puris on a pushcart. In a cauldron, golden yellow puris sizzled in hot oil. Aloo dum floating in red gravy filled a huge bowl. Chopped green coriander leaves floated in the gravy. Arif ordered a plate. His stomach full, he caught an autorickshaw to the Katihar station. The waiting hall for second-class travellers was full. On the platform, students were still wandering around waiting for their trains. The nine-thirty evening train to Patna was crowded. The students even got into the AC compartments and the police were called to get them out. A fight broke out with the police. Arif watched from a distance, ready to run away if it came to that. Three hours later, most of the students had left.

On the platform, near a closed bookshop, Arif found a place to sleep. He took out the bed sheet to make his bed and found it damp. In the morning, after taking a bath, he had pushed the wet towel into the travel bag and that had made the sheet damp. He folded the sheet and the towel and stuffed them in the side pockets of the travel bag. In the same bag, there was a set of ironed shirts and trousers wrapped in an old newspaper. He pulled out the newspaper and spread it on the floor. A front-page news item attracted his attention.

NEW DELHI: In a severe rebuke to Gujarat Chief Minister Narendra Modi, the United States has denied him entry to America.

> Taking a strong stand against the senior BJP leader and Hindutva icon, the US Consular division on Friday denied him a diplomatic visa, apparently holding him responsible for the communal riots in Gujarat in 2002, which claimed over 2000 lives.
>
> In addition, his tourist/business visa, which was already granted, has also been revoked under a section of the US Immigration and Nationality Act.
>
> A US embassy spokesman confirmed that the 'Chief Minister of Gujarat had applied for visa but was denied a diplomatic visa under 214 (b) of Immigration and Nationality Act because he was not coming for a purpose that qualifies for a diplomatic visa.'

'Saala George Bush! He's a bloody hypocrite. On the one hand, he supports the killing of Muslims all over the world, and on the other hand, takes the moral high ground in denying a visa to the Gujarat chief minister,' Arif muttered and spread out other pages of the newspaper. Placing his travel bag under his head, he lay on the floor. He kept thinking about his meeting with Sumitra, until sleep overpowered him.

In the morning, the waiting time at the Sulabh Shauchalaya was shorter. He had a quick bath, and then looked for a salon; he didn't want to face Sumitra with a rude stubble. He found an 'Italian' salon at the main entrance of the junction.

The barber, a thin old man with an Amitabh-like white French beard, informed him that he charged five rupees for shaving with cream. If he wished to use shaving soap then it would cost three. He chose the latter. He was made to sit on a small platform made by putting together six bricks. The word 'Italian' had nothing to do with Italy; it was Bihari slang for roadside salons. It was called so because 'ita' or bricks were used for seating the customer.

Shaving proved to be a painful process. Arif felt a burning sensation wherever the barber moved the razor on his face. He complained about it and the barber told him that this was because of his tough beard. After finishing the shave, he took a big chunk of potash alum dipped in water and rubbed it on his cheeks. Once again, his cheeks were on fire.

Before paying the barber, he looked in the mirror. He was presentable now. Smiling, he combed his hair.

The cobbler sitting next to the barber had already mended his sandal and was polishing it. Arif looked at his watch and said to him, 'Bhai, hurry up, I have to catch a train.'

The queue for the rail ticket moved leisurely as an old man at the counter struggled with the electronic ticketing machine. Arif was still thinking of Sumitra when he reached the counter. The old man almost shouted at him, 'Which station?'

Startled, Arif replied, 'Patna. Superfast.'

After getting his ticket, he moved on to platform one. He boarded the train and found seat no. 35 in A2. The train began to move but Sumitra had not come yet. A few minutes later, he saw a middle-aged man in a black blazer walking in his direction. He was the rail coach conductor of the AC two-tier coach.

The coach conductor adjusted his glasses and gave Arif a suspicious look. 'Please show me your ticket,' he demanded.

'I have come here to meet my bhabhi.' His throat started to dry up. Standing near seat no. 35, he looked around for Sumitra. But there was no sign of her.

Arif was surprised that he had referred to Sumitra as his sister-in-law.

'Where is your ticket?' the conductor asked in an agitated voice.

Arif pulled out a tiny white-and-brown ticket from his pocket.

'This is a general ticket. You are in an AC two-tier compartment. Don't you understand the difference?' he yelled.

'But . . .'

'Get away from the cabin. Stay near the door and get off at the next station. Pata nahin kahan kahan se chale aate hain.'

As Arif turned to leave, he found Sumitra standing just in front of him, holding her luggage. She was wearing a black sari with a yellow-and-red print and a full-sleeved matching blouse. She still looked stunning, even though some wrinkles on her face betrayed her age – she must be in her late forties.

'What seems to be the problem?' she asked the conductor.

'Nothing, madam, this boy is travelling in the AC compartment with a general ticket,' he said matter-of-factly.

'He's travelling with me. Please take the difference in fare and issue him an AC ticket. I believe seat no. 36 is empty.' Sumitra's voice was authoritative.

The conductor complied immediately. He took out a chart and a small calculator from his pocket. After some calculations, he spoke with a sheepish grin, 'If I issue you a ticket, it will be costly. I can allow your brother-in-law to sit in this AC compartment for two hundred.'

'No, please issue a proper ticket. We don't mind paying the fare, whatever it is,' Sumitra said.

'I'm in charge of this coach, madam. I'll go up to Patna. There'll be no inconvenience for you. Many passengers are travelling with a similar arrangement. I can make it one hundred and fifty for you.' There was a perfect Buddha smile on his face.

'No, please issue a ticket.'

'If you insist, I'll issue the ticket, but it will benefit neither you nor me. All the money will go to the government's coffers,' he said.

'Thanks for the offer. But I want a proper receipt. If you want something extra for chai-pani, over and above the cost of the ticket, I will give you that, too.'

'No, madam, I am not that shameless. If you are purchasing a ticket and paying the full fare, then I'll not charge anything extra.'

'Thank you very much for your kindness,' Sumitra said and opened her blue tote bag.

'Let me pay,' Arif said, pulling out his purse from his pocket. Then he remembered he had only two hundred rupees left and that was not enough for the second AC fare to Patna.

'No,' Sumitra said, and instantly offered a five-hundred-rupee note to the conductor.

'Okay,' Arif said and thanked God for saving him from a huge embarrassment.

The conductor smiled and accepted the money. Turning

to the coach attendant, he asked him to bring bed sheets and a pillow for Arif.

The occupancy in the compartment was very low. All the seats in the berth next to Sumitra's were unoccupied. Arif and Sumitra sat on the same berth as the train moved.

During the next one and a half hours, Arif told her about the ordeal he had gone through during the last five years. She had already heard about Zakir and was sympathetic when Arif related to her the series of events which had led Zakir to Delhi. She wasn't aware of Dadi's passing away.

'I was not in Patna. Ramesh had been transferred to Begusarai. Otherwise, I would have definitely come for her funeral. She was such a nice lady, pious and full of affection,' Sumitra said, wiping tears.

After about ten or fifteen minutes of leaving Thana Bihpur junction, the train halted suddenly. Arif and Sumitra learned from the coach attendant that the engine had developed some problems, and only after another one was brought from either Khagaria or Katihar would the train move.

The coach attendant could not serve any food. 'Madam, there is no pantry car on this train and both Narainpur and Thana Bihpur stations are a good distance away,' he said.

Hungry, Arif began to have a mild headache, which soon turned into a full-fledged one.

'Are you okay, Arif?' asked Sumitra.

'Massive headache!' he said, pressing both his temples with his fingers.

Sumitra pulled out her travel bag from under the seat, unzipped the side pocket and took out a bottle of Zandu balm.

'You lie on the berth, I'll rub some balm.'

Arif stretched out on the berth; Sumitra sat near him and rubbed the minty balm on his forehead. Since Zakir's disappearance and then Dadi's death, he had tucked away his desire somewhere inside him. Now as Sumitra touched him, it began to rear its head.

Minutes later, Sumitra and Arif sat cuddling and caressing each other. Sumitra said, 'You know, Arif, I always thought that our relationship would last forever but when you snapped all ties, I was heartbroken. I had become addicted to your company but then, somehow, I learned to live without you. Now you have come back, and I'm afraid of losing you again.'

'Don't worry, Sumitra, I can't do without you either. I've made up my mind to remain unmarried,' Arif replied in an impassioned voice. 'I'll be emotionally committed to you for life.'

Arif touched the end of the pallu of her sari as Sumitra continued, 'Arif! I have a plan for us. Why don't you open a book and stationery shop near Chitrakar Nagar Market? There are many schools there and you can run a profitable business. If you don't mind, I can help you with fifty thousand rupees. This way we'll be able to meet every day. This is an option, of course, only if you don't get through the Bihar civil services exam.'

'Sumitra, I can't think of any woman in my life but you,' Arif said, as he brought her hand to his nose and inhaled the fragrance of her palm.

The train whistled and started moving. They heard footsteps and swiftly separated from each other.

Around 1 a.m. at the Begusarai station, before bidding him goodbye with a soft kiss, Sumitra held Arif's hand and said, 'Ramesh will be getting a transfer order for Patna in the next two or three months. We can meet regularly then. In the meantime, do call me, please!'

From the glass window, he saw Sumitra getting down on to the platform and waving to her husband, who was standing a few yards away.

Hearing his wife's voice, Ramesh Kumar rushed over and grabbed the travel bag from her hands. Arif kept looking at her till she disappeared beyond the exit gate. He felt empty.

As the train began to move again, Arif sat propped against the glass window, his eyes closed, wondering if his decision to meet her had been a mistake. Reviving his discreet affair with her could get both of them into big trouble. What if Ramesh came to know?

He was not sure if he would be able to keep the promise he had made to her in a fit of passion. Should I have made a commitment to Sumitra for life?

Arif reached Patna the next morning.

At his Samanpura flat, nobody was at home except his sister Huma. She was weeping.

'Huma, what has happened?' Arif panicked, fearing some bad news.

'Bhaiyya! Abba has taken very ill suddenly.' Huma sobbed. 'Amma and Jameel chacha took him to the hospital.'

'Which hospital? How did they take Abba to the hospital?'

'Jameel chacha got an autorickshaw. They've gone to Getwell Clinic.'

Throwing his travel bag on the floor, he ran to the clinic in Raja Bazaar.

He saw Abba sitting on a bench at the clinic reception. Amma was by his side, looking anxious. Jameel Khan, their neighbour and Abba's former colleague, was holding a glass of water in his hand. He took out a pill from a packet and dropped it into the glass. Arif bent to lift the wrapper from the floor. It was Pepfiz, a popular antacid.

Abba beckoned to him and said, 'Beta, nothing to worry about, simple gas problem. Allah will set it right.'

But it wasn't a simple gas problem. Three days later, once again, in the middle of the night, Abba had pain in his chest, and the palpitations made his breathing uneven. He vomited twice. Arif couldn't figure out how to take his father to the hospital. In Patna, an ambulance took ages to come. He tried Firoz Taxi Service's number but the phone was switched off. None of his relatives or acquaintances had cars. His landlord, Shabbir Ali, only had an old Bajaj scooter. Jameel Khan still believed in the healthy habit of cycling and hadn't even bothered to buy a two-wheeler.

'Bishambhar bhaiyya!' he muttered to himself as an idea came to his mind. Bishambhar was Mritunjay's cousin. He was a lecturer of public administration at B.N. College. Years ago, Mritunjay had taken Arif to his house twice to seek guidance for the civil services examination. In the very first meeting, Arif had noted that he was a generous person. Later, he had also gone on his own to meet Bishambhar five or six times. Each time he had welcomed Arif and treated him with great affection. During his last visit, he had given him his mobile number. 'Whenever you need to visit me, just give me a call in advance,' he had said. That was two years back. Just around that time, he had purchased a car, a white Maruti 800.

Abba was vomiting again. Frantically, Arif looked for the book on public administration by Awasthi and Awasthi, on the back cover of which he remembered he had written down Bishambhar's mobile number. He found the book and the number, too. Grabbing the mobile from under the pillow on his bed, he dialled the number.

'Hello,' a woman's voice, drowsy and muffled, answered.

Arif said, 'Bishambhar bhaiyya!' The next moment he was on the line. Arif told him that he needed help to take his father to the hospital.

'Where do you live?'

'The house of Shabbir Ali, near the Old Mosque, Samanpura. It's just opposite a small provision store called 786 Kirana Shop.' Arif was about to explain the route to his house in detail but the phone was disconnected. He dialled again, but nobody picked it up. After three or four more attempts, he felt that he might not be interested in helping him. He was bewildered thinking of how to take his father to the hospital. Then he picked up his diary and searched for an ambulance number.

Fifteen minutes later, he heard a car pulling up outside his house. He rushed out to see Bishambhar emerging from it. He was still in his pyjamas.

~

Bailey Road was almost desolate; it took ten minutes to reach the Income Tax Chauraha. As they turned towards Museum Road and reached close to the Baptist Church of Chhajju Bagh, they saw the silhouettes of two men in the middle of the road. They were waving to stop.

'They look like robbers,' Bishambhar said in English.

'What should we do?' Arif said, panicking, and turned to look at Abba. He sat silently, his eyes closed. Amma was holding him. She was reciting some verses from the Holy Quran and blowing at him.

'Just sit quietly,' Bishambhar said, as he slowed down his car. Then he turned to Amma and said in Hindi, 'Chachiji, hold Chachaji properly. The roads are bumpy ahead.'

As they approached the men, in the light of a head lamp, they could see that there were five men, each of them had covered their faces with gamchhas. They were carrying hockey sticks in their hands.

The car was just ten yards from those suspicious-looking men when Bishambhar said, 'They are definitely robbers or carjackers.'

Suddenly, Bishambhar changed the gear and pressed the accelerator, and the car flew. It possibly hit two of the men who were in the middle of the road expecting the car to stop. Arif heard screams followed by Bihari swear words.

'Are they following us?' Bishambhar asked as they reached Gandhi Maidan.

'No!' Arif said.

Amma became alarmed when she heard the screams. 'What was that?'

'A street dog,' Bishambhar said.

'How much time will it take to reach the hospital?' Amma asked, worried, as Abba had begun to cough.

'Ten minutes, Chachiji,' Bishambhar said.

~

In the emergency ward of the Patna Medical College and Hospital, no doctor was available. The short stout nurse on duty informed them that the doctor would arrive in two minutes. When no doctor turned up for the next fifteen minutes, Bishambhar lost his temper. He yelled at the nurse.

The nurse replied curtly, 'My duty is to inform the doctor, which I have already done. Now it's up to the doctor whether he comes or not.'

Bishambhar dialled a number on his mobile. 'Am I talking to Minister Dwivediji . . .'

Bishambhar walked out of the emergency ward with the mobile stuck to his ear. Arif looked at his father who was lying on a bed still coughing and belching. 'Ya Allah,' he heard Amma praying.

Ten minutes later, an old man entered the ward and the nurse stood up immediately. She was taken aback to see him at this time.

'Where are the junior doctors?' the old man asked the nurse in an angry voice.

'Sir, the junior doctors are on strike,' she said in a trembling voice.

'But some doctor must be on duty in this emergency ward,' he said.

'Dr Sinha is on duty,' she said.

'Where is he? Call him and tell him that I am here.'

The nurse started dialling a number with her fumbling hands.

'Who is Mr Mishra?' he turned again to ask the nurse. Before she could reply, Bishambhar came forward.

'I am Bishambhar Mishra.'

'Mishraji, sorry for the inconvenience. Just received a call from the health minister. I was really shocked to know that no doctor was available in the emergency ward. By the way, I'm Doctor Thakur. Where is your patient?'

Bishambhar stayed till the morning when the doctor discharged Abba. They said it was a case of food poisoning, which might have happened due to contaminated water. They also diagnosed that he had a problem of severe gastritis which required long-term treatment. Bishambhar suggested that they consult the best doctor for gastritis in Patna, Dr A.K. Dutta.

~

The next day Arif booked an appointment with Dr Dutta.

The doctor was a short-tempered man in his late seventies. When Abba told him that at times he sweated excessively, had rapid heartbeat, felt faint or short of breath, had severe chest and stomach pain, and had foul-smelling bowel movements, Dr Dutta knew what the problem was.

He said angrily, 'Mr Khan, you have stretched your body too much during your service in the police department. Now it is time to rest. Rest means complete rest. I'm also going to put you on a strict diet, which you have to follow.

Otherwise, get ready to have your intestines chopped.' Then he turned to Amma and said, 'Make sure that your husband takes complete rest for the next three or four months. Don't give him anything to eat that I have explicitly forbidden.'

'Theek hain, Doctor sahab!' said Amma, pulling one corner of the pallu of her sari to cover a part of her face.

~

Abba had grown weak because of the continued illness and remained indoors all the time. The good thing about Abba staying at home was that Arif got a chance to spend time with his father.

In the morning, Arif left for the coaching classes quite early and returned late in the afternoon. He had started taking extra classes to make some additional money. It would be needed for Abba's treatment.

In the evening, Arif sat with Abba playing carrom, chess or cards. Arif would discuss almost anything a son could with his father. Sometimes, Abba would tell stories from his childhood, his years of dire poverty and his struggle to complete his education up to class eleven. The way he related stories reminded Arif of Dadi. Most interesting among Abba's stories were tales from their family history.

'In the 1930s my father had a flourishing timber business that brought him a large fortune. He had big houses in Jamalpura, in Motihari and in Patna. In Jamalpura, the haveli of Janab Ali Khan was famous. Two elephants were stationed at the door. A two-horse driven buggy was used to ferry the ladies of the family. There were dozens of servants and maidservants. He had married your Dadi after the death of his first wife, your Badke baba's mother. My father was the eldest among his brothers. In 1945, one of my uncles died suddenly. Before my father could recover, tragedy struck again.

'At that time the river used to be a fast and inexpensive mode of transportation. Wooden logs were tied together with ropes to form a platform. A person would sit on the platform to row the logs along with the stream of the Ganges to their destination. But it was very dangerous for those who sat on the logs. The river could get angry at any time and anything could happen. One of my uncles was a great adventurer and, despite his elder brother's orders, he secretly undertook a voyage with one of his retainers on the wooden logs. He drowned with the retainer and his body was never found. Three months later, my only surviving uncle was trampled to death by a mad elephant at Jamalpura.

'Unable to bear the loss of his three brothers in a very short time span, my father took ill and remained bedridden for almost three years. It was during this period that the country was divided into India and Pakistan. Many of our relatives warned my father of the danger of being slaughtered by Hindus and that it was better to migrate to Pakistan. My father refused, saying he would prefer to be buried alongside his forefathers.

'But destiny had something else in store for him. He died far away in Samastipur while being treated by a hakim for some mysterious disease. He was buried there.

'After him, the family had no surviving male adult.

'Though your Dadi tried to take control of things, she

was a purdanasheen lady who had no experience of worldly affairs. She sold off some of her land. In the absence of caretakers, distant relatives usurped the lands in the other villages. I tried to complete my studies despite all these constraints. I never forgot my father's words when I had been a child, that I should join the Indian civil services and become a district collector. For many years I carried the dream with me, encouraged by my mother. But, despite my first class matriculation, I couldn't continue my studies due to our limited means, and had to join the police department. Your Dadi was an iron-willed lady; she single-handedly brought up my brother and me.'

Whenever Abba talked about his mother, his eyes became moist with nostalgia.

Abba also told Arif how he got married to Amma.

'I was eighteen years old and had just returned from college, when your Dadi told me she had received a marriage proposal from a famous hakim in Inayat Nagar for his daughter. At that time, your mamu, Hakim sahab, was studying in Tibbiya College of Aligarh Muslim University to become a hakim like his father. The marriage was a grand affair, but your Amma, Hamida, was disappointed when she saw the old dilapidated ancestral house. She had grown up in the opulent house of a hugely successful hakim. But that was the first and the last day that she felt like that. She adjusted herself to the household. Our first child, a boy, was stillborn. Our second child, also a boy, died after six months of his birth. When the third child, a girl, died at the tender age of two months, Hamida went mad. Every now and then she'd run away from her room to the graveyard where our daughter was buried. How difficult it was to bring Hamida back to her normal self. In fact, it was your birth that set many things right. Hamida busied herself with you and gradually her smile returned. I was relieved. I was also promoted to the post of assistant sub-inspector the same year.' Abba turned to have a better view of his wife's face in the kitchen. Arif could see in his father's face a glowing love for Amma.

'Life has never been kind to me. I lost my father when I was just a kid. But I had a dream, my son. I wanted to see you as an IAS officer, but now it will remain a dream. It is my fault. I did not send you to a good school, nor did I provide you with the money required for joining coaching classes. My salary was just about enough to feed my family.'

'No, Abba, don't blame yourself. It was my mistake,' Arif replied. 'I should have worked harder.'

'What a good son you are. No complaints against your father. Quite different from sons of my friends who are always ready to find fault with their fathers,' he said in an emotionally charged voice.

During such discussions, Zakir's name would always come up and Abba's face would wrinkle in unbearable pain, tears welling up in his eyes. Arif would wipe his father's tears and in the process his eyes too would become moist.

One day Huma, who had completed her BA with distinction three years ago, told Abba she wished to do her MA. In Arif's presence, Abba had earlier stated his inability to support his daughter for further studies.

Arif knew he couldn't do anything for Huma. Whatever he saved from his salary was being kept aside for Huma's marriage. She was already twenty-six and their gossipy relatives had started asking Amma when she would arrange her youngest daughter's wedding.

Amid this the news of Abba's sickness reached their relatives. Many people came to see him. Amma cooked rice, dal and sabzi in big pots for the guests.

'Thanks to Allah, Hamida finally has a gas stove,' Arif heard Abba saying.

Hakim sahab came with his daughter, Farzana, and his wife.

'Farzana will be staying here to help Hamida baji with the household chores until Rashid sahab has recovered fully,' Hakim sahab said.

~

On a Sunday evening, Arif was sitting in his room, reading the newspaper, when he overheard Amma talking.

Amma and Abba were on the veranda.

'Arif ke Abba!' Amma began as she always did while addressing Abba. She followed the old tradition of not calling one's husband by name.

'Hakim sahab and his wife had telephoned again. They said that you should talk to Arif about the marriage. They can't wait any more.' They stopped talking as Farzana came to the veranda with a glass of water and medicines for Abba prescribed by Dr Dutta.

Arif noticed that during this visit Farzana not only helped Amma in the kitchen but also assisted her in cleaning the rooms and washing the clothes. The house hadn't been so spotless since Rabiya and Nazneen had been married. Amma was too old and weak to manage all the household chores alone. Huma took shelter in books to avoid household work. They could not afford a maidservant for five hundred rupees a month. Arif remembered the night he and Farzana had escaped from Jamalpura after the communal riots. He experienced a thrill when the image of a frightened Farzana clinging to his chest appeared in his mind's eye. He had begun to like Farzana. Lately, Farzana had also motivated Huma to join her in the housework.

What he liked most about Farzana was that she took such good care of Abba. The food she cooked was always less spicy, exactly as advised by Dr Dutta. She remembered promptly when and which medicines were to be given to Abba. In the morning, when Arif left for his coaching institute, Farzana was ready with his breakfast. And each day she prepared something different. Arif had started thinking seriously about Farzana. She would make a good wife. He didn't look at her any more as his semi-literate cousin but as a grown woman with big kohl-lined eyes, thick silky coal-black hair and generous breasts.

A week before Abba was to go to the doctor for his final check-up, he called Arif. Making Arif sit by him on his wooden bed, he cleared his throat and said, 'Beta, I know you love and respect your Abba very much. If I ask you for something, you won't disappoint me, will you?'

'Please tell me whatever you want me to do,' Arif said.

'Years ago, I had given my word to Hakim sahab that Farzana would be my daughter-in-law. My son, is it possible for you to honour my word and accept Farzana as your wife?' While speaking, his voice trembled. 'You only have to say yes if you feel Farzana will be a suitable life partner for you.'

'Give me the order, Abba,' Arif replied.

'Are you really ready to marry Farzana?' Abba asked.

'Yes, Abba, your happiness is supreme for me,' he said.

'Are you sure?' Abba asked again.

'Yes, Abba. But–' Arif paused. 'There is one concern though.'

'What is that?'

'I'm still not earning enough to support a family.'

'Don't worry about that. Even I wasn't employed when I married your Amma. Allah takes care of every living being on this earth.'

Arif's yes cheered Abba up. He got out of bed and called Amma to share the news. In the evening, Abba called Hakim sahab.

The very next day, Hakim sahab arrived in Patna.

When Arif greeted Hakim sahab with Assalam alaikum, Hakim sahab pressed a five-hundred-rupee note in his right palm, which Arif hesitantly accepted.

'So Arif got his first salaami,' Amma remarked with a smile. She was referring to the money Arif got from Hakim sahab, now his father-in-law-to-be.

'Where is my share in your salaami?' It was Huma, her hand outstretched.

Abba hugged Hakim sahab. 'Heartiest congratulations, samdhiji,' Abba said a bit loudly and laughed.

The bright smile on Abba's face gladdened Arif.

~

The following evening, as Arif entered his house, a familiar fragrance of Cuticura talcum powder told him Sumitra was visiting.

Inside the room, she was sitting on a chair talking to Amma, a cup of tea in her hand. Pretending he had not noticed her, he lifted the *Times of India* and settled on a folding chair in the veranda. Distracted by thoughts of Sumitra, he found it difficult to concentrate on the newspaper. He realized he still felt exhilarated by her presence. A few minutes later, Amma came out to see her off. Sumitra stopped where Arif was sitting. Arif greeted Sumitra formally and she smiled back.

Turning to Amma, who was just behind her, Sumitra said, 'Didi, see if I have left my mobile inside the room.'

'Take this,' she threw a letter at Arif as soon as Amma went inside the house. Arif grabbed it and pushed it into his pocket before Amma returned with Sumitra's mobile phone.

He opened the letter later.

Dear Arif,

I was really upset when you did not call. But day before yesterday I happened to meet your mother and Huma in Raja Bazaar and they told me about your father's illness. Then I understood why you didn't call me. I am happy to see your father is much better now.

As you know, I'm back in Patna and living in our newly built house in K block at Chitrakar Nagar.

I still relish the memories of the time we spent together. I enjoyed the time we spent on the train. One more thing to confess, this time I wasn't guilt-stricken for allowing you to touch my body or kiss my hands. I want that again. I want to take our relationship to another level. I want to get rid of all pretensions of purity and sacred love.

On the 24th, I will be alone at home. Ramesh will be leaving for a training course in Hyderabad.

I promise that night shall be something for us to remember forever. I'll give you everything a man expects from his wife and you'll give me everything a wife expects from her husband. That night, we will break all barriers between us. There will be no fear of sin or vice. And that night will decide the course of our lives. I will be waiting for you.

Yours forever,

Sumitra

Arif was stunned. He hadn't expected Sumitra to write something like this. He remembered how upset she had been years ago when they had gotten carried away once.

Arif was greatly tempted by Sumitra's offer. Joy permeated his body when he conjured up the possible rendezvous with her, before better sense prevailed. How long could he hide his clandestine affair from the world?

Get out of this relationship and marry Farzana. Otherwise your life will be spoiled and Sumitra's marriage too would be destroyed, Arif told himself. He couldn't imagine spending the rest of his life in a sinful relationship.

'On the Day of Judgement every individual will be presented with his deeds, good and bad. Accordingly, the individual will be allowed to enter paradise or hell,' he remembered Dadi's words.

'I don't want to die a sinner.' His lower middle-class Muslim upbringing affected him time and again, advising him not to be misled by the devil. Not to surrender to Nafs-e-Ammarah.

Arif heard the call for the evening prayer from the old mosque in Samanpura and then from the mosque built inside the campus of the Hai Medicare Research Institute. He decided to pray at the mosque inside the Hai Institute.

It was a night of indecision. He tore Sumitra's letter into pieces and threw it into the sewer. The stream of dirty water took it away. But each and every word of the letter floated in his mind.

The next morning, Arif woke up early and went to the old mosque to offer prayers. While walking back home, he decided the future course of his life. Sumitra had to go from his life forever. Farzana was now his destiny. As advised by Abba, he would wait for the BPSC examination result. If it didn't materialize, he would start his own coaching institute in Inayat Nagar.

The separation from Sumitra would be painful, but he was ready to bear that pain.

TWENTY-ONE

Arif couldn't clear the BPSC prelims. He didn't know what had gone wrong.

Sitting in the veranda, he went through the result published in the newspaper again and again, but his roll number was not there. He placed the paper on a stool nearby, stretched his legs and closed his eyes. The optimism which he had experienced for the last six months dissipated like a dewdrop in the hot summer sun. Again, he began to feel lonely and depressed; he felt a void in his heart.

'Bhaiyya!' It was Huma.

Arif opened his eyes, smiled, a smile tinged with sadness, and saw a cup of tea in his sister's hand. He accepted it, drank a little and placed it on a plastic stool in front of him. Arif picked up the paper again and started going through it desultorily. On the last page, the result of another examination was published.

Bihar State Subordinate Service Selection Board
Final Result for Junior Urdu Translators
(Result published as per the directive of the Honourable Supreme Court)

Below the heading were the names and roll numbers of the successful candidates. With his heart beating fast, he placed his index finger on the page and started moving across the columns to go through the names. Aayesha Perween, Abdul Hamid, Abdul Haque Ansari, Adil Siddiqui, Arif Khan . . . Arif's name was there at serial no. 5. His lips curled in a smile. He tried to speak, but his voice choked, then he began coughing. Huma, who was removing clothes from the clothes line, turned and looked at her brother in surprise, and then ran to fetch a glass of water.

Five years ago on the eve of the election, a special recruitment drive had been announced for Urdu translators to consolidate the M factor of the chief minister's social engineering agenda, the 'MY' or Muslim–Yadav equation.

After Partition, Urdu had virtually become a language of north Indian Muslims, so every unemployed Muslim youth in Bihar with a bachelor's degree had lined up at the board office to submit his application.

Fresh from the failure of the IAS exam, Arif had been forced by Abba to sit for the examination. But the result had not been declared as some candidates had filed a writ petition in the Patna High Court alleging corruption in the recruitment. Finally, after so many years, the case had been decided by the Supreme Court of India and the result had been published.

There was a time Arif wouldn't have accepted anything less than an IAS position, but the situation had changed. Even this humble offer seemed like a godsend. How dreams change with the passage of time and with change in circumstances!

Arif remembered a poem he had written years ago.

A Workable Dream

I set out on a boat of memories
Into the ocean of imagination
In search of my dreams
That had drowned years ago

The dark clouds of doubts
The terrifying storm of hopelessness
And the high tides of fear
Discourage me to go ahead

The oar of my courage
Is about to slip away from my hands
When I see
The lighthouse of hope

It is the shore of an island
An island of wishes and desires
There is a forest on it
Thick with the trees of imagination

And on this strange island
I may not get my lost dreams back
But I can find a dream surely
A tiny but workable dream

Arif had found a tiny but workable dream. He shared the happy news with his family.

Abba hugged him. Amma offered nafil namaz to thank Allah. Strangely enough, Huma laughed aloud (after so many years) while congratulating her brother. The news travelled to Inayat Nagar and Hakim sahab and his wife telephoned him, offering their best of blessings. Farzana cooked the most delicious chicken biryani. She also congratulated him, but Arif observed that her voice lacked enthusiasm.

'Farzana's hands have magic,' Amma said as Farzana ladled out another helping of biryani on her plate. 'She is Arif's lucky charm. Within a fortnight of the engagement, Arif has got a government job.'

Abba smiled and then added, 'Allah is very merciful.'

Arif wished to share his happiness with Sumitra. But he forced himself to think of Farzana instead.

The first thing he decided to do the next morning was to write a letter to Sumitra and hand-deliver it to her.

Dear Sumitra,

You'll be surprised to get this letter. Believe me, I am equally surprised writing it. This relationship has brought much misery to me. And if it continues it will also destroy your family. Think of what would happen if your children come to know about us; how would they react? And God forbid, your husband would die of shock. I know he loves you very much.

I've decided not to meet you on the 24th. I know you'll not relish the news that I'm going to marry my cousin Farzana. The date hasn't been finalized yet. I'm doing this to make my parents happy.

You'll be happy to know that I have got a job as an Urdu translator in the Bihar government. I will leave for Bhagalpur in a few days. After that, we may not see each other ever again. Our separation is good for both of us. My entire family is moving to Jamalpura.

I've purchased some small gifts for you. I hope you'll like them. There's a small payal, the runjhun of which I will not be there to hear. And a nose pin. You will look stunning with the nose pin.

If I have hurt you by writing this letter, I apologize. I owe a lot to you. I don't think I will ever be able to pay you back.

I will miss you.

Yours forever,

Arif

~

Arif visited the Bihar Military Police Colony with a whole bunch of his certificates to get photocopies of all them and have them attested by a gazetted officer. They had to be attached with the joining letter when he reported for duty at Bhagalpur. When Arif returned, he found Farzana alone at home. She informed him that Abba had gone to the doctor with Huma and Amma. It was the final check-up before Arif's family left for Jamalpura in a few days.

The previous week Abba had decided that there was no use living in this rathole in Patna when they had an airy two-story ancestral house in Jamalpura. By moving to Jamalpura, he would also save two thousand per month in rent. Huma's marriage had also been fixed. Abba planned to sell part of his agricultural land for the dowry. Abba would start looking for a suitable match as soon as he moved to Jamalpura. Arif, too, would be able to save something during the year.

It would soon be the last day for his family in Patna, the city where he had spent the last eighteen years, Arif reflected, standing on the veranda. It was painful to think of being separated from the city; it was painful to think of being separated from Sumitra.

He thought of Dadi and Zakir, too. And that saddened him. Brushing aside all the bad memories of the past, he tried thinking of his impending marriage to Farzana.

Farzana was sitting inside the room with an old issue of *Grih Shobha*. Her dupatta had slipped and he caught glimpses of her cleavage. For the first time in his life, he experienced desire for Farzana. When Farzana lifted her gaze from the pages, he flushed and turned his eyes away.

Remembering that he had to buy a pair of trousers and a shirt from the market, he rose to leave.

'I'm going to Raja Bazaar. Tell me, do you need anything for the kitchen?' Arif asked.

'No bhaijaan,' she replied without looking at him.

Foolish girl, she still calls me bhaijaan, Arif thought.

He walked down the backstreet on to Madrasa Road, and had almost reached Magadh Vikramshila Apartments when he realized that his wallet was missing. I must have left it at home, he said to himself and turned back. The door was ajar and nobody was on the veranda or in the adjacent room. Entering the room, he spotted his wallet on the bed.

He heard somebody sobbing in the other room, which was followed by a whispering voice. It was Farzana talking to someone on the mobile phone.

'You don't understand, everyone is so happy. I can't say that I don't want to marry Arif bhaijaan. How can I say that?'

Then there was a pause as the person on the other side spoke.

'He says that he respects Arif bhaijaan a lot. He can't come in the way of his happiness.' Farzana started sobbing again. 'I have no option but to marry Arif bhaijaan and spend the rest of my life in misery.'

Arif felt as if some bolt out of the blue had hit him. He stepped back on to the veranda and sat on the edge of the charpai, holding his head in his hands.

'Why is this happening to me?' he murmured, looking up at the sky. 'Whenever I try to make peace with my life, it creates new hurdles, throwing me into the throes of misery.' Arif had always believed Farzana secretly loved him and by marrying her he was doing her a favour.

But who was the 'he' Farzana was referring to? The identity of Farzana's lover intrigued him.

It was getting darker; mosquitoes were buzzing in the air as Arif went out on to the road. He kept walking for hours without knowing where he was headed. Soon he found himself standing before the peepal tree. The same holy fig tree that had been witness to his dreams, seen him falling in love with Sumitra, and also seen him failing in life. Two and half millennia ago, under a holy fig tree, Siddhartha

Gautama had received enlightenment. Under the shadow of this sacred tree, could Arif find the answer to the jigsaw puzzle of his life? His lips curled in an empty smile.

At home, Abba had returned from the doctor. Arif was relieved to know that the doctor had said he was perfectly fine now.

~

There was no direct train from Patna to Inayat Nagar and the bus journey would have been very tiring. So the following morning an autorickshaw was hired to take Arif's family to the neighbouring town of Hajipur. From there they were to catch the train to Inayat Nagar. The luggage and other household goods had already been sent by a minitruck. Abba sat on the front seat next to the driver. In the back were Amma, Huma and Farzana. Arif looked at Farzana and knew from her swollen eyes that she had been crying.

Abba seemed to be satisfied.

As Arif came closer to the autorickshaw, Abba took out his mobile phone and put it in his hand.

'Abba, I think there should be a phone at home. I don't need a mobile phone; you can call me at my office,' Arif said.

'But there is no network coverage in Jamalpura. It will be of no use there,' Abba replied, smiling. He added, 'It's the first time you're going to be away from home. Take good care of yourself. Haan! Call me when you reach Bhagalpur. Call on Hakim sahab's number. We'll be in Inayat Nagar for the next four or five days.'

'Okay, Abba.'

'Baua, I have packed some homemade sweets and namkeens for you,' Amma said.

The genial-faced, bearded landlord of the house, Shabbir Ali, a retired engineer from the irrigation department and Abba's ex-colleague, Jameel Khan, were also present to see them off.

'Rashid bhai, I'd like to ask your forgiveness for any discomfort or inconvenience during your stay in my humble house,' said Shabbir Ali while shaking Abba's hand.

'Engineer sahab, you are such a nice person. We will always remember the wonderful time we spent in your house.'

'Shukriya! Thank you very much!' Shabbir Ali said.

'Haan, Arif will leave for Bhagalpur to join office tomorrow evening. So you'll get the keys of the house then.'

'That's okay, Rashid bhai,' Shabbir Ali replied.

Abba looked at his wristwatch and said, 'The train for Inayat Nagar leaves at eleven from Hajipur. We have to start now. You know at Gandhi Setu Bridge you can get stuck in traffic.' Once again Abba shook hands with Shabir Ali and Jameel Khan.

'Fi Amanullah,' Shabbir Ali said.

'Khuda hafiz,' said Jameel Khan.

Abba said, 'Khuda hafiz.'

The autorickshaw lurched forward and disappeared down the street, but Arif stood there for a while looking intently at the road, as if he was searching for something he had lost. Was he trying to find his lost happiness? A wave of melancholy hit him.

Back in the solitude of his room, he began to pack things in a travelling bag. As he lifted his old diary, a black-and-white photograph slipped out of it. It was of Arif and Zakir when they were children, Arif ten and Zakir nine. The photograph was taken on the tenth day of Muharram by Nazo uncle. Though the photograph was black-and-white, he vividly remembered he was wearing a red kurta pyjama and Zakir a green one.

Holding his brother's hand, Arif had gone towards Karbala, which was an open field on the outskirts of his village where the tazias from all four villages gathered to commemorate the martyrdom of Hazrat Hussain. He had lied to Amma that he was going with Badke baba, for he had known they would not be allowed to go to Karbala on their own. Karbala had been crowded, so Arif had held his brother's hand and stood at some distance. He could see people with pickaxes, spears and swords; he could hear the marsiya being sung and the cry of Allahu Akbar or Ya Hussain Ya Hussain.

A riot had broken out between Jamalpura and the neighbouring Shamshad Nagar. Both the sides had started pelting stones and bricks at each other. People had run helter-skelter. Arif too had run towards a mango orchard near Karbala. But then he had realized that Zakir was not with him. Frantically, he had called out his name loudly but he didn't get any reply from his brother. He looked around but he was nowhere to be seen.

An hour later, the police had intervened and the rioting crowds were chased away. Arif had stood at the corner of Karbala, weeping, as his eyes still searched frantically for

Zakir. A policeman standing there had scolded him and had asked him to go home. He had turned around crying, reciting verses from the Holy Quran. He had also promised that he would offer special namaz if he got his brother back. Not even a minute had passed, when he saw Zakir emerging from behind a bamboo grove inside the orchard. He had held his brother in his arms and started to wail. He had prayed loudly, thanking Allah, the most merciful.

Arif recalled the precise moment he had hugged his brother and had cried without saying anything to him.

Confused, Zakir had asked him, 'What happened, bhaiyya?'

Arif heard Zakir's words from that day. He prayed and hoped that this time too his brother would emerge from somewhere. That he could hold him again in his arms and weep to his heart's content.

~

The next evening when Arif was to leave for Bhagalpur, a storm hit Patna. Dust from the unpaved footpaths of the city rose and hung in the air. Then a brief spell of rain washed the sky clean. When Arif came out of the room to start for the railway junction, the weather was pleasant and a cool wind blew incessantly. But that didn't cheer him up. His face still had gloom written all over it.

Arif again thought of his brother, Zakir. A round but strong face marked with a chiselled jawline, and a curly mane kissing broad shoulders came to his mind. Arif exhaled deeply as his chin trembled and tears streamed down his cheeks. He wiped the tears with a white handkerchief before going to his landlord to return his flat keys.

The landlord was at the mosque for the night prayer. Arif handed the keys to his younger son, who was gossiping with a couple of boys on the road. Pocketing the keys, he continued to talk to his friends, ignoring Arif.

On the way to Raja Bazaar to catch an autorickshaw to Patna junction, Arif stopped near Magadh Vikramshila Apartments where a shamiana had been erected. Two halogen lights shone at the far corners of the canopy. Men and women occupied more than a hundred plastic chairs. At the end of the canopy was a makeshift stage, which was covered with a green carpet. Dr Abdul Hai, a well-known surgeon of Patna, was on the stage with a microphone in his hand.

'We have gathered here to honour Shahla Khan who has made our community proud . . .'

Arif knew that the ceremony had been organized by the Muslims of Samanpura and Raja Bazaar to honour Shahla Khan. She lived in the same neighbourhood and had topped the civil services examination that year. A Muslim girl and an IAS topper. He saw Shahla sitting on a chair on the stage in her turquoise salwar suit, her face shining with a sense of fulfilment. Arif thought of his own IAS aspirations and felt a pain piercing through his heart. What if I were in her place, he thought. It was unbearable for him to stay there for too long. Each and every word that came through the loudspeakers seemed to be mocking his failures.

TWENTY-TWO

As Arif looked at himself in a washroom mirror at Patna junction, a stranger stared back at him. His puffy eyes and receding hairline made him look older and he thought he looked ridiculous in his old blue baggy jeans and a full-sleeved blue shirt. Expressionless, he continued to stare at himself.

Returning to platform no. 1, he placed his bag on the floor and settled down with a sigh on a slightly dusty steel bench. Leaning against the back of the bench, he shut his eyes tightly and went back in time, to when he was a thirteen-year-old boy sitting on the edge of the arched veranda of his ancestral house in Jamalpura. Dadi was sitting on a low wooden stool, ready to tell a fantastic story, with Zakir standing next to her looking expectant.

A loud clap of thunder startled Arif.

The electricity supply at the station immediately went off. He groped in the dark for his travel bag. In this city, one never knew when pickpockets and thieves would decamp with one's belongings.

The incidents of the last two days disoriented him.

Farzana's phone call had confused him. Sumitra's invitation continued to seduce him. Abba's hopes forced him to silently accept whatever came his way.

Arif felt his brain become as light as a feather.

A firefly perched on his bag distracted him. It flew and landed on his shoulder as if consoling him for whatever mockery life was making of him. He felt better for a moment. The power was restored, the firefly lost its glow, and he slumped down again.

He lay down on the bench, stretched his legs and placed his bag near his head. The cool breeze lulled him into slumber.

Sumitra was naked, except for the mangalsutra around her neck, kajal in her eyes, blood red lipstick and a black thread around her waist. She was walking across freshly irrigated paddy fields, the tiny saplings submerged in water. Deep footprints formed on the slushy fields.

A hairy bare-chested masked man, covered in just a red loincloth, appeared from nowhere. He grabbed Sumitra's hand, pulling her towards him. She stretched out her other arm and called to Arif. Arif ran after them and tried to stop the masked man, but he was strong. He pushed Arif hard and as Arif hit the ground, he felt an excruciating pain in his head.

Arif woke up and found himself on the cemented floor of the platform, his head spinning. Holding his head, he got up and sat on the edge of the bench wondering what kind of dream it was.

A celestial dream, khwab-e-rahmani?

A satanic dream, khwab-e-shaitani?

Or was it a psychological dream, khwab-e-zehani?

Whatever it was, the after-effect of the dream was that he began to crave for Sumitra, wanting to hold her in a tight embrace, to tear off her clothes, throw her on the bed and make love to her till they were totally exhausted.

Should I go back to Sumitra? As he debated with himself, a couplet from Ghalib about a man who had to choose between vice and virtue popped up in his mind.

Iman mujhe roke hain to kheenche hain mujhe kufr
Kaba mere peechhe hain, kalisha mere aage

(Faith restrains me, temptations attract me
The holy Kaba is behind me while the idols are in front of me)

Should I tell Abba that I don't want to get married? Or should I tell Abba I don't want to marry Farzana because she doesn't want to marry me? Or should I marry Farzana pretending to know nothing?

All three choices were difficult, but he had to choose one. He didn't have the luxury of a 'none of the above' like he did in the civil services exam.

Undecided, Arif cracked his knuckles. Then suddenly, he picked up his bag and quickly walked out of the junction. The air outside was cool. The city was dark, except for a few dappled spots near street lamps.

He looked at his mobile. It was quarter to twelve. He was tempted to dial Sumitra's number, but he didn't. Walking past the Hanuman temple and the showpiece rail engine, he crossed the road to reach the auto stand. He found three autos parked under a big cut-out of a smiling Nitish Kumar, Bihar's newly elected chief minister. He got into the first auto.

'Ninety rupees,' the auto driver said. Arif agreed, despite knowing that the driver was overcharging him. He was in no mood to bargain and waste time.

Suddenly, Farzana came to his mind and anger burnt him from the inside.

To get rid of the uneasy feelings, he thought of Sumitra. He thought about the day he had seen her for the first time. He thought about the night he had spent with her on the train. Soon, he found himself in the vortex of love, desire and a strange longing. Closing his eyes, he imagined Sumitra dressed in all black, bedecked with the finest jewellery and reciting to him from her favourite Urdu poet, Ghalib.

Sumitra, he whispered to himself, and asked the auto driver to speed up.

The driver stopped the vehicle on one side of the road inside Chitrakar Nagar.

In the headlights of the vehicle, Arif saw the flooded lane that led to Sumitra's house. He paid the auto, took out a pen torch from his pocket and began walking gingerly on the makeshift bridge of stones placed along the side of the flooded road.

Once in front of Sumitra's house, Arif discreetly pushed open the iron grille gate. For the next few minutes, he stood there without moving. Then he turned to look at Sumitra's newly built house.

Milky white light escaped through the half-open window

of one of the rooms. He walked closer to the window and peeped into the room. Inside, on the bed was Ramesh, one of his legs in a plaster cast. His forehead was covered with a white cloth bandage which had some brown patches where some liquid antiseptic had seeped through it. Sumitra sat by him, holding his hands, sobbing.

'For me, you are everything, Ramesh,' Sumitra said.

'Don't cry, Sumitra, please,' Ramesh said in a low voice and Sumitra rested her head on his chest.

So I have lost Sumitra too. Ramesh has rightfully reclaimed her. Arif felt a sudden wave of sadness hitting him as he turned to leave.

It had begun to drizzle again. He turned around and walked out of the gate. His bag felt heavy but he didn't care. The main road was desolate, and it was unlikely that he would find a cycle rickshaw or an auto for the station. He decided to take the shortcut through Bank Colony to Naya Mor from where he could take an autorickshaw. Avoiding the potholes and slushy part of the road, he walked slowly, following the narrow stream of light emerging from his pen torch. He walked past the colony, and followed the road leading to the Phulwari Sharif–Naya Mor Road.

The peepal tree lay on the road, uprooted. Arif stood there, focusing the torch on the tree, mourning its death. He felt like he had lost one of his friends. The tree had been a witness to his love for Sumitra and when he had lost everything, it was also gone.

His mobile rang. He noticed that it had stopped drizzling. It was Abba.

'Hello Ab–'

'Zakir is alive!' his father exclaimed.

One of Arif's childhood friends, Sadaqat, claimed to have seen Zakir at Kurla junction in Bombay, boarding the Kurla Patna Express, dressed in a white kurta and jeans.

'So the anonymous letter we received years ago was genuine.'

'Yes beta! Where are you?

'Just outside Patna junction,' Arif lied.

'Hurry inside and check if the Kurla Patna Express has arrived. Call me immediately.'

'Yes Abba!' Arif said as he placed his bag on his shoulder and broke into a run.

Arif felt as if he was flying.

~

Seated on a cold bench, Arif looked at the black electronic clock hanging from the corrugated steel ceiling. Its blood-red display said 2.43. He rose and walked to the enquiry booth and knocked on the glass. The man at the counter was asleep, his head resting against a table, his mouth agape. He knocked again and the man woke up with a start. Rubbing his eyes with the back of his palm, his other hand reached for a bottle of water; he took a couple of swigs and gave Arif an angry look.

'See mister! I've already told you that we'll announce it as soon as we get information about the arrival of the Kurla Patna Express.' Arif moved away without a word, trudging back to the same bench, his steps heavy with anxiety. Two railway porters were pushing a cart full of parcels.

Restlessness seized Arif. *Ya Allah! Please give me my brother back, and I'll never ask anything from you*, he prayed silently.

Stretching himself, he lay down on the bench again, the travel bag serving as a pillow, and closed his eyes. A nightmare troubled him: he saw his brother's bullet-ridden body lying in the compartment of a train. Screaming, he jumped off the bench. 'Zakir, my brother!'

When Arif realized where he was, he sat down on the bench, holding his head.

At 3.45 a.m., the loudspeakers announced that the route to Mughalsarai had finally been cleared. Then, after a pause, the announcer added that the Patna Kurla Express had reached Danapur station and would be the first train to reach the platform. Arif stood up, trying to hold back his tears. He walked up to the edge of the platform and looked westward for the incoming train. Far away, the signal light had turned green. The sky was morose and starless. He recited the Surah Al-Ikhlas, the verses of the divinity and oneness of God, from the Holy Quran.

Inside him hope and despair played hide-and-seek. Was Zakir alive and aboard the train Arif was waiting for? Arif's spirit soared in anticipation of unexpected joy, and then he felt abysmally low fearing that the news about his brother might just be false. The headlights of the engine were now visible. Arif could hear the train whistle. His heart raced, and his recitations became desperate.

The train slowly chugged into the station and pulled to a stop. Arif saw a small motley crowd disembarking from the train. He scanned each and every face exiting the station;

none of them was Zakir. Soon the platform was as empty as it had been before the arrival of the train.

Maybe Zakir had exited the platform from the other gate and was trying to hire an autorickshaw for Samanpura. He thought of this possibility and hurried towards the autorickshaw stand.

An hour later, he returned to the platform disappointed. He couldn't get rid of the hope that his brother was somewhere around. He moved around the platform frantically, hoping to find his brother.

Had Sadaqat mistaken someone else for Zakir? Arif felt his legs lose their strength and his knees went weak. He placed his bag on the floor and sat on it. The sky was beginning to be lit with the promise of dawn.

His anxious eyes scanned the entire expanse of the platform. He decided to call Abba and was about to dial the number when he observed a bearded man splashing his face with water at the drinking water tap which was barely ten to twelve yards away. He looked like his brother.

Is that Zakir? Is that not Zakir? For a moment the hope smothered the despair, and he found himself invigorated. He got up and walked with uneven heartbeats and hurried steps, and almost stumbled over sleeping beggars before he jumped aside to avoid stepping on them.

The bearded man was in front of him, but Arif couldn't see clearly; his vision was blurred by his tears. He could, however, make out that the man was dressed in a white kurta and faded blue jeans. There was a scar on his forehead. His untidy hair had a few strands of grey. It was surely Zakir. The man had said nothing and was looking at Arif quizzically. Then he began to smile. Arif knew that smile. The man started to walk towards him.

Arif blew his running nose, wiped his tears, but couldn't contain the excitement brewing inside him. He coughed uncontrollably, holding his tummy, and sat down on his haunches. He couldn't believe his eyes. He couldn't trust his senses. Was it a dream? Was he hallucinating? He tried to get up as his legs trembled. The entire world spun around him. He rubbed his eyes as hard as he could.

The man continued smiling as he approached Arif.

Of course he was Zakir. How could Arif forget his brother's face? He slapped his cheeks gently to make himself believe it was not a dream. Then he slapped his face repeatedly. He had gone out of his mind.

Zakir rushed to Arif, throwing his tiny travel bag away. He held Arif's hands and shouted, 'Bhaiyya, I am Zakir. Your brother.'

'Zakir! Mere bhai!' Arif howled, as he wrapped his arms around Zakir.

Acknowledgements

I offer my sincere gratitude to:

Daniel Thomas, for giving me my first writing break.

Renu Agal of Juggernaut Books, for guiding me to make my novel better and for championing *Patna Blues* from day one.

Sivapriya, for accepting to publish *Patna Blues* and then working on it relentlessly to make it shine.

Chiki Sarkar, for starting Juggernaut Books.

Janani Ganesan and Cincy Jose of Juggernaut Books, for their sharp editorial eye and for making sure that my novel was perfect before it was sent to press.

Amitava Kumar, for giving me important tips at the beginning of my writing career.

Amit Chaudhuri and Romesh Gunasekara, for their valuable writing tips at University of East Anglia Writing Workshop.

Noah Lukeman, for sending his remarkable books on fiction writing all the way from New York.

Anees Salim, Albert Alla, Anirban Bose, Hirsh Sawhney,

Kanishka Gupta, Lexi Revellian, Marcy Dermansky, Mariam Karim Ahlawat, Michelle Cohen Corasanti, Rahul Soni, Samit Basu, Siddharth Chowdhury, Sriram Karri, Sumana Roy, Usha Sanyal and Zafar Anjum, for their great moral support, encouragement and editorial feedback.

Atul K. Thakur, Asma Anjum Khan, Kishore Ram, Manu Dash, Mohammad Farhan, Ruchi N.P. Singh, Siddharth Banerjee, Suneetha Balakrishnan, for reading my early drafts and their constructive criticism.

My friends Bishambhar Nath Mishra, Bisheshwar, Digvijay, Murthy, Manish, Naginderpreet, Reyaz, Satish, Subhash and Unaib, for boosting my morale whenever I felt low.

My father, Mohammad Quadir Khan, for gifting me a storybook when I was five.

My sisters, Nikhat and Ishrat; my brothers, Ziaullah and Rezaullah; and my sister-in-law, Musarrat, for being enthusiastic early listeners and readers of my story.

My daughters, Sanaa and Ayanaa, for their love and for continuously asking me about the progress of my novel.

Tarannum, my wife, for her unconditional love and support and for making many sacrifices to see this novel completed.

A Note on the Author

Abdullah Khan is a Mumbai-based novelist, screenwriter, literary critic and banker. Born in a village near Motihari, Bihar, Abdullah was initially educated in Urdu-medium and madrasa schools. His writings have appeared in *Brooklyn Rail* (New York), *Wasafiri* (London), *The Hindu* (India), *Daily Star* (Bangladesh) and *Friday Times* (Pakistan), among other publications. *Viraam*, his debut film as a screenwriter, was released in 2017. *Patna Blues* is Abdullah's first novel and is being translated into several languages, including Arabic, Hindi, Urdu, Kannada, Marathi, Malayalam, Bengali, Telugu and Tamil.

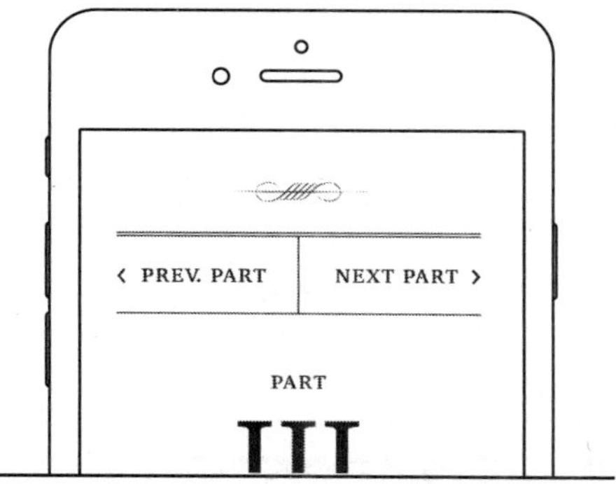

Beautiful Typography

The quality of print transferred to your mobile. Forget ugly PDFs.

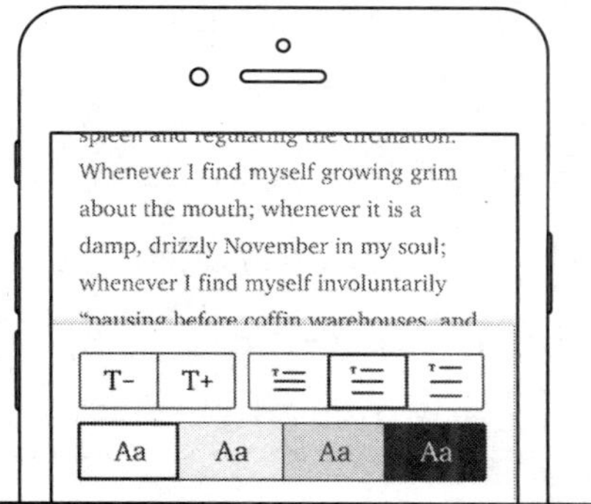

Customizable Reading

Read in the font size, spacing and background of your liking.

AN EXTENSIVE LIBRARY

Including fresh, new, original Juggernaut books from the likes of Sunny Leone, Praveen Swami, Husain Haqqani, Umera Ahmed, Rujuta Diwekar and lots more. Plus, books from partner publishers and loads of free classics. Whichever genre you like, there's a book waiting for you.

juggernaut.in

Ask authors questions

Get all your answers from the horse's mouth. Juggernaut authors actually reply to every question they can.

Rate and review

Let everyone know of your favourite reads or critique the finer points of a book – you will be heard in a community of like-minded readers.

Gift books to friends

For a book-lover, there's no nicer gift than a book personally picked. You can even do it anonymously if you like.

Enjoy new book formats

Discover serials released in parts over time, picture books including comics, and story-bundles at discounted rates. And coming soon, audiobooks.

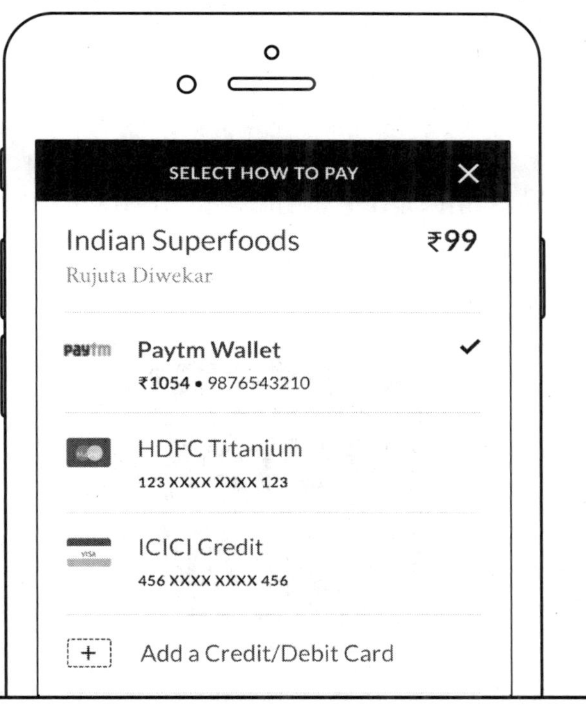

Paytm Wallet, Cards & Apple Payments

On Android, just add a Paytm Wallet once and buy any book with one tap. On iOS, pay with one tap with your iTunes-linked debit/credit card.

Click the QR Code with a QR scanner app
or type the link into the Internet browser
on your phone to download the app.